The Poudre Canyon Saga
Book 5

Shifting Trails

The Poudre Canyon Saga
Book 5

Shifting Trails

By

Dave P. Fisher

First Edition

Bottom of the Hill Publishing
Memphis, TN
www.BottomoftheHillPublishing.com

ISBN: 978-1-4837-9936-0

10 9 8 7 6 5 4 3 2 1

TABLE OF CONTENTS

Cover Art
A Detail of the Painting

DOS BOVINE AMIGOS

By

Don Weller

As a young man, western artist Don Weller was drawing horses and cowboys. He also was gaining experience as a cowboy roping calves in high school and college rodeos. After graduating from Washington State University, Don sold his horses and moved to Los Angeles, California, where he spent decades creating graphic design. He illustrated posters for the Hollywood Bowl, Warner Brothers Records, the NFL, covers for TV Guide, Time Magazine, stamps for the U.S. Post office and more. His career took him to teaching, first at UCLA and then for a decade at the Art Center School in Pasadena.

Finally, with children grown and gone and realizing he had seen all the cement and palm trees he could stand, he and wife Cha Cha moved to rural Utah. There, Don creates beautiful western paintings and enjoys riding his cutting horses. To view more of this outstanding artist's magnificent artwork, visit his website:

www.donweller.com

Don Weller Western Art

CHAPTER ONE

The two men pinning the struggling calf to the ground and the third with a red hot running iron in his hand stared up at the four mounted vaqueros as they silently scowled down on them. The small fire crackled as wisps of smoke drifted off the running iron in the dead silence. Two of the vaqueros held rifles aimed at the three men. The second pair of riders each held a rawhide reata in their hands. No one was moving.

The calf broke the silence with a long pitiful bawl as he kicked to escape the hands and knees holding him against his will. The horses under the vaqueros shifted their weight as their tails switched at the flies buzzing annoyingly around their legs. A ways off the weaned calf's mother let out a call to her offspring.

The man at the calf's head reacted out of habit before his brain had a chance to catch up to his muscles. Jumping up, he jerked out his pistol and died violently as two rifle shots resounded off the hills, throwing him violently to the ground. The calf landed its hooves in the middle of him as it leapt up and ran for freedom.

Dropping the running iron, the remaining two men jumped up and futilely ran. Like striking rattlers the reata loops shot out without an effort from the ropers. Snapping the loops tightly around the fleeing cattle thieves, the men dallied the rawhide around the saddle horns and then jerked the runners off their feet.

The two vaqueros with the reatas backed their horses, dragging the captured men through the dust while the two with the rifles nudged their horses forward until their mounts stood to either side of the dust-coated men. The weather etched brown faces under the sweat stained sombreros glared at the captives, their eyes hard and black as obsidian. No movement stirred the mustaches above the lips of the riders. Up to this point no words had been spoken, none needed to be.

One of the vaqueros with a rifle, a middle aged wire-lean and tough Mexican, addressed the men on the ground. "*Buenos dias, banditos* or should I say Anglo outlaws. *Gracias* for solving our mystery. You see, we have been finding mother cows all over the hacienda that should have calves and they do not. So, I look at these poor cows and say to myself, Juan Quintana, why are all

these cows missing their calves? Then I think, because some coyotes are stealing them. It seems we have caught the coyotes."

The men bound by the taut reatas were young, no more than
early twenties in age. The dead one was a bit older. They stared up
at the four mounted men. The eldest of the two glared his hatred
at Juan Quintana, "You best let us go if you know what's good for
you."

A broad humorless smile split Juan's face showing his white
teeth, "Tell me, what is good for me?"

"Letting us go, you peppergut."

"Why?"

"Because Milo Taggard is our pa, that's why."

Juan had stopped smiling, "Oh yes, Milo Taggard the cattle and
horse thief." He gave a mocking snort, "Yes, I am frightened down
to the rowels on my spurs."

Juan looked around and then settled his eyes on the two men
holding the reatas. He jerked his head indicating they should drag
the captured men after him. They understood and began dragging
the two across the sand following Juan and the other rifleman.

"Hey, what do you think you're doing?" the eldest shouted out.

Juan moved his horse slowly ahead of the riders dragging the
thieves. Juan called back to the captives, "It was very courteous
of you to have made your fire so close to such a fine tree. Look at
this tree with a good strong limb."

Cruz Herrera stepped off his horse and kicked out the fire. He
dug two lengths of rawhide pigging string out of his saddlebag and
then followed behind the dragging men until the riders stopped
under the heavy limb extending out of the ancient gnarled tree.

With his boot Cruz shoved the talker over on his face forcing his
mouth into the sand as he knelt on his back and tied his hands
behind him. He did the same with the second young man who was
now crying. His brother spit sand and snapped at him, "Stop crying you big baby; don't let these greasers see you crying."

"Billy they're going to *hang* us," he almost screamed.

"Shut up!"

Juan looked at Cruz as he stood up from his tying. "Bring their
horses and use their own ropes."

Cruz walked to the outlaws' horses and jerked the reins loose
from the bushes where they were tied. He led them under the
tree limb and pulled the grass ropes off the saddles. He threw the

ends over the limb. Mounting his horse, he rode under the limb and stopped. Standing on his saddle he adjusted the ropes to the proper height and tied them fast to the limb. Sitting back down in the saddle he moved his horse out from under the limb.

Juan remained mounted with his rifle on the two thieves. The ropers dismounted, roughly yanked the crying one to his feet and pushed him up on one of the horses. He was blubbering openly while Billy glared defiantly from the ground at the men.

Then they each grabbed one of Billy's arms. He cursed and tried to spit on them, but they kept his face forward. They attempted to push him up on the horse against his struggling and fighting without success. They deliberately dropped him back to the ground. He landed on the back of his head which momentarily stunned him. The two vaqueros then yanked him back up and onto the horse.

Cruz rode up to them and slipped the loops over their heads, then pulled the nooses tight around their necks. Without a word he slapped his sombrero across the rumps of the two horses causing them to bolt out from under the Taggard brothers. The ropes snapped tight with a pop and swung with the sound of hemp creaking against wood.

The four vaqueros watched the lifeless forms as the ropes spun digging deeper into the thick bark of the limb. They were hard men who had fought the Apaches until the warriors, along with their entire tribes, were forced south or onto reservations. These were not the first cattle thieves they had hung and they felt no remorse or pity. Steal from Don Sebastian Ruiz and his vaqueros would eventually shoot or hang you.

Unseen by the four vaqueros was the youngest Taggard hiding in the brush watching the entire episode with revulsion and gaping fear. Eighteen-year-old Marty was the youngest of the infamous Taggard family of outlaws. He had been away finding more calves to run to the fire when the Ruiz men surrounded his brothers. He left the calf he had been hazing toward his brothers and took cover.

Old man Taggard raised his eight sons to be killers and thieves. They stayed to the hills above Elizabethtown across the mountain range from the Ruiz hacienda. The family had managed to escape ropes and bullets for years, the sons were all still alive and active in the family business. Their latest venture had been stealing Ruiz cattle and putting a running iron to as many weaned unbranded calves as they could find. The animals were then driven into the mountains to fatten up on the grass rich meadows surrounding their home cabin.

Juan told the men with him to catch the thieves' horses. They rode out returning with the horses as instructed.

"Cut them down," Juan indicated the bodies. "Tie them on their horses. We will send a message back to *Señor* Taggard about stealing Ruiz cattle."

The bodies were cut down and thrown belly down over the saddles of their horses. In a few minutes the two dead men were tied in place. The vaqueros pulled off the bridles and slapped the rumps of the horses, sending them east into the mountains.

"They will go home," Juan stated. With that the men headed back towards the house to tell Don Sebastian what had happened.

Reaching the great adobe house, Juan told Cruz to accompany him after telling the other men to return to their work. Tying their horses to the railing, the two men walked to the patio that led to the open doorway. Removing their hats, Juan and Cruz stepped inside the door and waited.

Ignacio, the houseman and Don Sebastian's personal attendant, met them at the door. Juan looked at him, "We must see the *patron*."

Ignacio nodded and turned, an action they understood meant they should follow. Ignacio stopped in front of an open room, "*Patron*," he called softly. "Juan Quintana and Cruz Herrera wish a word with you."

Sebastian rose from his chair and walked out of the room to meet his men. Ignacio bowed slightly to the Don and walked away. Juan bowed to Sebastian in the same manner, "*Patron*, we caught three men in the act of stealing your cattle. We believe they are the ones we have been looking for."

"*Bueno!*" Sebastian exclaimed. "What have you done with them?"

"One tried to fight and we shot him. The other two we hung."

Sebastian nodded his approval. "Well done. Do you know who they were?"

"*Si*, the sons of the Anglo outlaw, Milo Taggard."

Sebastian scowled, "Taggard, yes, a bad one, a very bad man."

"It is my belief, *patron*, that they are holding the stolen cattle and have not sold them yet. The missing cattle are mostly young, just weaned or yearlings at the oldest, some were animals missed at the branding. They will hold them somewhere and allow them to age and fatten before the sale. If we can find the place we can recover the stolen cattle."

Sebastian nodded, "Yes, I agree with your idea. Tomorrow you and I will take a ride and you show me what you have found. I have been too long in the house, sitting like an old man. It is good to get out and ride, no?"

"*Si, patron,* it is good."

"Then, tomorrow, you and I, we shall ride."

"I will be here, *patron.*"

Juan and Cruz bowed slightly as they left the house.

Marty Taggard ran his horse up and down the mountain trails until he was afraid he would kill his horse, leaving him on foot in the mountains with night drawing on. The vision of his brothers swinging limp from the tree was locked in his mind's eye and he couldn't shake it. He had come close to sharing the limb with them, if he had been five minutes faster in driving the calf to them he would have. The idea made him want to cry with fear. What they were doing was dangerous and wrong and he wanted out of it, but he could never voice such an idea to the old man unless he wanted a beating. His father would consider it cowardice and he had no room for perceived weakness in his sons.

Reaching the home cabin hidden in the pines and aspen he stripped the tack from his sweat soaked exhausted horse and let him loose to graze. The cabin yard was strewn with debris, chunks of firewood, empty liquor bottles, and tin cans. An axe lay on the ground beside the scattered woodpile that sprawled out into the pine pole corral with the broken, wired together poles. It was a shoddy affair, what better men would call a 'haywire outfit,' yet in its familiarity he did not notice the mess as he ran with shaking legs to the cabin.

Lamplight reflected with a dull glow through the oil soaked paper that served as glass in the window frames. He pushed the door open to smoky lamplight, his brother burning some meat on the stove, and his father sitting in a lopsided chair with his feet up on a round of firewood, nursing a whiskey bottle. The sight of the old man caused Marty to cringe inwardly, he was always worse when drinking and anymore he was always drinking.

His remaining four brothers looked at him as did his father. He had planned to relate the story in a controlled manner, expressing his rage at the Mexicans, however, the strain had taken over his mouth and he blurted out like a frightened child, "Them greasers killed Billy, Kit, and Joe."

All activity ceased in the cabin; the bottle frozen an inch from Milo Taggard's pursed lips. He lowered the bottle, "*What?*"

"We was over on that greaser Ruiz's ranch and his men caught 'em runnin' a calf. They shot Kit and hung Billy and Joe."

Taggard lowered the bottle and placed it on the floor beside his awkward chair. He stood up weaving a bit. He shouted at Marty, "Stop your blubberin' and talk boy."

Marty wasn't sure how else to tell it so he began to repeat the same sentence only to be cut off mid-word. "*They killed my boys?*" Taggard shouted louder.

Marty nodded.

Taggart glared at the boy, his bloodshot eyes and whiskey reddened face was scrunched up above his dirty, scraggly beard. He snarled, "Where were *you* when all this happened?"

"I saw it afterwards."

He advanced toward the boy, "And you didn't jump in and help 'em? You cowardly little whelp." The old man ended the accusation by slapping Marty hard across the face.

The boy was staggered by the blow. He retreated and put his hands up, "I saw it after they had done it. I found them, Kit shot, and the others hung. The greasers was ridin' away. There was nothin' I could do except get me killed too."

"You're still a cowardly little pile of mule marbles," the old man snorted.

Taggard glared at the door as if trying to assemble thoughts in his liquor soaked brain. He turned and looked at the other boys. "Tomorrow we ride over there and kill that Ruiz. Him with his high and mighty greaser nose in the air. I'll teach him to hang Milo Taggard's boys."

His sons fidgeted without response. They had no conscience as to their criminal actions, but there was a matter of self-preservation. Going up against Ruiz's vaqueros was kin to suicide. That was one tough outfit.

Taggard noticed the hesitation. He curled back his upper lip like a dog, "Well, if I didn't raise a bunch of lily livered, milk suckin' mama's boys. You're all too yella to avenge your brothers?"

They looked back at him, there was no love lost between the brothers. They had been raised to fight each other for the old man's amusement to see who was the toughest. Billy had, at one time or another whipped them all unmercifully and the fact that he was dead was appreciated by them.

Taggard cursed them all soundly and violently. "You'll go and do this or I'll shoot the lot of you myself."

The bottom line was they feared the old man more than the vaqueros who rode for Sebastian Ruiz. It never occurred to the sons that a bullet between the old man's eyes would end the tyranny; it was too ingrained to fear and obey him. They would ride with him to the Ruiz ranch in the morning.

The sun was spreading a brilliant canvas of pinks and blues across the eastern sky as Sebastian finished his breakfast in preparation for his ride. He was feeling vibrant and happy. It was time he rode his hacienda again, he had been too long out of the picture leaving the running of the stock operations to his son Pablo and his most trusted *jefe*, Juan Quintana. Juan was doing an excellent job of it and Sebastian was generous in his rewards to his head vaquero, yet, he needed to see for himself what had been going on with the thievery.

Pablo walked with a brisk step into the dining room. He kissed the top of his father's head, "Good morning, Papa."

Sebastian studied his son as he sat down, "You are late for breakfast Pablo. Do you think the servants and cook have nothing to do but wait all day for you to get out of bed?"

Pablo grinned. He had heard the chastisement many times before. "It is only six o'clock in the morning, Papa."

"The sun is up and so should you be."

Pablo held the grin, "But I am up."

Sebastian grumbled under his breath, "Have you been drinking tequila with the men again?"

"No, Papa . . . not this time. I was looking out my window admiring this beautiful day."

"Are you in love Pablo?"

Pablo shook his head, "Only with life Papa."

Sebastian snorted, "When are you going to fall in love and give me more grandchildren?"

"Angelina has given you two beautiful grandchildren," Pablo's grin widened. "How many do you need?"

"Many. Get busy."

Pablo laughed. "You are wearing your riding clothes today, are you going out on the hacienda?"

"Yes, Juan and the men hung two cattle thieves yesterday. I wish to see what has been going on out there."

"Juan and Cruz told me last night."

"I thought you were not drinking tequila with the men last night?"

"I wasn't, I merely spoke to them. We are *compañeros* you know."

Sebastian smiled, "Yes, Juan and Cruz are fine comrades."

"Papa, I will ride with you."

Sebastian shook his head, "I have a job for you."

Pablo gave his father a wry grin, "Will I like this job?"

"You will like it. It is a trip to Taos."

Pablo's smile split his face.

"I want you to talk with our attorney Beckett. It is a most vital business matter."

Pablo turned serious, "What is it about?"

"The Lucien Maxwell Grant has been taken over by a syndicate called the Santa Fe Ring. There has been fighting over the land. I wish to know how solvent our grant is or if there are going to be problems with the United States Government over the old Spanish Grants."

"It is my understanding that Maxwell sold his grant."

"Perhaps, however, it may not have been sold, only taken over. I need to know that and how we stand with the new government."

Pablo nodded, "Yes it would be good to know."

Sebastian shook a finger at Pablo, "Business, Pablo. No cantinas, no tequila, no senoritas."

Pablo placed his hand over his heart feigning a heart attack. "Papa, what is a trip to Taos without my favorite pastimes?"

"You will live without your pastimes for once."

"You do me an injustice, Papa."

Sebastian stood up and dropped his napkin on his plate. "Yes, in your broken heart I am sure you see it that way. Too bad."

Sebastian walked across the room. Stopping, he turned and looked at Pablo. "Pablo, this is very important."

"I know Papa, I was only joking. I will see to it properly."

Sebastian nodded, "I know you will. I love you Pablo, have a safe trip."

Pablo smiled, "*Si* Papa, I know. I love you, too."

The Ruiz hacienda ran one township wide east-to-west and two townships north-to-south. The mountains formed the eastern border and the Rio Grande del Norte ran from Colorado through the length of the hacienda and on to the Mexican border. The land was a mix of mountains with pine and aspen giving way to a sand, sage, and prickly pear valley hemmed around by rimrock before rising up to the mountains in the west.

The Grant had been given to Sebastian's father, Felipe, by the King of Spain. The country was ruled by the Apache at the time but they did not recognize the King of Spain. Felipe had his hands full fighting off the marauding Indians as he built his small empire. He was a Spaniard and a warrior; he soon showed the Apache that he had come to stay. Yet, not without paying a bitter price as Felipe's sons Francisco and Jose were killed by them.

Felipe had married a Mexican woman of good blood from a respected family in Mexico City. When Mexico revolted against Spain he and his wife rode out the war on the hacienda seeing no change as the land went from Spanish control to Mexican. When Felipe died, and soon after his wife, Sebastian, the sole living heir, inherited the hacienda.

Another war was fought between the United States of America and Mexico. The land again changed governing bodies and was now the New Mexico Territory of the American victors. With American ownership came the rush for free land and the herding of Indians onto reservations. Sebastian saw the tricks that various Anglo governments and their representatives played to take what was not theirs to take. He was justly concerned about his Grant.

Sebastian buckled on his revolver and picked a rifle off the hall rack as he left the house. Juan was waiting by the corral with a horse saddled for him. Sebastian greeted him, "*Buenos dias, Juan.*"

"*Buenos dias, patron,*" Juan replied.

"Fine day for a ride."

"*Si patron,* a fine day indeed."

"Show me first where you hung the cattle thieves and then where you believe the cattle might have been taken."

Juan nodded, "As you wish."

The two men mounted their horses and rode out of the yard.

Arriving at the place where they had hung the thieves, Juan explained how they caught the thieves in the act of using a running iron on the calf. The iron still lay where it had been dropped by the cold ashes.

They rode up a trail following it east into the foothills. They looked over the country and searched for tracks. Sebastian pointed to the east, "Elizabethtown is due east of us and it is the place of many outlaws. Could it be these men are living in the mountains between here and there?"

"That is my belief," Juan answered.

"Then, let us go further into the mountains and see what we can find."

An eruption of gunfire suddenly broke out escalating quickly into a crescendo of rapid fire. The reports filled the aspen groves and echoed off the old pines then stopped as suddenly as it had started. The bullet riddled bodies of Sebastian and Juan lay on the ground among the rocks, pine cones, and sand.

Milo Taggard rode casually up to the bodies with his sons trailing behind him. He stopped and looked down at the dead men. Taggard snorted, "You greasers ain't so smart now, are yuh?"

CHAPTER TWO

Pablo returned after dark from Taos. His meeting with their attorney, Samuel Beckett, had gone well. The Grant was legal and all was in order. Beckett did not anticipate there would be any problems regarding it. The issue with Lucien Maxwell's Grant, Beckett had explained, was that Maxwell sold his holdings to Colorado Senator Jerome Chafee and his friends two years before. The government officials instantly turned around and sold the property to a Dutch consortium for double the price they had paid for it.

The trouble began when the Dutch consortium hired men to run off the residents occupying the land composing the Maxwell Grant. Many had bought their property from Maxwell or had it given to them. Maxwell had not issued Bills of Sale or Deeds to those he sold or gave land to as they were verbal deals based on Maxwell's well respected word. The Dutch were calling those claims invalid and the residents holding them squatters.

Outlaws and hired guns, under the control of an organization referred to as the Santa Fe Ring, backed by the Dutch consortium, were being hired. The Ring intended to remove all inhabitants from the former grant, using guns if necessary to force them out. The residents were standing firm and hiring their own guns. A fight between the two sides was rapidly brewing which would eventually involve all of Colfax County.

Beckett further explained that the United States was anxious to buy up other grants so the land could be sold in sections and opened up for settlement. Since Don Sebastian had no interest in selling, and he was the legal owner, he was in a favorable position and had nothing to worry about. Beckett was an Anglo; however, he was quick to defend Mexican rights in the new U.S. Territory.

Pablo's walk was slow as he entered the house, he was exhausted and hungry. Ignacio hurried to him, "I am worried, Don Sebastian has not returned from his ride."

Pablo raised his eyebrows, "From his ride this morning with Juan?"

"*Si*, he has not returned."

"Has Juan returned?"

"I do not know. I have not seen any of the vaqueros today."

"Ignacio, please find me some food while I go see Juan."

"*Si*, I will have food for you."

Turning on his heels Pablo headed out the door. He was fearful that something bad had happened to his father. There was no reason that they should still be out on the hacienda. There could not have been that much to see.

The fatigue he felt earlier was gone as he moved briskly toward Juan's small adobe house that he shared with his wife and three children. He reached the house and called into the open door for Juan.

His call was answered by Juan's wife Lucia running to the door. "*Patron*, Juan is not home from the hacienda yet?"

Pablo nodded, "He rode out with my father early this morning and he is not home yet. Has Juan been home at all today?"

"No, *patron*. I am worried. There has been trouble with *banditos*."

Pablo smiled at her, "Do not worry, I will find them. My father can be a stubborn man at times and may have kept Juan out late." He didn't believe that to be true, but he didn't want to scare Lucia.

"*Gracias, patron*."

He left the adobe and next went to find Cruz in the long bunkhouse where the vaqueros lived. He walked in the open door to the surprise of the men. They were all friends and Pablo never acted above them because of who he was. They, however, did treat him with the respect due his station, a respect he had earned with them.

"Has anyone seen Juan?"

Cruz stood up from a table and met him, "Juan has not returned; we have been talking about it, that we should go search for him."

"That is what I came for, to see if you or any of the men have seen him since this morning."

"No, none of us have."

"My father was with him, he wanted to see where the outlaws were hung and if it was possible to figure out where the missing cattle have gone."

Cruz nodded, "We did see Don Sebastian riding out this morning with Juan. We believed he had returned. We were all out on the hacienda working and did not see him after this morning. If they are both still gone, it is a bad sign."

Pablo frowned, "Yes, a very bad sign."

"We had thought to go out and look, but in the dark . . ." Cruz shrugged.

"It is useless to search in the dark. We will have to wait until morning. I will ride out at first light, I wish you to ride with me Cruz. In Juan's absence you are *jefe*, assign work to the men and pick two to ride with us. If there are Anglo outlaws or *banditos* on the hacienda we must all be vigilant." He directed the last statement to the men as a whole.

Cruz nodded his understanding as did the rest of the men. "We will be ready at dawn."

Pablo left the bunkhouse and returned to his house. He was filled with dread. Ignacio had left food on the table for him. He sat down and ate slowly thinking of all possibilities as to what could have happened to his father and Juan.

Ignacio stopped in the entranceway of the dining room. "What did you learn *patron*?"

"Juan is gone also."

The servant's eyes were heavy with worry. Ignacio was ten years older than Sebastian. His father Benito had been Felipe's houseman. Ignacio had started as a stable boy and worked his way into the household. His father had served Sebastian after Felipe died and Sebastian become patron of the hacienda. When his father died he became Sebastian's houseman and friend.

Pablo loved the old man who was always gentle and calm no matter what the crisis. He had grown up around Ignacio and sometimes, as a boy, vexed him with his mischievousness. However, Ignacio never lost his temper with such a bad boy. If caught causing mischief to Ignacio, Sebastian was not slow to deal out a spanking to him. As a man Pablo came to respect the old servant for the good man he was and to see him as a friend.

"You look tired Ignacio, why don't you go to bed?"

The old man nodded, "*Si, patron.*" He turned to leave and then stopped and looked back at Pablo, his eyes welling with tears. "I love Don Sebastian as if he were my own brother. I am afraid."

Pablo nodded, "My father is a wonderful man and we all love him. We will find him. *Gracias* my old friend, go to bed and rest."

Ignacio nodded, turned, and shuffled slowly away.

Pablo slept little that night. He rose every hour to look outside to see if the sun was peeking yet. The fact that his father had remained gone through the night verified that there had been trouble. If he were injured Juan would not leave him. If Juan was injured his father would have come in to get help for him. If they both were injured or worse, the thought plagued his mind...yes, they could be dead.

He was standing outside in the cool of the morning when the sun broke the eastern horizon. He turned at Ignacio's footfalls behind him. "The cook has made breakfast for you *patron*. We knew you were riding out early."

He wasn't hungry, but they had made a special effort for him and he would not belittle that by refusing to eat. "*Gracias*, Ignacio." He followed the old man into the dining room.

Concern and worry over Sebastian spread through the hacienda. He had always treated all his people well and fairly and they loved him for it. He knew their names and their children's names and cared about each of them. When Pablo left the house, the stable boy had his best horse saddled and waiting outside the patio.

Pablo smiled at him, "*Gracias*, Jesus."

Jesus handed him the reins, "You will find the *patron*?"

"I will," Pablo assured him as he stepped into the saddle.

Cruz and two vaqueros rode up and met Pablo by the corral. "My father said he wanted to see where the outlaws were hung. I want to go there first."

Cruz nodded, "It is the place at the western base of the mountains where the old pines are and the trail that leads to Elizabethtown."

"I know the place. Who was it you hung? Did you know them?"

"Yes, it was three Taggard brothers."

Pablo frowned, "Taggards. They are a bad lot. They have always kept to the east side of the mountains with their robbing and killing though. I wonder how long they have been coming this way."

"We started seeing the cows without calves about two weeks ago. Juan and I believe, after catching them, that it had been the Taggards all along."

They rode to the site of the hanging and moved around the area. "There are fresh horse tracks here," Cruz pointed at the ground.

Pablo rode up beside him and looked down at the ground. Two sets of freshly shod horse tracks were visible around the area. Pablo knew the Ruiz horses were regularly shod to prevent hoof and leg problems. Horseshoe tracks from Ruiz horses always made distinct impressions as the shoes were never on long enough to wear down.

Cruz pointed, "The tracks are heading up the trail to Elizabethtown."

They rode for half an hour before seeing two saddled horses grazing along dragging their reins. Pablo rode up to the horses with the others following. "This is my father's black," he said as he caught up the trailing reins.

"And this is the *rojo* gelding Juan preferred," Cruz added as he moved alongside the horse and picked up the reins.

Cruz ran his hand over the saddle's pommel; feeling something on the dark leather he scratched it with his fingernails. He examined the substance under his nails, "Pablo, blood." He held up his hand to show the dried dark residue.

The sound of ravens fighting further along the trail and on the far side of an upgrade drew their attention. They rode toward the birds. Topping the upgrade, they spotted several ravens on the ground ahead of them. Pablo spurred his horse into a run at the gathered scavengers scattering the ravens as they protested loudly. On the ground were two men.

Pablo jumped out of the saddle and ran to the prone figures. One was face down; however, he recognized the clothes that his father had worn the morning he left. The second man was face up, it was Juan Quintana.

Falling to his knees, Pablo turned over the stiff body and stared into his father's cold, dead face. With a burst of anguish he screamed and fell across Sebastian's body and wept. Cruz and the other men were on the ground looking Juan's body over. They allowed their friend his grief.

The men spoke low observing the number of bullet holes in Juan's body. Without removing his clothes they counted ten places that bullets had torn into his flesh. They suspected that Sebastian's would be similar.

After several minutes Pablo lifted his upper body while he remained kneeling beside his father. His face was twisted with grief, but the tears had stopped. The others stood silently by, hats in their hands.

Pablo finally looked up at them without words.

Cruz spoke softly, "Juan has been shot at least ten times."

Pablo stared at Cruz for a moment and then looked over his father's body. He nodded his head, "Many bullets."

"They were shot by more than one man for that many shots," Cruz commented. "Juan's gun is still in his holster, as is Don Sebastian's. They were ambushed by several men."

Pablo's pain filled eyes narrowed as they took on a new intensity of rage. "*Taggards,*" he growled.

Cruz nodded, "*Si.* Shall we ride to Elizabethtown and kill them?"

Pablo stood up. "Yes, but not right now. Now, we must get my father and Juan home and then to Taos so the undertaker can prepare them for burial and put them both in fine coffins. We will bury them on the hacienda with Padre Flores to say the mass, and I must wire my sister and Jean Pelletier and tell them. They will want to come for the funeral. Then, my friend, we will ride and kill the Taggards. Burn Elizabethtown to the ground if we have to, but there will be no Taggard left alive when we finish."

Cruz's face was set like stone with angry determination. "No finer *patron* ever lived than Don Sebastian Ruiz, and I had no better friend than Juan Quintana. He was my *jefe* yes, but he was my friend as well. I will kill those who did this."

Pablo nodded, "Juan was my friend as well."

They were all silent for a minute before Pablo looked at Cruz, "You are *jefe* now."

Cruz lifted his chin, "*Gracias,* and you are now the *patron.* I will serve you as I did your father."

Pablo looked back at the body of his father as the realization of his being the head of the Ruiz hacienda sank in. "Yes, and we will ride together very soon and give them justice."

CHAPTER THREE

Jenny Pelletier dismissed the children from the classroom at the end of the school day. The boys and girls of varying ages ran out the door with excited shouts. Jenny shook her head and smiled at their exuberance as she began to clean the room. She wiped off the lessons written on the blackboard pausing to look at the date she had written, May 1. It was exactly eighteen months since she and Jeb had been married. It had been a cold day, yet she had only felt the warmth of the event. They had a good life together and she enjoyed teaching at the school.

She was respected in the town for her position as the only school teacher for their new school. The women spoke well to her and the men met her with tipped hats and polite greetings. Her husband, Jeb was equally respected as the deputy sheriff. He worked closely with Sheriff Paul Lander. One day when Paul moved up to bigger positions Jeb would easily win the election as the new sheriff.

As she finished cleaning the single room, then straightening the tables Jenny was bending over placing her lunch pail and shawl in her carrying bag. She heard one of the double doors open and then close, followed by the sound of heavy boots shuffling on the wooden floor. Looking up she saw a man watching her. With alarm she noticed two things at once, the menacing leer on the man's face and the holstered pistol on his hip.

"What do you want?" Jenny demanded, hoping her voice didn't reveal her fear.

The man continued to smile his leering unspoken taunt. He took a step closer, "I saw you on the street this morning as I rode in and couldn't believe my eyes. Then, I found out you were the *school marm*. So, I had to come and see for myself."

An ember of recognition flamed in Jenny's mind, something about that face and voice. "I do not know who you are, sir."

"Sure you do little Jennifer. Denver, Madam Min . . . Alex Cassidy."

Jenny blanched at the name. Alex Cassidy, Madam Min's enforcer and murderer. He was the one who cut Nancy to pieces with a knife when she tried to run away. Why was he here?

Cassidy grinned taking pleasure in her obvious fear. "You got away, but lucky for you that old China bat is in prison so there's no pay for me to bring you back."

"Then why are you bothering me?" Jenny's voice came out in a whisper.

"Old times' sake."

"We never had any 'old times'."

"We can start now."

Jenny moved so her desk was between her and the man. "Leave me alone."

Cassidy looked around the room, "You know, I wonder what the folks in this square-head town would think if they knew their beloved school marm used to be a Denver whore?"

Jenny began to hyperventilate with fear and anxiety. She began to cry. "I never was. You're a filthy liar. I was a prisoner."

Cassidy only grinned.

"My husband is the deputy sheriff here. Leave me alone."

"*Husband?* Does he know what you are?"

"I'm not anything you say I am and he knows what happened to me."

"I'll bet the rest of the town doesn't though." He laughed enjoying his bullying position. "They don't have to know though."

Jenny tightly gripped the back of her desk chair draining the blood from her knuckles. "What do you want from me?"

"You."

Jenny's eyes opened wide with realization and horror. "Never! I never would."

"Well, you think it over and what your reputation is worth to you in this town. After all, it ain't any different than what you did before."

"I never did anything before. You're a liar."

"Think it over, I'll be around."

"There is nothing to think over. I would never."

Cassidy shrugged, "Suit yourself."

"Why are you doing this to me?"

"Because you got away, and I don't like to lose one. Besides that," his grin widened, "it's fun." He turned and walked back out the door closing it softly behind him.

Jenny sat down heavily in her chair, trembling and staring with shock at the door. Tears welled up in her eyes and she buried her face in her hands and wept. "Will it never end?" She sobbed behind her hands.

She sat crying and worrying until she thought of going home. It was already late, Jeb would be wondering what happened to her. She had threatened Cassidy with Jeb; then she realized that Jeb must never know this happened. He must never hear what that man said to her, his demand of her to remain silent. She knew Jeb would go after him, and as brave as Jeb was, Cassidy was a professional killer. He would kill Jeb.

She absently chewed her bottom lip, how could she hide this from him? Her demeanor alone would let him know she was upset and then he would want to know why. She didn't know what to do, but she *did* know that Jeb must never find out Cassidy was in town.

She stood up and walked on weak legs to the closed doors and paused in front of them. Was it safe to go outside? She concluded that there would be enough people around that Cassidy would never bother her in daylight. She opened the left door, took a single step, stopping inside the door frame and looked to the right and left. Taking a second tenuous step outside, she scanned the area around her again. Seeing no sign of the man, she closed the door. Too frightened to turn her back to lock the doors she left them and walked quickly home.

Jeb was in the bedroom with his Remington buckled on practicing a fast draw. A year ago he had asked his friend, Clint Rush to teach him how to fast draw and handle himself in a gunfight. Clint had hesitated at first, but relented when Jeb said that as a lawman, his life might one day hang on his ability to get a gun into action fast. Should he be challenged by a gunfighter, he would have to stand up to the challenger. There was no backing down and if he didn't know how to gunfight, he would be killed.

Clint realized that Jeb was right and what he could teach him might well save his life. Jeb remembered that the first thing Clint had explained was the proper placement of the holstered gun. Show offs wore it down low, drawing from that far down wasted valuable seconds in reaching down and then swinging the gun up level enough for a killing shot. There were no old show offs. Too high, like dudes wore a gun they never used, and your arm was in the wrong position to draw. The proper position was in between and he wore his gun every day exactly where Clint had decided was right for him.

After that Clint showed him how to get the revolver into action fast. Thumbing back the hammer while drawing, leveling it before pulling the trigger, and most important, not hesitating to shoot. "Do not think about it, do not draw a breath, just draw and shoot all in one fluid motion," Clint had emphasized over and again.

He practiced constantly when no one was around to see him. He went out in the hills and shot until he could draw, point, and hit. After a year Clint told him he was as fast and accurate as anyone he had ever seen. He didn't want Jenny to know that he was working on his gun fighting skills as she would be worried about him more than usual.

Hearing the door open, Jeb quickly unbuckled the gunbelt and hung the rig on a wall peg. He walked out of the room to see Jenny busying herself in the kitchen. "Hey, pretty girl," Jeb said from behind her. "Got a kiss for a lonely lawman?"

Jenny turned around forcing a smile and threw her arms around his neck and kissed him. "Sorry I'm late," she said trying to hold her voice steady. "I was working on some things in the school and forgot the time."

Jeb looked in her eyes, "Have you been crying?"

"Oh, no. I got some cleaning water in my eyes and it irritated them."

Jeb didn't believe the excuse, but chose to let it drop. His married brothers and father had told him that women sometimes cried for no good reason, or at least one no man could see. It was one of those things about women that they could never understand. He figured this was one of those woman things they had talked about.

"Well, you need to be careful. Sure don't want to damage those pretty blue eyes."

Jenny smiled at him, "I'll make supper."

"Want some help?"

"Oh no, thank you all the same though."

"Okay, I'll get out of your way then."

Jenny turned back to the counter and began to peel potatoes. Jeb watched her. He knew her well enough to know that something had disturbed her. He also knew that if she didn't want to tell he couldn't pry it out of her. He left the kitchen and sat down to read a week old Denver paper he had found.

The next school day ended with Jenny fearful of another unwanted visit from Cassidy. She was cleaning the blackboard as fast as she could in order to get out of the room. With her back to the doors, she heard one of them open and the voice she feared spoke. She jumped, dropping the eraser as she spun around. Cassidy closed the door and sauntered into the room.

"Afternoon teacher, made a decision yet?"

Jenny stood rigid with fear and stared at the man seeing the same leering grin on his face. She struggled to control her panic. Taking a deep breath she replied in a quivering voice, "I told you never. *Please* leave me alone."

"But, I don't want to leave you alone." He swaggered toward her in a taunting manner. "Give me the key. I'll lock the door so it's just you and me, and no one will disturb us. I doubt that any of the little rug rats will want back into a school."

Cassidy stopped at the desk that was between them and laughed. Without warning he suddenly made a lunge for her. In an involuntary act of self-preservation, Jenny grabbed up the long wooden pointer stick from the desktop and swung it with all her strength landing it soundly across his face. The stick broke in half, the pointer end flying across the room.

With a surprised yelp of pain Cassidy slapped his hand to his face. He pulled his hand back to see blood on it from the long bleeding welt running from his mouth to his ear. He cursed her violently and made another lunge, "I'll fix you good," he snarled.

As he lunged, Jenny stabbed at him with the broken end of the stick that was still in her hand. The sharp point took him in the throat. Cassidy instantly fell to his knees gagging and hacking as blood ran down his neck. After several minutes he staggered to his feet gripping a hand around his throat.

He glared his hatred at her and whispered in a hoarse voice, "Fine, you had your chance."

Feeling strengthened by her actions and the resulting end to the attack Jenny said in a harsh tone, "And I told you *never.*"

Cassidy stumbled out of the room gripping his throat.

Jenny's legs began to shake, forcing her to sit down until she felt strong enough to stand and walk. She had protected herself and was safe for the moment. Her worry now was whether Cassidy would make good on his promise to tell the town about Denver. It would ruin her if he did.

The next school day ended with Jenny fearing another visit. Her anxiety increased as the school day drew to a close, finally bursting into full panic as the last child ran out the door. She sat in her chair watching the doors, too frightened to turn her back to them. After fifteen minutes she hurried across the room and locked them. Walking backwards she reached her desk. She organized her school supplies and cleaned the blackboard.

With the cleaning chores finished and her bag in hand she stood at the doors and took a deep settling breath. She slowly slipped the key in the keyhole and turned it. Opening one door she hesitated looking out and all around. She stepped out closing the door behind her and half running, headed for home. Reaching her house she hurried inside locking the door behind her. As the next day was Saturday with no school, she cried in her relief of being home safe and not having to worry about Alex Cassidy for two days.

———

Clint Rush drove the ranch wagon into town Saturday morning. He had been busy day and night with calving season and had not left the ranch in weeks. Today necessitated the trip in for supplies. He pulled the team to a stop in front of the Evans' store.

Jeb was on the street talking to one of the new farmers who had recently migrated to Larimer County from the east. He listened patiently as the man wanted to know what the sheriff's office was going to do about the coyotes that killed his milk cow's calf. Jeb tried to make the man understand that the sheriff had no control over the predation of coyotes. The farmer was unhappy with the answer.

Clint stepped off the wagon and looked toward Jeb and the farmer. Jeb looked at Clint with a pleading expression to give him a reason to leave the conversation. Clint took the hint and marched angrily toward Jeb. When he got within hearing of the one sided conversation Clint couldn't believe what the farmer was griping about. He barked at the farmer, "Then shoot the durn coyote, you fool. I have important business with the deputy; get back to your cow."

The farmer stiffened with indignation and began to speak when he thought better of it after seeing Clint's hard face and tied down six-gun. He huffed and stomped angrily away.

Jeb sighed, "I owe you a big one for that Clint."

Clint laughed, "Idiots. What's the east doing? Purging out the fools and idiots and shipping them all to Larimer County?"

"I'm thinking so lately. There are a lot of immigrants moving into the county and town. They don't understand the country or the customs of the west. They want everything to be like in the east where they go and snivel to a policeman to fix whatever their stupid problem is."

"I don't envy you your job"

Jeb gestured with his head, "Come on, let me buy you a cup of coffee."

"Okay, a quick one, I've got to get back to the calving."

As they walked toward the café Jeb asked, "So, how are things going out on the Rush and Webster ranch?"

"Good, better than good actually. Joe's turning into one first rate cattleman."

Jeb remembered the boy, Joe Webster, still seeing him that night in the Webster barn after the Rebel renegades had murdered his father. "That's good to hear, you've had a solid influence on him."

"I like to think so."

"How is Mrs. Webster doing?"

"Smiling and happy again. It's been over a year and a half since her husband was murdered."

Jeb could tell the statement was leading somewhere. "That was an ugly night all around."

Clint nodded, "It was that. Anyway, Ida and I have talked a lot, and with Joe to consider, we are going to be married."

Jeb grinned, "I figured as much."

"Oh, you did, did you?"

"Sure, it was only a matter of time. Widow in need of a strong man. Ex-gunfighter in need of settling down. Two-and-two makes four."

Clint laughed, "Pretty smart for a tin star."

Jeb laughed in return, "If I was so smart I would know how to stop coyotes from being coyotes and eating milk calves."

"I'll let you in on a secret . . . you can't. No more than you can teach pilgrims to fix their own problems."

"Oh, that was simple. I should hang around you more often." They stepped into the café.

After finishing their coffee the two went their separate ways. Clint returned to the store and made his purchases. After loading the supplies in the wagon he climbed on the seat and moved the team down the street to Reed Hall's blacksmith shop and livery to pick up some horseshoe iron.

Stepping off the wagon he looked around for Reed. Not seeing him, he made his way into the livery. Two men were engaged in talk laughing over some subject. Clint ignored them until he overheard one of the men say, "That's what he said, that cute little blonde school teacher was a Denver sporting girl."

Clint froze in his tracks as he stared at the men. There was only one blonde haired school teacher he knew. He walked up to the men. He looked at the man who had made the comment, "What are you talking about?"

The man grinned, "That cute little blonde haired, blue eyed school teacher."

"You mean Jenny Pelletier? What about her?"

"Fella in Pruitt's last night was sayin' how he knew her in Denver, she was a sporting girl in a fancy cathouse."

Clint's temper flared, "That's nonsense. Jenny is a friend of mine."

The man chuckled, "Sounds like she was friends with a lot of men."

Clint's hands were down at his sides. By the time the right fist made it to the man's face it was carrying all his muscle and anger with it. The punch landed solidly under the man's chin slamming his teeth together and snapping his neck back. He fell to the dirt floor unconscious.

The second man stared at Clint in fear, holding his hands out in front of him. "I was only listening, that's all. I ain't never even been in Pruitt's."

"Who's spreading these lies about Jenny?"

"He," pointing at the prone man, "said a man name of Cassidy was talking it up in Pruitt's last night."

"Cassidy? Alex Cassidy?"

The man shrugged apologetically, "I don't know his first name. Who is Alex Cassidy?"

"Scum of the earth, fancies himself a gunfighter."

"All I know is what he told me."

Clint set a hard eye on him, "You better not spread this gossip around or I'll find you and you won't be doing any talking for a long time."

The man turned and ran out of the barn.

Reed Hall walked into the livery and looked down at the unconscious man. "What happened to him?"

"He talked too much."

"That can be dangerous."

"I'll be back." Clint walked out of the barn. He felt the need to tell Jeb about the rumors so he could nip the lies in the bud. As he walked he wondered why the likes of Alex Cassidy would be in town talking bad about Jenny.

Clint spotted Jeb standing in front of the telegraph office and made a beeline for him. "Jeb, I need to talk to you."

Jeb turned his attention to Clint at the same time the telegrapher hurried out of the office. "Jeb," he called out. "I got this wire for your pa yesterday. Don't figure he'll be around for a spell so maybe you can take it to him. Sounds kind of important." He handed the paper to Jeb.

Jeb took the paper, "I'll get it to him."

Clint stopped as Jeb read the message. Jeb's face dropped as he reread the message. "Oh, my Lord," he whispered.

"What is it?" Clint asked.

Jeb looked up at him, "Don Sebastian Ruiz has been murdered. I have to get this to my folks right now." With the shock of the message filling his thoughts Jeb forgot that Clint wanted to talk to him. He ran off leaving Clint standing.

Clint stared after him and wondered what he should do about the rumors. Maybe he should talk to Jenny or maybe that would be a bad idea. Something had to be done to stop the lies. He could look up Cassidy and confront him on it.

He knew Cassidy from his travels. They had butted heads and he had backed Cassidy down in Denver. Then, again, if he was spreading such talk it was Jeb's right to call him out. It wasn't his place. He would wait and talk to Jeb first.

CHAPTER FOUR

Gossip spreads like wildfire in a small town where there is little news to liven up the day. The more sullied the subject of the gossip, the faster it spreads and the more it grows and becomes enhanced for the better telling. The news that Jenny Pelletier had been a Denver prostitute before moving to Fort Collins was juicy gossip. The women spreading the tales acted appalled at hearing the enhanced stories yet not so appalled to not listen intently and quickly tell it to the next person in line. The men telling the tales winked and laughed thinking of the blonde school teacher in an entirely different light.

Jeb had returned home only long enough to tell Jenny the news of Sebastian's death and then made a fast ride to the Poudre Canyon. Jean had taken the news hard and Angelina wept. Jean and Catherine along with Henry, Angelina and their children were loading the wagons that afternoon to leave the next morning for the Ruiz hacienda.

Jeb had returned home late to find Jenny sitting up unable to sleep. He had questioned her about what was troubling her and received only that she was feeling a bit ill. He knew she wasn't ill and the anxiety in her eyes went well beyond some womanly need to cry. Still, he couldn't and wouldn't try to force it out of her and let it go, hoping she would talk eventually.

The next morning Jeb and Jenny walked to church. Jenny's eyes flickered everywhere as she clung tightly to Jeb's arm. As they approached the little church the people were outside talking in groups separated by gender. As they walked by, men suddenly stopped talking and gave the couple nervous greetings. Jeb eyed them with suspicion as he nodded his acknowledgement to their awkward greetings.

The groups of women stopped talking as well, casting disapproving glances at Jenny. Whispers behind hands directly into gossip hungry ears brought a range of theatrical expressions from the gossipers. Most of the people gathered in the church yard were eastern newcomers. The original residents of the town, who were its founders and made its history, were quickly being outnumbered.

Ben Evans and Alice greeted Jeb and Jenny as normal. Alice gave Jenny a pained look of sympathy. She had heard the rumors and knew them to be vicious lies. One of the recently arrived women made the mistake of telling Alice the *news*. She received a severe tongue lashing for her indiscretion. The old time residents knew how much Alice Evans despised gossip.

Mrs. Kelly walked up to Jeb and Jenny and gave Jenny a hug. "How is my little colleen this morning?" She had heard the talk as well. She and Paul were the only people outside of the family that knew of Jenny's wretched experience in Denver.

Jenny warmly hugged the old Irish woman who was like a grandmother to her. "A little ill feeling, Mrs. Kelly."

The Irish woman gave her a smile, "Hope you feel better soon."

Mrs. Kelly looked up at Jeb who stood a foot taller than her. "There's business for you to attend to Mr. Pelletier."

Jeb gave her a confused look which telegraphed to Mrs. Kelly that he had not heard the talk. "You and I will talk."

Jeb nodded, "Yes, ma'am." He was more confused than ever now. He looked at Jenny who was glancing nervously at the women who were studying her. Jeb whispered to Jenny, "What is going on?"

Jenny shook her head and made her way into the church. They knew, they had heard. Alex Cassidy had made good on his threat.

The two sat up front in their usual place. Mrs. Kelly sat at the rear of the church as she wanted to spot the wagging tongues and who they belonged to. She was a wise woman who understood the destruction gossip sowed. She would identify the worse of the gossipers and take them to task.

During the service she watched as women leaned their heads toward each other and whispered. The whispers were followed by gaping expressions and then looks at the back of Jenny's head. Mrs. Kelly fumed. Gossipin' instead of listenin' to the sermon she thought to herself, disgustin'.

At the conclusion of the service the congregation filed out to rejoin their little groups. The minister shook hands with Jeb and Jenny smiling warmly at them. Clergymen were never included in the gossip as they would surely disapprove, ruining the fun.

The men Jeb usually spoke to tried to ignore him. Sensitive to the moods of others he quickly assumed that he was the subject of the cold receptions. He also noticed that none of the women welcomed Jenny into their little klatches. His temper was rising as he was already displeased with the direction the town was going with the immigrants.

Jenny leaned against Jeb, "Take me home, I don't feel well."

Jeb looked around him with disgust, "I don't feel so good myself."

As they walked away Mrs. Kelly marched up to the group of women who were known to be the worse gossip mongers in the town. She heard them talking about Jenny with disparaging remarks and arrogant self-righteous expressions. In her strong brogue she lit into the women. "For shame on yuh, you dirty foul mouthed gossips. Speakin' so vile against a lovely child like my little colleen."

The women were taken aback by the sudden attack. They stared at the angry old woman unable to speak.

Mrs. Kelly continued to berate them. "You sit in church pretendin' to be a-worshippin' the Lord and all the while your poison tongues are a-waggin' like so many snakes. Shame on yuh, malignin' such a sweet child and you knowin' nothin' of her except the lies you've heard. If I wasn't a lady I'd beat you all to an inch of your filthy lives. Now, get off this holy ground and take your poison to the devil."

With that Mrs. Kelly stormed off, her face bright red. She had spoken loud enough for all to hear and their eyes followed her. Once the threat was removed the attacked women showed their indignation. "Well, I *never*," huffed one. "*Who* does she think she is?"

Alice Evans walked up to the women and glared at them, "Mrs. Kelly is one of our pioneers and I can say her perspective of the situation is keen and I applaud and second her comments to you. Take your filthy gossip home and stay there with it." Alice lifted her chin and walked back to join her friends.

As Jeb and Jenny walked back home Jeb was irritated and continued to mention about how odd the people were acting. "What a queer bunch," he growled. "I suppose I didn't exactly say the right thing to one of those fools whining like a dog about some petty problem. I'm getting tired of this place and the changes I'm seeing around here. It's not like it was even two years ago."

They walked into the house and closed the door. Jenny immediately burst into tears, "It's not you."

Shocked by her sudden burst of emotion Jeb was momentarily stunned. Recovering quickly he put his hands on her shoulders and looked in her flooding eyes, "Jenny, it's time you told me what is going on."

Jenny bit her bottom lip and nodded. They went into the bedroom and sat beside each other on the bed. In tears and choking sobs she told Jeb everything that had happened since Alex Cassidy threatened her.

Jeb sat listening, his emotions running from shock to a driving urge to walk right out and kill this Cassidy. Jenny finished by whispering, "And he has told everyone that I am . . . I am a whore." She burst into tears burying her face in the bed.

Jeb kissed the back of her head and helped her sit up. He looked her directly in the eyes, "You listen to me, you are not . . . I refuse to even say the word. I know what happened to you, as does the family, and Mrs. Kelly. What a bunch of dirty people think is not important."

"Oh, but Jeb it *is*, it is very important to me." The tears continued to flow.

Jeb considered that and realized it would be the same as if men said he was a coward and liar, something that could not be dismissed as unimportant. In Jenny's case it was far more serious and personal. He nodded, "Yes, I know it is. I didn't mean to make little of it."

"I know you didn't, but do you think the town will want the kind of person they say I am to be teaching children?"

Jeb could only look at her knowing she had a valid concern. "They had better not fire you because of some gossiping lies."

"Besides that, how am I supposed to ever hold my head up in this town again if everyone believes the gossip?"

Jeb hugged her, "We can hope that most of the people won't believe it."

Jenny pressed her face against Jeb's chest and cried. "I don't know," she mumbled.

Jeb began to focus his thinking on Alex Cassidy. Jenny had said he was a murderer and thug. He was obviously a bully as most of his ilk were. "Jenny, do you know where I can find Cassidy?"

She shook her head, "I don't know." Realization of what she feared struck her and she looked at Jeb with tears streaming down her face. "Why?"

"You don't think I'm going to let him get away with this do you? He threatened you, said what he did to you, and then tried to attack you. Do you really think I won't go after him?"

Jenny stared in his face and slowly shook her head, "No, I know you too well."

"If Ian heard about this I'd have to tie him to a tree to get ahead of him."

Jenny wiped her face with the palms of her hands, "Pa would too. Oh, Jeb that is what I'm so afraid of, that you or Pa will go after him. Alex Cassidy is a killer, a professional killer. He will kill you."

"I don't kill so easy. You should know that."

Jenny recalled the long watch over Jeb when he had been shot by the Confederates. She had learned from Catherine and from experience that it was futile to argue with a male Pelletier when honor was on the line. She had to accept their code and trust that Jeb was able to defeat Cassidy. She nodded her acceptance of how Jeb stood on the matter.

Jenny took a deep settling breath and wiped her face and swollen eyes. "I guess we will find out what happens tomorrow when I go to the school."

"I will walk you there and be waiting when school lets out."

Jenny put her arms around Jeb's neck and whispered, "I love you."

"I love you, too. Why didn't you tell me right away when Cassidy first approached you?"

Jenny sat back. "I was afraid you would go after him and be killed. He kills people like swatting flies. You are brave, Jeb, but I'm afraid for you." She said no more, not wishing to insult Jeb by saying she feared Cassidy was more experienced with a gun than he was and would kill him.

Jeb looked in her eyes, "Don't worry, I can handle him."

———————————

Monday morning Jeb walked with Jenny to the schoolhouse. She had not slept the night before and now looked and felt exhausted and sick to her stomach with fear and nervous anxiety. The closer they got to the school the worse she felt. Jeb held onto her arm and hand to show his support for her.

Reaching the school there were no adults outside as Jenny had feared. The children ran around the school playing games. The boys stared at Jeb, the star on his shirt, and the revolver on his hip. The little girls came up to Jenny and wanted to hold her hand as they went into the school.

Jeb let go of Jenny's hand, "Looks like you will be alright today."

Jenny smiled at the little girls, "Yes, it appears so. Thank you for walking with me."

"I'll be here when school lets out. If I'm delayed wait for me."

Jenny gave him a hug and walked up the steps to the doors and opened them. She called to the children to come inside. They all obeyed and ran for the open door. Jeb watched until he saw the doors close.

He wanted to talk to Paul about all this. Paul had been out of town handling a farmer feud to the east, but had returned the night before. He walked away from the school bound for the Grout Building.

Paul was sitting at his desk sorting through some paper work. He grinned at Jeb and shook his head, "When Mr. Evans talked me into this job he never said anything about all this paperwork. I spend more time writing than sheriffing."

"Part of the job," Jeb replied without humor.

Paul studied him as he laid down the papers in his hand, "You look like a man worrying a problem."

"Yeah. Got a few minutes?"

"For you, all the time in the world. Sit down."

Jeb explained all he knew about Jenny's confrontation with Cassidy, the gossip, and Jenny's fears. He concluded by saying, "I know you'll understand, what with the problems you and Two Moons have endured."

Paul listened without comment until Jeb had finished. "I do understand. There are some mighty good folks in this town and then there are some bad ones. You can't get away from that anywhere. Do you want us to go out and arrest Cassidy?"

"For what? There's no law on the books for malicious gossip. It's no crime to be a liar. If we brought him in we'd just have to let him go again."

"What about his threats to Jenny?"

"All he has to do is deny it all. It would be her word against his and he's done a pretty good job of making her look bad."

"So, what do you want to do?"

"I figure a worm like Cassidy would hang out with the rest of the worms."

Paul gave Jeb a sardonic grin, "Pruitt's worm hole?"

Jeb nodded. "I want to see if he's there and just what he has to say for himself."

Paul held the look as he watched Jeb, "What he has to say for himself? Sounds pretty mild for a Pelletier, almost like cold dishwater. You plan to hand him a daisy too? What do you really intend to do?"

Jeb held his friend's eyes for a long moment before answering. "I intend to kill him."

Paul leaned back in his chair and let out a sigh, "That's more what I thought. I have to tell you that you can't do that . . ."

Jeb snorted cutting him off, "This coming from the man who had a .45 stuck up Gyp Crawford's nose for calling Two Moons the same thing Cassidy called Jenny."

"I was going to say . . . while wearing that badge."

"Then, I'll give it back to you if that's what it takes."

"I don't want that and you know it. Let's go on down to Pruitt's and play it by ear." He stood up from his desk.

The two rode across the expanding town to the area that had once been the center of town. Larry Pruitt's whiskey hole was in a dilapidated area, a back alley that the town had grown away from. Tying off their horses they walked up to the door and stepped inside.

There were several unkempt deadbeat men sitting around the dirty tables already drinking at this early hour. Larry Pruitt was behind the bar as usual. He sneered at the two lawmen as they walked in. "What do you want?" Pruitt hissed.

Paul looked around and with a sarcastic tone said, "I see you've fixed up the place."

"What do you mean?"

"You cleaned the month old vomit off that table. You'll be a high class establishment before too long."

Pruitt put his hands on the bar and leaned over it, "You got a purpose here?"

"I'm looking for Alex Cassidy," Jeb said as he looked around the room.

Pruitt grinned, "Oh, now I see."

"See what?"

"Why you're here." Pruitt chuckled, "Makes me almost want to go to school."

Jeb growled and took three giant steps toward Pruitt.

Pruitt backed up to the wall and held up his hands, "What, you're gonna beat me up for sayin' I want to go to school. A man should have an education and a certain teacher can give me that." He laughed.

"Where's Cassidy, you pile of horse manure," Jeb snarled at Pruitt.

"Don't know him."

Jeb started to jump over the bar when Paul caught his arm. "Beating him won't find Cassidy."

Jeb settled his feet back on the floor. "One of these days Pruitt."

Pruitt laughed, "I'm all a-tremble."

Jeb glared at him, "Tell Cassidy that I'm looking for him and when I find him he'd better be wearing a gun!

CHAPTER FIVE

The two wagons carrying the Pelletier families pulled into the Ruiz yard after a week of travel. They were dust covered and trail weary. Catherine was feeling her age in stiff muscles and sore bones from bouncing for days on a hard wagon seat. Jean was tired, but a lifetime of hard work and rugged living had steeled him to hardships even in his seventies.

Henry and Angelina were young enough to withstand the rigors of the journey. Their children, Marcus and Alicia were bored and anxious to be set free to run and play. They had made the journey the past spring before the weather turned hot and had spent a month with Sebastian much to the old man's delight.

Angelina's tears for her father had ceased after the second day, however, a doleful pallor hung over the family. Henry had seen Sebastian as a second father, and the children had clung to him. They looked forward to seeing Pablo, yet the hacienda without the immense presence of Sebastian would not be the same.

Along the way, once the children were asleep in the wagon bed at night, Jean and Henry would quietly discuss Sebastian's murder. They speculated as to the cause of his death. The wire had been brief, just enough to let them know the old man had been the victim of foul play. The wire, though vague, was enough to put them on the road to Taos immediately. It didn't need to be said aloud, there was simply an understanding that there would be a debt to collect from the murderer. Jean had sent Jeb back to town with a message in reply to Pablo that they were on the way.

Jesus quickly rushed from the barn, along with another young worker, to take control of the wagons. Jean stepped down, thanked the young man who held their team, and assisted Catherine to the ground. Henry climbed off the wagon seat and patted Jesus on the back as he held their horses and thanked him. Henry helped Angelina down while Marcus and Alicia jumped from the wagon bed.

Angelina walked up to Jesus and ruffed her hand across his rough shorn head of black hair and smiled, "Jesus, look how you have grown. You will one day be in charge of much more."

The boy smiled proudly, "*Gracias, señora*, I am happy to see you again.

It was not common practice for members of a patron's family to be friendly with the servants, seeing them only as bodies to put to work. Sebastian had not been like that, nor had his wife in her lifetime. These were his people and he treated them as such. Pablo and Angelina were raised to be respectful of them, they were never to abuse the workers or belittle them. As a teen, Pablo had once haughtily belittled a stable boy within his father's hearing and spent the next week cleaning stables to see how hard the work was. It was a lesson he never forgot.

Pablo appeared from the open doorway of the big adobe and made his way to the family. He first hugged his sister, "Angelina, it is good to see you."

He then gripped Henry's hand and threw his other arm around his brother-in-law's shoulder. "*Hermano,* glad you could come."

Henry returned the gesture, "You think we would not drop everything for Papa?"

"No, I would never think that."

Pablo then turned his attention to Jean and Catherine. He bowed slightly to Catherine, "*Señora* Pelletier, a pleasure, *mi casa es su casa.*"

Catherine smiled at him, "Thank you Pablo, you are gracious as always."

Pablo turned to face Jean and extended his hand, "A pleasure *señor* Pelletier. It has been much too long since we last stood face to face."

Jean shook his hand, "Yes, much too long. I should have come more often to see Sebastian like a proper friend."

Pablo smiled sadly, "Papa spoke often of you, he knew you were his good friend."

Angelina stepped up beside Pablo, "Where is Papa?"

"In a cool room. I had the undertaker prepare him and seal the casket as I refused to bury him until you arrived for the mass and funeral. Juan's casket is next to Papa's. He died with him and I honor him as our good friend. We will bury them at the same time."

"Thank you, Pablo. How is Lucia?"

"In great grief, she visits Juan's casket every day. She was concerned as to where she and the children would live now. I told them they would stay right in the house they are in and I would care for them. Juan was my good friend."

Angelina smiled, "As it should be, yes."

At that moment Lucia walked slowly out of the adobe, her head down and mantilla draped over her head and down her shoulders. In her hands she held a wood bead rosary. She looked up and saw the family. Angelina walked toward her.

Lucia bowed slightly, "*Señora*," then she began to cry.

Angelina put her arms around the grief stricken woman. "Juan and Papa, it is a great loss to us all."

"*Si*, the *patron* was such a good man and Juan such a good husband. Who would do such a horrible thing?"

"I don't know, but if I know Pablo and the other men they will find them."

Lucia nodded, "It may be a sin, but I hope they kill who did this evil thing."

"It will not go unpunished, Lucia."

"*Gracias, señora.* I must feed my children now." Lucia walked slowly back to her small adobe.

Ignacio was standing at the entrance to the house watching the group. Pablo called to him, "Ignacio, please prepare baths for the *señoras*."

Ignacio nodded and turned on his heels disappearing through the doorway.

Marcus and Alicia ran up to Angelina, "Can we go play in the barn with Jesus?" Marcus asked, excited to be free from the confines of the wagon.

"Jesus has his work to do and you both need baths."

Marcus made a face, "A *bath! Ma!*"

"Yes, a bath, both of you. You look like little puppies who have been rolling in the dirt. Tomorrow you may go to Lucia's house, her children could use playmates."

Marcus swung his eight year old head like a colt and kicked the dirt. In a tone of surrender he agreed to the bath. "Alright, if I have to."

Younger Alicia squealed with delight, "Ma, I want a bath."

Angelina smiled at her, "That is because you are a lady and will present yourself as one." She then ruffed Marcus' hair, "And this one wishes to be like his Uncle Pablo."

Pablo heard the remark and answered, "I take a bath."

"Not until you were thirty years old."

Pablo shrugged and winked at Marcus, "Better late than never, hey *compañero*?"

Marcus laughed, "Uncle Pablo reminds me of Uncle Ian, only not so grumpy."

Angelina laughed, "Yes, they are both dangerous men, especially if you make them take baths."

Pablo led the way to the house, "Let me show you your rooms." Jean and Henry removed the bags from the wagons and followed him.

Once in their rooms, Catherine and Angelina found that bathtubs had been filled with warm water. Jean ran his hand through the water, "That's service. You'd better jump in there while it's still warm."

Catherine put her hand in the water and smiled, "Oh that is going to be heavenly."

Jean began to leave the room, but Catherine stopped him, "How about you mountain man? Bath?"

Jean grinned, "It's not my month."

Catherine shook her head, "And we wonder where Marcus gets it from and our boys are no better."

"I'm just a bad influence, I know."

"Well, at least go outside and knock the dust off before you deposit it on the furniture."

Jean left the room and met Henry and Pablo between the rooms. Pablo looked to the right and left. "You can take your baths in the *baños* where the vaqueros take theirs."

Jean nodded, "Good. We have our reputations to protect." They followed Pablo out of the house.

Everyone came back together at the dinner table. Catherine, in her clean dress and scrubbed face eyed Jean and then gave a slight head gesture to Angelina in regards to Jean and Henry. Both men had dusted their old clothes and put them back on, however the fact their hands and faces were clean and their hair damp tipped the women off to the fact the men had secretly bathed.

Catherine commented, "My Jean, you managed to dust yourself off quite well."

Jean nodded, "I had Pablo take a corn broom to me."

"And your hands and face are clean."

"I splashed a little water on them to make you happy."

"And your hair, you must have gone wild splashing your face because your hair is wet too."

Jean frowned at her.

Angelina broke in, "Henry must have used the same basin or *maybe* they went to the vaquero's *baños.*"

Catherine grinned, "Sneaky." She looked at Angelina, "So, how exactly do *you* know about the vaqueros *baños*?"

Angelina gave a sly smile, "When I was a young girl I snuck up to see."

Catherine covered her mouth, "You didn't."

"I did. Pablo saw me and snitched to Mama. She gave me *such* a spanking."

"Was it worth a spanking?"

Angelina tipped her head side-to-side and turned her eyes to the ceiling, "I learned some things I had been wondering about."

Marcus and Alicia walked into the room bringing the subject to a close. Both children were shining clean and dressed in their best clothes. Jean looked at himself and then to Henry, "I've got better clothes."

"Me too," Henry agreed. They both left the table to change.

Pablo walked into the dining room dressed for dinner. "Where are Jean and Henry?"

Catherine smiled, "They decided that their frontier look was a little out of place and went to change."

"Ah," Pablo lifted his chin and then sat down.

Angelina studied her brother, "You look different, Pablo."

"How so?"

"Matured. Like the *patron* of a great hacienda."

Pablo nodded, "It is interesting how my outlook changed when I realized I was now *patron*. I am responsible for the financial success of the hacienda and I hold a great obligation to our people working here. It is a sobering thing."

"It looks good on you, *hermano.*"

"Thank you. I will do my best."

Jean and Henry returned to the table dressed in clean appropriate clothes. They sat down to the approving smiles of their wives.

Pablo smiled at his guests, "You all looked refreshed."

"We are," Catherine smiled. "Thank you."

"You will all stay for a long visit I hope."

Jean looked across the table at Pablo, "Andrew and Andre and his boys have got the place handled, we can stay for a spell."

"Good."

"Besides," Jean added, "there's business that needs attending to."

Pablo knew he was referring to hunting the killers of his father and Juan. "Yes, we will discuss it further after dinner."

Ignacio walked in carrying a wine bottle and began filling glasses. Angelina smiled at him, "So nice to see you again Ignacio, you are looking well."

Ignacio bowed slightly as he looked at Angelina, "*Gracias, señora*, it is so very good to see you back at the hacienda again."

"Yes, I wish it were under more pleasant circumstances."

The old servant frowned, "*Si*, it is so tragic. To lose so great a man as Don Sebastian." He shook his head and stopped talking as he continued pouring the wine.

Angelina saw tears glistening in the old man's eyes. "We will all miss him my old friend," she said in a comforting tone.

"*Si*, however, I know Pablo will be as good a *patron* as his father."

Pablo gave him a slight smile, "Thank you for your faith in me Ignacio, I will do my best."

"You are your father's son. You will do well."

After dinner the family filed into the room that solemnly held the sealed caskets. Angelina laid her hand on Sebastian's casket with tears rolling down her face. The others stood stone still in remembrance of the man.

Alicia whispered to Henry, "Is Grandpa Sebastian in there?"

Henry bent over so his face was next to the child's, "Yes."

"I remember I used to sit on his lap. I loved Grandpa."

"Yes, we all did."

Marcus asked his father, "Was Grandpa a great man?"

Henry nodded, "Yes, a very great man."

"Like Grandpa Jean?"

"Yes, they are men from a time that made great men."

After several more minutes the family filed out of the room. "Let us go to the sitting room and discuss matters," Pablo said.

Angelina wiped tears from her eyes, "I believe I would like to be alone this evening."

Pablo nodded, "I have spent many hours in there with Papa since that day. I ask him questions regarding what I am to do. He answers me in my heart."

Henry bent down toward his children, "Why don't you two go change into your night clothes and make ready for bed. We are going to be discussing grown up things." Marcus and Alicia walked to their room knowing better than to argue the point with their father.

Angelina turned back into the room with the caskets while the others walked to the sitting room. Taking chairs around the room they sat down. Pablo held up a bottle of bourbon and one of tequila, "A drink?"

Jean accepted the bourbon, Henry the tequila. Catherine abstained with a raise of her hand. Pablo poured the drinks and passed them out. He sat down with his and sighed.

"I guess we should start at the beginning," Jean remarked.

Pablo took a sip from his glass. "We have been having a rash of cattle thefts over the past several weeks. We have always had some, but in the last month it has become a serious problem. The vaqueros were noticing an absence of young animals, yearlings and weaned calves, some unbranded. The mother cows were out there showing they had been nursing recently, but there was no calf with her."

"Didn't you have a branding this spring?" Henry asked.

"Yes, but on a rancho this size we always miss some calves whose mother's hide them in the brush and then come back out when the roundup is finished.

"The thieves were using a running iron then?"

"Yes, putting a running iron to them and driving them away. Last week Juan and his vaqueros caught three thieves with a tied down calf ready to brand it. They shot one of the thieves and hung the other two. The next day Papa and Juan rode out to look over the situation and see if they could figure out where the stolen cattle were being taken. They never returned from the ride.

"The next day Cruz and I went in search of them and found them both dead. They had been shot many times each, by several men we believe."

"Any idea who?" Jean asked.

"We have an idea. Cruz, who was with Juan at the hanging, said the thieves were Taggard brothers. Before he was hung, one threatened that if the vaqueros harmed them their father would take care of us. The Taggards are one of those families where the father is an outlaw and has taught his sons to be outlaws as well. They are known in the area of Elizabethtown and Cimarron and have a reputation for murder, robbery and thefts of all kinds, especially cattle and horses. They have never been caught at it so they are still alive."

"But, now there are three less," Jean concluded. "How many are there supposed to be?"

"From what we have been able to learn it seems there are eight sons and the father."

"That leaves five sons and the father," Henry put in. "Any idea where they hide out?"

"My vaqueros tell me that word has it they are seen in and out of Elizabethtown most often. The trail Papa and Juan were killed on was the trail across the mountains to Elizabethtown. The Taggards, we believe, are holding the cattle in the mountains near there to fatten them up for sale."

"Elizabethtown, that's a gold strike town isn't it?" Jean asked.

"It's an outlaw town," Henry answered.

Pablo agreed, "Yes, a lot of outlaw activity going in and out of there. Colfax County is a powder keg ready to blow into war over the old Maxwell Grant. Hired guns are moving in for both sides."

"Does that leak over this way much?" Jean asked.

"Only as far as cattle thieves are concerned. The range war is pretty much confined to Colfax County. Our attorney in Taos assured me that the Ruiz Grant is not affected."

Jean gave Pablo a curious look, "Why would a range war in Colfax County affect your grant?"

"At this point the effect is only a spillover of outlaws into Taos County, however, it has come to me that the United States Government, or at least members of it, are seeking to obtain the old Spanish Grants for resale to settlers."

Jean snorted, "Well, that don't surprise me."

"It is inevitable," Catherine put in. "People are moving west and want land. The Indians have been moved off and the government is selling the land they once occupied. Look at how much land has been sold around us and Larimer County. I hardly recognize Fort Collins anymore."

Jean agreed, "People want land. If any loophole can be found by those wanting to make a profit they will slip their fingers in and pry it open. I'm sure they are looking for finger holds in these old grants."

Pablo agreed, "Times are changing rapidly. Hopefully they will continue to squabble over the Maxwell Grant's two million acres and leave my small hacienda alone."

"Fifty thousand acres isn't that small," Henry said.

"Smaller than many still in Mexico."

Henry pursed his lips as he thought, "It's something to be aware of though. Better make sure there are no loopholes in your grant with all the vultures hanging over the land."

"Attorney Beckett says we are fine, however, I will keep my eyes open."

Jean returned to the original discussion, "So, what do you want to do about this Taggard business?"

Pablo cast a nervous glance toward Catherine.

Catherine picked up on Pablo's hesitation. "Pablo, I spent years going to rendezvous with Jean and building a home in the wilderness. I have seen my share of violence and frontier justice. After our episode with Justin Hornsworth I have no sympathy for murderers, brigands, and outlaws. A bullet or a rope is acceptable to me where such men are concerned. Feel free to speak openly in front of me."

Pablo bowed his head toward her, "Of course, I should have anticipated that."

"Is there a sheriff in Colfax County?" Catherine asked.

"Yes, but from what I gather he is corrupt."

"Then, you have no other choice."

Pablo shook his head, "No, we will do what needs to be done."

Pablo looked back at Jean, "To answer your question, simply put, I intend to hunt them down and kill them."

"When?"

"After the funeral."

Turning his attention to Henry Pablo said, "I have promoted Cruz Herrera to Juan's position."

Henry nodded, "Very good choice."

"I have asked Cruz to send a man to Taos in the morning to bring back Padre Flores for the funeral mass to be held here so the workers can attend. I have given them all the day off. The vaqueros' cook and our house cook, Teresa, have volunteered to cook for all in attendance. The day will be spent in remembrance of Papa and Juan."

"That sounds proper," Jean agreed.

"Then," Pablo narrowed his eyes and took on an ominous expression, "the next morning we ride for Elizabethtown."

CHAPTER SIX

Cruz had sent his chosen vaquero down to Taos to pick up the priest in the seldom used buggy. It did not seem appropriate to him to pick up someone as important as Padre Flores in a buckboard. The vaquero had cleaned the buggy inside and out and set out before daylight. It seemed odd to see a hard eyed vaquero with a large pistol on his hip driving a single horse ladies buggy, yet those hard eyes were enough to stop any who would laugh. He was on an important mission.

Covering the twenty miles to Taos and returning brought the buggy carrying Padre Flores back to the hacienda in the early afternoon. There was a great deal of excitement as the priest stepped off the buggy and the people greeted him. The old padre smiled, blessed them all, and spoke kindly to the children.

Pablo quickly rushed out to greet his honored guest. "Padre Flores, thank you for coming. I know it is a difficult journey." He took the small suitcase the priest carried.

Padre Flores chuckled, "Pablo, in my youth, as a young padre, I used to walk many miles through the desert to visit my children. A ride in a comfortable buggy with the excellent company of my son Miguel is certainly no hardship. Sebastian was my good friend and this is an important day for us all."

Pablo introduced Flores to Jean and his family, and they all shook hands. Flores smiled at Jean, "You are French?"

"Yes, Father, from Trois Rivieres, Quebec."

"Catholic?"

"Yes, however, it has been many years since we have lived by a Catholic Church."

Flores nodded, "Such is the way of the frontier."

"Would you like to freshen up Padre?" Pablo asked.

"Perhaps a bit."

"Where would you like us to set up the altar, Padre?"

"Under those trees looks nice."

"You will honor my house by staying the night with us?"

"It is a time consuming return to Taos and I am sure Miguel

would like to enjoy his day off. Yes, he told me you have granted all the workers the day off. It is something Sebastian would have done, it is kind of you. Yes, I will spend the night."

"You honor me, Padre." Pablo led the priest to his room.

Henry glanced at Angelina, "Who is that man?"

"You mean Padre Flores?"

"No, the other one."

Angelina laughed, "You mean the one who drank too much tequila, chased the senoritas, and got into fights? The one named Pablo Marquez-Alvarado Ruiz?"

Henry feigned shock, "Is that my brother, *Pablo*?"

"Yes, your brother, *patron* Pablo Ruiz."

Henry grinned, "That's going to take some getting used to."

Angelina looked toward the direction Pablo had gone with the priest, "I think that under the manners and clean suit you will still find much of the old Pablo."

Pablo came back out of the house and began directing a couple of his men in the setting up of the altar and preparing for the mass. He picked out several other men to be the pallbearers for the caskets. The sound of an approaching horse caught Pablo's attention. He turned to see Samuel Beckett riding in.

Pablo walked over to him with a greeting.

Beckett stepped off the horse and shook hands with Pablo. "I saw your man leaving town with Father Flores and figured the funeral was today. I wanted to be here for it."

"Thank you Mr. Beckett, you are most welcome. We are getting all set up now, if you will excuse me."

"Yes, I will wait with the others outside here."

Jesus ran up to Beckett, "I will care for your horse *señor*."

"Thank you, young man." Jesus led the horse away.

When Padre Flores came back out of the house he was wearing his vestments and all was in readiness. The chosen men went into the house and returned solemnly bearing the caskets. Juan's friends, led by Cruz, carried his, and Pablo along with Jean, Henry and three other men carried Sebastian's.

There were many tears and anguished sobs from the women throughout the mass. Lucia wept continually for her husband. At the conclusion of the mass, the caskets were placed on a wagon bed and slowly escorted by the people to the family cemetery where lay Felipe, and his wife and sons. Sebastian was placed in a grave dug beside his wife. Juan was also interned with the family because he died with Sebastian in his service.

The caskets were lowered into the graves at which point Pablo wept without shame. The vaqueros stood in silent grief holding their sombreros in their hands. None thought their new *patron* weak for his tears, rather they saw how much he loved his father and would be like him.

Four men had volunteered to fill the graves as the others made their way back to the houses. Pablo thanked the men and followed the group. They all gathered together at the long table where the lunch was laid out, filled their plates, and then broke off into their own groups to talk.

Padre Flores joined Pablo, who was with the Pelletier's and Samuel Beckett. Pablo thanked the priest for the service and gave him a donation for his church. He spoke with them and then wandered about to mingle among the workers.

Pablo watched him, "Padre Flores is a good man; he truly cares about the people."

"As do you," Angelina added.

Beckett gave Pablo a pained look, "This might not be a good time Mr. Ruiz, but I need to speak to you regarding an urgent matter."

Pablo's expression turned to concern, "Alright."

Beckett looked around him, "Privately."

"In the house then." The family stood as Pablo began to walk with Beckett. Pablo turned and said, "Come, what concerns me concerns you as well."

Beckett frowned at the others being invited. "This is a rather sensitive issue for your ears alone."

Pablo looked directly at Beckett, "I appreciate that Mr. Beckett, however, my sister is part of this hacienda, as is Henry who is my oldest friend. Mr. and Mrs. Pelletier are old friends of my father and we have done much business together. What needs to be said to me needs to be known by them as well."

Beckett relented, "As you wish."

They all walked into the sitting room and took seats.

Beckett paced across the room and back wringing his hands together. He sighed heavily and faced Pablo. "There is a problem with the Grant."

Pablo leaned back in his chair, "You said there were no problems with the grant."

"There wasn't . . . until your father's sudden death."

Pablo eyed him, a hint of caution in his tone, "And that is?"

"Your father did not leave a will naming you as heir to the Grant, the property. Under U.S. law it does not automatically pass down to you."

All faces in the room registered alarm. Pablo leaned forward in his chair, "What do you mean?"

"Sebastian was the heir to the Grant from his father. Spain, and then Mexico, recognized that the eldest or last living son inherits on death of his father. The United States does not recognize that rule. The U.S. government requires that a will stating the heir, and what is passed on to that heir, be written and retained by an attorney. Your father never made a will."

"You are saying the Ruiz grant is not mine?"

Beckett shook his head, "It reverts back to the United States upon the death of Sebastian."

Pablo's eyes flickered back and forth as he tried to understand. "How could my father inherit from his father and not me from mine?"

"Who owned this country when your grandfather died?"

Pablo sagged a bit in his chair, "Mexico."

"Who recognized the inheritance rule."

Pablo sat speechless.

Angelina asked, "Why did my father not make a will. Did you not advise him?"

"Oh, I did, many times. He thought it was unnecessary. He was old school and believed in the inherent right of succession from father-to-son. I tried to explain that the United States required a will. He said he would think on it. He didn't expect to die as he did."

Angelina sighed, "Yes, my father could be stubborn at times."

Pablo looked at Beckett confused and repeated, "But, you said all was well with the Grant."

"At the time I told you that it was. There were no issues of ownership as long as Sebastian was alive. None of us expected him to be suddenly murdered."

"So, the Grant, the hacienda, belongs to the United States Government now?"

Beckett nodded, "Yes."

"What becomes of my people who work here? Many of them have had no other home. They would have nowhere to go."

Beckett shook his head, "I don't know."

"What will happen with the property now?" Jean asked.

Beckett turned his attention to Jean, "The government is anxious to take control of these old grants so they can open the land to settlement and sell the tracts off."

"Then, it could be bought back from the government right?"

Beckett pondered on the idea. He slowly nodded his head, "That is possible."

Pablo's face showed a ray of hope. "Can you find out and let me know?"

"Yes. Yes, I can do that. I will make inquiries, I have government connections."

"You know what my bank accounts look like, if I can purchase the hacienda back I will. Please start the procedure, I will pay it."

Encouraged, Beckett said, "I will head back to Taos right now and begin my inquiries." He hesitated and then asked Pablo, "Do you know who murdered your father?"

"I have a pretty good idea."

"Who is it?"

"The Taggard outlaw family."

"Milo Taggard, yes, his name is being cast about quite a bit. Would you like me to start legal procedures against him or inform the law?"

Pablo shook his head, "We will deal with Milo Taggard."

Beckett's jaw slacked as he took in the meaning of Pablo's statement. He looked into Jean and Henry's faces seeing the accepting expressions of what Pablo meant. "In that case, I don't think I should hear anymore. I will be working on your case."

Pablo stood up and shook the attorney's hand, "Thank you, Mr. Beckett."

"I only hope I can find a way to save the hacienda for you."

"I have faith in you Mr. Beckett, thank you."

Pablo walked with Beckett out to the patio. Seeing Jesus, Pablo waved him over. Jesus came on the run. "Jesus, please bring Mr. Beckett's horse."

"*Si patron*," the boy ran off toward the barn.

Beckett glanced at Pablo, "These people love you as they loved your father."

"They are my people," Pablo responded, "I must do all I can to keep them in their homes."

"I will do all I can as well."

Jesus walked quickly toward them leading the horse Beckett had ridden in on. "He is fed and brushed," Jesus said as he handed the reins to Beckett. Beckett thanked the boy and mounted. "I will be in touch." He nudged the horse with his heels and rode out of the yard.

The evening dinner was small and somber. Teresa had refused to let her *patron* and his guests go hungry. Pablo told her to make it a simple meal and then go be with her family.

The news of the government's future actions on the grant filled all their minds. Padre Flores studied the silent group, he knew there was grief, yet this was much more. "It was good to see how the people loved Don Sebastian," he said it more as an opening than a statement.

Pablo looked over at the priest who sat in the honored seat to his right. "Yes, Pablo, he was greatly loved." He fell silent again.

Knowing that directness was the best approach to men like Pablo he asked, "I sense a problem beyond the expected grief. Would you care to tell me Pablo?"

Pablo lifted his eyes and looked into the open, honest face of Padre Flores. He paused for several seconds and then related all Beckett had told them.

Flores nodded his head, "I see. It is a desperate situation, however, you say there is a chance to buy the hacienda back."

"Yes, it is our hope."

"Then, you must not lose that hope. If there is a chance, then there is a chance, which is far better than no chance at all."

Pablo's downcast expression lifted into a slight smile, the padre had put it so simply. There was a chance and in there lay hope. "You are right Padre, I must look to the chance and the hope it offers and not give in to fear."

Flores smiled, "And, I know you Pablo, there is no fear in you."

Angelina joined in, "Pablo, we must wait and see what Mr. Beckett tells us before we lose hope."

"We will make something work," Henry said, his tone reflecting confidence.

"You have friends," Jean added. "You don't have to shoulder this alone. We will find a way to save the hacienda."

Pablo cast his eyes over all of them, "Forgive me, in my distress I failed to remember my good friends and family."

Flores fixed an eye on Pablo, "Now, there is something I wish to discuss with you." He glanced toward Marcus and Alicia sitting quietly beside Angelina. "Perhaps it would be best if the children went out to play."

Angelina understood and excused the children who did not hesitate to escape the dull adult conversation on matters in which they had no understanding.

With the fading sound of running feet Flores looked at Pablo. "What do you plan to do about the men who murdered your father and Juan?"

Pablo did not hesitate or shift nervously in his chair. "I intend to hunt them down."

"And kill them?"

"Yes."

"I cannot condone such an action Pablo."

"I know that you cannot and I do not ask you to. However, I will not let murderers like the Taggards roam free laughing at what they have done or to kill again. I will put an end to their evil."

"One evil cannot cancel out another evil."

"I do not see bringing justice down on the heads of these murderers as evil."

"Revenge is my mine, says the Lord."

"Excuse my directness Padre, and meaning no disrespect to God, but the Lord did not live in the New Mexico Territory where outlaws and murderers are free to run and commit their crimes unchecked and unchallenged except for the men who step forward to stop them.

"The Holy Book also tells that Goliath mocked God's army and killed all who came against him. Goliath was a murderer and proud of it. God sent David against him and David killed Goliath and God honored David for bringing justice against His enemy. Milo Taggard has mocked and murdered my family. Is it so different?"

"What of the local law then? Should they not deal with these men?"

"There is no law in Colfax County, Padre. Elizabethtown and Cimarron are nests of criminals, and the only law is corrupt and on the side of the criminals. Who then is to bring my father's murderers to justice if not me?"

Flores listened patiently. He had been in this country all his life. He knew that hard, yet honest men, dealt with outlaws on their own terms. There was no effective law, he understood that. He also understood that men like the ones who killed Sebastian and Juan would never be brought to an accounting and would likely kill again.

"How much grief should these men be allowed to spread before they are stopped?" Pablo asked. "How many widows, how many orphans will they be allowed to create before they are stopped? You have met our little Jesus, he was such an orphan. Papa found him hiding with his murdered parents, murdered by *banditos* for the few coins and horses they had. Papa brought him here and gave him a home. I am sorry Padre, but I will not let the Taggards go free."

Flores nodded, "Yes, I know. In this land it is a very fine line good men must walk. What is right and what is wrong. When do men take God's right into their own hands because it is the only way to protect the innocent?"

"If I may," Catherine said softly.

Flores turned his attention to her, "Please *señora* Pelletier, go ahead."

"My father was a Methodist minister; he and I came west together from Tennessee. He felt a calling to work among the Indians and white settlers. I too held to the belief that all justice belonged in the hands of the law or God. This was long before the war and there was law and order in that part of the country.

"Upon arriving in the west it was a shocking revelation for me to see how different it all was. There was no law, no ordered society, no one to turn to when men killed or robbed. I saw how the good men rose up against the bad and carried out their own justice. I came to understand that it was the only way, as some men left to their own devices, with no checks or balances, no laws to control their behavior, became animals and committed all manner of horrible crimes. There had to be control where no official control existed.

"I believe the greatest lesson I learned in the frontier was that evil will perpetuate itself until no one is safe if good men do not stand against it. When good men stand idly by doing nothing, evil will thrive. This is the same situation here. How long do good men of the New Mexico Territory stand by while men like the Taggards boldly murder at will?"

With a smile Flores nodded toward Catherine, "Well put *señora* Pelletier. As I said, good men here walk a fine line. It is true, good men must stand against evil and sometimes to the point of breaking the Commandments. I am not a naïve babe in the desert. I do understand the hardness of this country as I understand its unwritten laws. As a priest I am obliged to speak against such actions. As a man I know what must be done."

"And what is that, Padre?" Pablo asked.

Flores looked Pablo in the eyes, "You must stop these men before they kill again."

CHAPTER SEVEN

Throughout the week Jenny heard nothing from the school board which consisted mostly of new immigrants who had school age children. The children of the original residents were grown and gone. Alice Evans and a few others took part for the benefit of the town's future. The control lay in the hands of the eastern transplants. The majority of those saw the Pelletier family as ruffians who lived with savages.

Afraid of what she might see or hear Jenny had not gone into the town proper since the stories began. Her life consisted of walking to school with Jeb as escort and returning home immediately after the children were dismissed, once again with Jeb at her side. She neither saw nor heard any more from Alex Cassidy.

Jenny still suffered with fear and anxiety over the gossip and its result on her life. She couldn't stay isolated forever as she enjoyed the company of others, yet the haughty looks she received from the women and the leers from men were too much for her to endure. It was a week filled with relief in not encountering Cassidy again, but also one filled with pain and worry.

Jeb had continued his work in the town and county. He overheard comments in regards to Jenny and received cold shoulders from women and nervous greetings from men. Not one for towns to begin with, he was quickly becoming fed up with the place. He also kept his eyes and ears open for Alex Cassidy, but there was no further sign of him. He had done his damage and departed much to Jeb's frustration. He wanted to confront the man.

He had spoken often with Ben Evans and George Mason during the week. They had heard the talk as well. Not caring if it was true or not they remained his friends and treated him and Jenny as such. He had asked Ben why it should matter so much to everyone anyway. Ben could only shake his head and say he didn't understand it either. To men like them it was about the kind of person you were today, not yesterday, and rumors carried no weight with them.

Easterners judged by a set of standards heavily weighed on social standing, which were generally double standards depending on who the subject was. An action overlooked in one person because of an elite social standing was grounds for persecution for another of a different social status.

The lid blew off Jeb's internal powder keg at the end of the week. Friday night Jeb had escorted Jenny home. After supper, Jenny discovered that she had left some things in the school and asked Jeb to walk her back. As they approached the school building they could see light shining out of the windows.

Jenny stopped and clung tighter to Jeb's arm. "The board is having a meeting," she whispered.

Jeb scowled, "Haven't you always attended their meetings?"

Jenny nodded, "I update them on the school's progress and the needs."

"Then there's only one reason for them to be holding a meeting without you."

Jenny wiped a tear from her eye, "Because it is about me."

"Let's find out," Jeb began to step forward.

Jenny pulled back on his arm, "No, I don't want to go in there."

"We won't . . . not yet."

They walked a safe distance out to the side of the building to where they could see in the windows without being seen. There were a large number of people in the seats. Peter Anderson, the board's president, was standing in front of the people appearing very animated as if in heated argument.

Jenny whispered to Jeb in a voice choked with tears, "Take me home."

Jeb's temper could stand no more. He walked Jenny home and once inside the safety of their small house she broke down in tears again. Jeb helped her sit down in a kitchen chair.

Jeb hunkered down in front of her, "Jenny, you have to pull yourself together. You have been in fear and tears all week over these lousy people. Letting them control your life is not how you or we want to live."

Jenny looked in his face and sniffed, "You're right." Her eyes searched his, "I don't want to live here anymore, Jeb."

"I don't either. I was raised up in the canyon and never cared much for towns. Taking the deputy job forced me down here, but to be completely honest with you I hate it here. I'm tired of the sniveling complaints, arguing farmers, and being crowded in."

"Would we go back to the canyon, to Pa and Ma?"

Jeb shook his head, "We need to leave Colorado behind and make our own home. Remember when Ian and Anne came down for that visit and Ian said that if I ever got tired of wearing the badge he could sure use my help in building up their ranch?"

"You want to go to Wyoming?"

"Yes. People in Wyoming look at folks differently, they don't care what happened in your past, they look to see what you can do now. You and Anne got along wonderfully I thought."

Jenny passed a hand over her face wiping away the tears, "Yes, we got along very well, and now she has the baby and I am sure could use some help."

"Yes, I'm sure she could. Owl has moved up with Ian, and Will and Pete go up to help, but their antics drive Ian nuts. Ian and me are more the same temperament and he treats you like his kid sister."

Jenny smiled, "I would like that. I would like that very much."

"Besides, it can only be a matter of time before Sweetwater County needs a school teacher."

"Yes, that is a possibility. When would we go?"

"Tomorrow. I'll take you up to Andrew's. We'll go horseback and I'll come back with him and a wagon to get our things."

"What about the house, everyone put so much work into it, what will your Pa and Ma say?"

"Pa would say exactly what I'm saying, he doesn't put up with anything from these people. Ma would be down here in a heartbeat giving these women what-for. Pa owns the house; he can always sell it to one of these new people."

Jenny's whole countenance turned happy and refreshed. "Thank you Jeb, for doing this for me."

Jeb gave her a teasing smile and winked, "I'm doing it for me too. I've had a belly full of this place."

Jeb stood up, "Why don't you start packing."

Jenny gave him a concerned look, "Where are you going?"

"To do what Andrew, Ian, or Pa would do. I'm going to crash that meeting and give that outfit a double piece of my mind." Leaving Jenny sitting in the chair he turned and walked out the door.

Jeb paused outside the school doors and listened. The voices were loud with occasional angry outbursts. He heard references to 'that woman' and other derogatory remarks concerning the un-named 'woman' who he was certain was Jenny. Peter Anderson's voice, along with Alice Evans', shouted in response. He pulled open the doors and the voices ceased with the turning of their heads to look at who had come in. The room turned quiet as the church.

Jeb looked over the gaping expressions of the seated men and women. There were far more in attendance than the board members. There were few in the room that had been in the county longer than two years. Alice and one or two others were the only faces ranked among the original Camp Collins settlers.

Jeb cast an angry glare over the crowd who continued to stare silently at him. "Well, I see the gossips of the county have assembled for the condemnation meeting. I'm surprised you don't all have hoods over your heads to hide your cowardly faces."

A skinny man in a suit began to shout at him, "Now, see here . . ."

Jeb barked at him, "Shut up...or I'll shut you up!"

The man's jaw snapped shut like a steel trap. He sat meekly back down.

"Look at you pathetic wretches, a lynch mob for a twenty-one year old girl who never did one of you a lick of harm. *Pathetic*, you're all a pathetic collection of spineless worms."

Jeb looked at Peter and then Alice, "With the exception of a couple of you who I heard defending Jenny." He cast his withering glare over the group again, "Yes, that's right, Jenny, *that woman* has a name. You have all been fed a pack of lies and being from the east where lies are taken as truth you eat them up and spit them back out as truth."

"I have the *facts* from a reliable source," one woman haughtily croaked.

"Name your reliable source?" Jeb demanded.

"Oh, well, well . . . I'd rather not say."

Jeb snorted, "You'd rather not say, how convenient."

"Let me tell you something about your *reliable* source. His name is Alex Cassidy, he is a professional killer for hire, a murderer and general degradation to the world."

"Why would he say such things if they were not true?" a man challenged.

Jeb looked the man square in the eyes, "Because she refused his advancements. He tried to molest her in this very room and she fought back driving him away. He's getting even by telling lies about her."

A general gasp passed over the assembled. "I told you people there was no truth to the rumors," Peter Anderson snapped at the crowd.

"It doesn't matter," a rotund short woman beamed triumphantly. "We have voted."

"On what?" Jeb snapped at her.

"We have voted that little trollop out. I won't have my little Sydney taught by such a woman."

Alice Evans shouted at the woman, "You disgusting *cow*, how dare you call that sweet girl a trollop. Did you not hear what Mr. Pelletier just said?"

The rotund woman's face turned red with rage as she glared at Alice who never slackened her own angry stare.

"Enough!" Anderson shouted out.

The room turned silent, yet the heated glares and tempers remained. He looked at Jeb, "I have fought for Jennifer, as has Mrs. Evans, and a couple others."

"But, it's out of your hands. I understand," Jeb finished Anderson's sentence.

Anderson nodded with pained resignation, "I'm sorry, it seems I have been outvoted and . . ." He cast an angry eye on the fat woman, "Outweighed on the matter."

The woman began to respond to the insult, but Anderson cut her off, "Oh, shut up, I've heard enough from you for tonight, for a lifetime actually."

"It doesn't matter," Jeb said to him, "we'll be leaving town in the morning."

Peter Anderson's face fell. Alice Evans' mouth dropped open in surprise.

"My folks came into this country when there was nothing here except prairie, buffalo, and the Utes. We watched this town start out as a makeshift army camp, to a fort, to a town, a good town with good people," he looked directly at Alice when said the last part. He turned his eyes back on the group with a scowl, "Now, I don't even recognize it." He turned and walked out the door.

Paul Lander was opening his office in the Grout Building the next morning when Jeb walked up to him. Paul smiled at him, "Morning Jeb."

Paul pushed the door open and walked to his desk. Jeb followed him. When Paul turned around Jeb was holding his badge out to him. Paul looked startled, "What's this?"

"My badge, I'm done."

"Why?"

Jeb told him what happened at the meeting and concluded with, "Jenny wants out of this town and, nothing personal Paul, but I do too."

Paul sighed with disgust, "I hate to lose you."

"We're still family, you lost a deputy, not a friend."

Paul sat back against the desk with his legs stretched out in front of him. "I can't say I haven't thought of the same thing more than once myself with the way Two Moons gets treated around here."

"Then leave," Jeb said point blank.

"Nathan offered me a position with his office, but I can't see where Denver would be any better for her, likely worse. Besides, I'd have to be gone for weeks at a time and Two Moons left alone. That's not what I want."

"We're going to Wyoming, to Ian's. He wanted me to come up and help him rebuild the ranch. Jenny wants to go too."

"Can't say I blame her with all that's been said about her. Whether it's dispelled or not that kind of talk will always hang a cloud over her head if she stays here."

"That's what I figure. Break completely away is what's best."

Paul was silent in thought for several seconds, "Cattle, huh?"

"It's the future of the west."

"When my term is up in November I might give Wyoming some serious thought."

"We'll be there." Jeb put out his hand to Paul who took it heartily. "I'm taking Jenny up to Andrew's and coming later for our things."

"I'll get ahold of Clint and we'll give you a hand."

"Thanks. Watch for me tomorrow some time."

Ben Evans suddenly appeared in the doorway, "I thought I heard you two down here." He looked at the badge in Paul's hand and frowned. "Alice told me about the meeting last night and that you and Jenny were leaving."

"You heard right, Ben."

Ben shook his head, "I don't know what to say. How can I tell you to stay when so much ugliness has been directed at Jenny?"

"There are still some good people in this town. All the old timers and even some of the new folks are decent and will fit into the country. It's the others that make it intolerable."

"You're right there. We started with a little store outside of Camp Collins and eventually expanded it to what we have today. The town is growing, however, one of the drawbacks to growth is an influx of unsavory people and you will find that anywhere."

Jeb agreed, "Yes, you will. In a big city they can be absorbed, but in a small town they stand out too large. Bad talk and gossip can be ignored in a bigger town, but in a small town talk like what has been heaped on Jenny can't be. It'll constantly float to the top like grease on water."

Ben nodded, "Unfortunately that is true. What I don't understand is where this all started from? Alice said you made reference to a man, a known murderer, who attempted advances on Jenny. Is he the one who started all this and where did he come up with those kinds of ideas?"

Jeb felt that Ben and Alice deserved to know the background behind Jenny's confrontation with Cassidy. "Ben, close the door."

Ben stepped back and closed the door and then looked at Jeb.

Jeb began at the beginning, of Sarah and the women being kidnapped and finding Jenny a prisoner at Madam Min's. How she was beaten when she tried to escape and kept in fear for her life. He told of Andrew's recue and adopting her, Mrs. Kelly's taking her in, and Jenny's struggles with fears and sense of worthlessness. He finished by telling how she had finally come out of it and was enjoying her life here and teaching."

"My Lord," Ben whispered, "that poor girl. And then this has to happen."

"Outside of the family, Paul, and Mrs. Kelly you are the only other one to know and I want it kept that way."

"Of course. I can tell Alice though, can't I?"

"Yes, Alice would understand."

"Where does this Cassidy character fit into all this?"

"He was the enforcer at the house. He tracked down the girls who escaped and killed them. Jenny told me of one girl who Cassidy cut to pieces with a knife."

Ben was appalled, "This animal is in our town now?"

"I don't know. I've been on the lookout for him. He tried to attack Jenny and told her if she didn't give in to him he would tell everyone she had been a Denver sporting girl. She busted a pointer stick across his face and he made good with his promise to ruin her."

"And all these fools are attacking Jenny based on this monster's lies."

"That's the sum of it."

Ben shook his head with disgust, "I will have Paul arrest him if he shows up."

"We already discussed that. There is nothing to charge him with. There are no laws against lying."

"We could charge him with slander at least."

"That would require a hearing and . . ."

"And, open up Jenny's tragic experience to the gossips in this town," Ben concluded.

"I intend to take care of Cassidy," Jeb said without emotion.

Ben stared at him.

Jeb met his eyes, "What would you do in my place?"

"The same thing I told you to do with the Confederate renegades."

———————

Jeb went to the livery where he kept his two horses. He began to saddle the first one when Reed walked up to him wearing his leather blacksmith's apron. "Heard you told them pilgrims off but good last night."

Jeb smiled, "I let 'em know what they were."

"It's intolerable what they're saying about Jenny, but what can you expect out of folks from back east."

Jeb pulled the cinch on his saddle, "Not much."

Reed watched as Jeb threw his other saddle on the second horse. "Leaving town?"

"Yup. Taking Jenny up to my brother's and then coming back for our things."

Reed pushed the chew of tobacco to the opposite cheek with his tongue. "What about Alex Cassidy?"

"Haven't forgotten about him, he's not been around."

"He will be. Want I should keep my ear to the ground for him?"

"Yeah."

"Likely hanging with the Pruitt crowd, I'll poke my nose in there once in a while."

"Thanks Reed, I'd appreciate that."

Jeb stepped into the saddle, Reed handed him the reins to the second horse. "After you kill Cassidy where do you figure to light?"

"Wyoming, Ian's ranch."

Reed chuckled, "Lord a'mighty, the two of you in the same place. I heard what Ian and your brothers did to that fella up in Sweetwater. Never seen a town blowed up before."

Jeb grinned at Reed, "Ian's full of surprises."

"Not really, just figure the most direct way to get something done and you'll find Ian."

"That you will. See you later Reed." Jeb rode out of the barn.

Jeb tied the horses in front of his house and went inside to find Jenny dressed in a riding skirt and putting some of her clothes in a large carpet bag. "Got what you need in there?" He asked.

"For a few days, until we get the rest of our things up to Pa's."

Jeb studied her, "You doing alright?"

Jenny nodded as she folded her last dress and laid it carefully in the bag. "I'm sad that it is ending this way. The Evans and Mrs. Kelly are my friends, among others, and I will miss them. I will miss teaching, I did enjoy that. I won't miss a lot of other things though."

A knock sounded on the door. Jeb walked to it and opened the door to see Mrs. Kelly standing there. "Mrs. Kelly, please come in."

Jenny walked out of the bedroom with her bag.

Mrs. Kelly looked sad, "You weren't thinkin' of leavin' without sayin' goodbye were yuh now?"

Jenny's expression was sad, "I am sorry. I guess I forgot in all the trouble."

The old Irish woman embraced Jenny tightly, "It's okay, darlin' I understand. I wish you all the best and I will miss you. Will you come and visit me?"

Jenny returned the embrace, "I will, I promise."

Mrs. Kelly stepped back and set her jaw in an angry clench. "I'll be hauntin' some of our fine hypocrites at church tomorrow mornin'. I heard about the meetin' last night from Alice. I've some words for a certain woman and she's sure to choke on 'em too."

Jenny smiled at her, but didn't respond.

Mrs. Kelly looked up at Jeb, "You take care of my little colleen you hear, Mr. Pelletier."

"I will, always."

"Well, I'd best be gettin' out of your way." She turned for the door and then spoke over her shoulder, "And I'll be listenin' for the obituary on that snake Cassidy, Mr. Pelletier. You do what's needful here."

"I'm not finished with him," Jeb answered.

"I certainly hope not." Mrs. Kelly strolled down the street back to her boarding house.

CHAPTER EIGHT

Jeb and Jenny rode into the Pelletier yard of the main house with its beaten trails that led to the houses of the family members. With his parents in New Mexico, Jeb chose to go directly to Andrew's house and followed the trail to the home. They pulled the horses to a stop in front of the house. Jeb had rigged Jenny's bag on the cantle of her saddle so she could lean back against it when she got tired. He dismounted and lifted Jenny off the saddle as she could not swing her leg over the bag.

Sarah and Rebecca opened the door and walked out to greet them. Rebecca threw her arms around her adopted sister and they embraced. Little Jennie, ran out of the house and wrapped her seven year old arms around Jenny's waist. Jenny stroked her dark hair and told her how big she was getting.

Sarah smiled at Jeb, "What is the occasion for the visit?"

"We left Fort Collins."

Sarah's smiled slowly vanished, "What happened?"

"Jenny, I'm sure, would prefer to tell you herself."

Sarah turned her attention to Jenny. Jenny, with her arm around little Jennie's shoulders, replied, "There is a lot to tell."

Jeb looked around, "Where's Andrew?"

As Sarah looked back at Jeb she said, "He and Tom are at the barn, one of the mares is having a difficult birth."

Jeb untied Jenny's bag and handed it to her. "I'll be back."

He mounted and rode down to the barn leading Jenny's horse. There he tied the horses to the corral adjacent to the barn and walked around to the open door. In the big birthing stall fresh meadow hay had been laid down and the Palouse mare was lying on her side. Tom and Red Horse were holding the mare's head and talking gently to her. Andrew had his hands up inside the mare's birth canal and Jacque was kneeling beside him ready to lend a hand.

Andrew was breathing hard as he spoke to Jacque, "It's not breached, but its head is turned funny. I think the cord's around it." He continued to talk to himself as he worked. "Muzzle, neck, come on Andrew figure it out. There!" he said in a satisfied gasp.

Andrew pulled the nose of the foal out of the birth canal. The mare pushed from within and the foal slid out into Andrew's lap, placenta and all. Andrew quickly wiped the mucus out of the foal's mouth and watched for the long legged little horse to breathe. The foal sucked in a breath and let it out.

Tom let go of the mare allowing her to lift up her head to look back at her baby. Andrew moved the foal up next to the mare's head. The mare sniffed the newborn and began to lick it clean. The men all congratulated each other on the successful birth.

"It's a stud," Andrew said. "We needed a new one for the batch of fillies."

Red Horse looked up to see Jeb watching them. "Look who gets here when the work is all finished."

Jeb grinned as Tom smiled at him and Andrew turned around to him. "I know how to time it," Jeb answered.

Andrew stood up flinging the clinging mucus off his hands and examining the wet mess of his clothes. "I'd shake hands Jeb, but . . ." he held up his dripping hands.

"That's all right, I know you love me," Jeb said in a joking tone.

"Guess I should get cleaned up."

Jeb cringed, "I wouldn't try the house though; Sarah will run you out with a shotgun."

"Think so?"

"Know so. You might want to jump in the river."

Andrew nodded, "Probably safer than dripping this all over Sarah's clean floor."

Tom laughed, "Yeah, Ma would kill you if you got that on her floor. Then you'd have to listen to Becky nag you about it."

"Tom, you know she doesn't like to be called Becky," Andrew said with a hint of sarcasm.

Tom grinned, "Yeah, I know."

Andrew looked at Jeb, "See what I put up with."

They all watched as the mare stood up and the spindly legged colt tried his legs.

Falling with his first two attempts, he managed to stay up on the third try with his skinny legs spread wide apart and trembling. The mare continued to clean and groom him.

Andrew closed the stall gate leaving the mother and her new colt alone. The men walked out of the barn. "Just come up for a visit?"

Andrew asked.

"We left Fort Collins."

Andrew looked at him with surprise. "You quit your job?"

"Yeah."

"Jenny's not teaching school?"

"Not anymore."

"What happened?"

Jeb lifted his chin toward Andrew's slimy self, "You don't want that to dry on you."

Andrew turned to his son, "Tom, will you ride to the house and get me some clean clothes."

"Sure, Pa." Tom ran for his horse.

Jeb watched Tom jump into the saddle and hit the trail at a gallop. "Turning into one heck of a horseman ain't he?"

Andrew's face reflected the pride he held in his son, "Turned sixteen this year. He's a man and I treat him like one."

The four men walked to the river. "What's going on?" Andrew asked.

Jeb told him the full accounting of Cassidy and the town gossip about Jenny. He related his clash with the people at the meeting and the result of the meeting was Jenny being fired.

Andrew's face turned dark with anger as he listened.

Jeb concluded, "This morning I quit and we rode up here. Figure to stay in the folks' house for a bit and then head on up to Ian's. He wanted me to help him with the ranch."

"Will and Pete are up at Ian's right now lending a hand, and Owl moved up there permanently."

Jeb nodded as an acknowledgement.

"Moving to Ian's? Is that what Jenny wants too?"

"Yes. She wants out of that town, and she and Anne are friends. So, it will be a good change for her."

Andrew accepted that. "A clean break, under the circumstances, is probably the best course of action to protect her."

"That's how I feel. That sort of talk would hang over her head forever."

Andrew looked disgusted, "It would too. Who all stuck up for Jenny?"

"Ben and Alice, Mrs. Kelly, Reed Hall, a few others. It was all those lousy easterners who turned on her."

Andrew frowned, "I don't care much for them at all."

"So, it is not only Indians they hate," Red Horse commented.

Jeb shook his head, "No. It's anyone they decide not to like based on some stupid eastern standard that I don't understand or care to understand."

"What about this Cassidy?" Andrew asked.

"What about him?" Jeb responded with an icy tone.

"What are you going to do about him?"

"What do you think? I'm going to kill him. He tried to rape my wife, no man lives after trying that."

"If you don't I will."

"Stand in line big brother, I've got him first."

The pounding of Tom's galloping horse was heard before he was seen. Riding up to the group he pulled the horse to a sliding stop. "Take it easy on him," Andrew chastised.

"Sorry, Pa." He handed Andrew a roll of clothes. "Jenny's up at the house and she's crying and the whole bunch of them females are blubbering. What happened?"

"Show some respect for your mother, you're not to refer to her as a 'female'."

"Yes sir. What happened?"

Andrew gave his son a quick version of the story.

Tom listened and then said, "That makes sense as to why the women are all upset. What about Cassidy? You can't let him just get away with this."

"He's not getting away with anything," Andrew answered.

Tom looked at Jeb, "You going to shoot him?"

Jeb glanced at Andrew, "Apple doesn't fall far from the Pelletier tree does it?"

"You expect it not to?"

"I hope I never see the day when it doesn't." Jeb turned his face to Tom, "Cassidy took off, but Reed Hall is keeping an eye out for him. I'll deal with him."

"What now?" Andrew asked.

"I figured to get the ranch wagon and head back down in the morning to pack our things out of the house. There's not all that much, Paul said he'd get Clint and lend a hand."

"Pa and Ma took the ranch wagon, but we can use ours. Tom and I will go along and give you a hand. Besides, I might see some people I want to have a word with."

"I will ride along as well," Red Horse volunteered. "You might get into a fight and I would hate to miss it."

Jeb smiled, "Shouldn't take too long with all this help."

Andrew held his arms up, "Well, I'd like to stay and visit and all, but this stuff's starting to dry on me and I need to go jump in the river. I'll see you back up at the house."

Jacque and Red Horse went to their cabin while Jeb and Tom returned to Andrew's house.

The next morning Andrew drove the wagon while Jeb, Tom, and Red Horse rode alongside. It was mid-morning when they reached the little house Jeb and Jenny had occupied. They had drawn curious looks from the townspeople as they passed through to the far end where the house sat.

Setting the brake on the wagon, Andrew stepped down as the others dismounted. They went into the house and looked it over deciding how best to load. There wasn't much; a few chairs, a table, the bed and Jenny's kitchen. A clothes chest and a few wooden boxes of assorted items completed the contents of the house.

Paul stuck his head in the open door, "Okay, Clint and I are here. Where do we start?"

The men came together in the front room for a bit of conversation before beginning the work. Clint cast his eyes around the house, "I guess you found out about the talk against Jenny. That's what I was going to tell you that day you got the telegram and rushed off."

Jeb apologized, "I'm sorry about that. I was half way up the canyon when I remembered you had something to talk to me about."

"Yeah, I had just busted the jaw of some dude who was talking bad about Jenny."

"Well, I appreciate that," Jeb grinned.

"No problem, I enjoyed it. There were two of them together. The one still conscious said the man he heard it from was Alex Cassidy."

"Jenny finally told me about him. He came into the school room and threatened her the first time. The second time he tried to attack her. She busted a stick across his face and jammed the pointed end into his throat."

Clint grinned, "Good for her."

Jeb nodded, "She put up a fight. He said he was going to tell everyone that she had been a Denver sporting girl. He made good on it." He made the last comment with disgust.

"Sounds like it. Alex Cassidy is scum, always has been."

"You know him?"

"I backed him down once in Denver. He's a hired gun and a fair-to-middlin' gunfighter. Bottom line is he's a killer and not particular about how he gets it done."

"You backed him down though," Paul remarked.

Clint grinned, "I said a fair gunfighter, not a good one."

Jeb considered what Clint had said, "He's not just a bully then."

"He is, but he's a killer."

"I'll keep that in mind."

The men set to work, in a couple of hours they had the wagon loaded and tied down. Jeb looked over the loaded wagon. "I sure appreciate all the help, let me stake you all to a meal at the café, it's the least I can do."

"I never pass up free food," Clint laughed.

The men walked into town aiming for the cafe. They ignored the unpleasant looks they received from the new residents and waved back with cheery hellos to old friends who greeted them. They walked into the café and sat down to the unpleasant looks of several patrons.

Aggie Ansel, the young waitress with red hair and freckled nose, walked to their table. Her father owned the lumber yard that was one of the original businesses in town. She and Jenny had become friends, even though Aggie was only sixteen. She smiled pleasantly at them all. "So, nice to see you all again." She gave an extra-long look and smile at Tom who smiled back at her.

The men all gave her a warm greeting. "What's the special today?" Jeb asked.

"Chicken pie and it's good."

"I'll bet it is." He looked at the others, "Chicken pie?"

The men all agreed. Jeb smiled at Aggie, "Chicken pie and coffee all around."

Aggie left the table and walked to the kitchen. A moment later she returned with a coffee pot and cups. As she poured the coffee she said to Jeb in a low voice, "I've heard the talk about Jenny; it's so vile and disgusting. I'm so sorry for her, she's my friend."

Jeb nodded, "It's been pretty hard on her. We're leaving Fort Collins and going to Wyoming."

Aggie sighed, "I'll miss Jenny, but I can't say I blame you. Pa says a lot of these new people are very unpleasant."

"Tell me about it," Jeb replied.

"If it helps, our family is on her side."

"It does help, thanks."

"Pa says there's no better folks in Larimer County than the Pelletiers." She glanced at Tom again, an action not missed by the others.

Andrew chuckled, "Not everyone thinks so."

"Oh, what do they know!?" Aggie left the table and returned to her work.

"She's a sweet kid," Paul said. Then he grinned at Tom, "Isn't she?"

Tom blushed red, "I guess so."

Clint leaned toward Tom, "I've noticed that the prettiest girls all seem to gravitate toward Pelletier men." He winked at the young man as his red deepened.

They ate and then made their way back out to the wagon and horses where they stood talking.

A man pulled his horse up in front of the group. He was wearing dirty clothes with long greasy hair hanging out from under his hole-riddled hat that was as dirty as the rest of him. They all looked up at him without a trace of friendliness. They could smell him from eight feet away.

The rider cast his bloodshot eyes over them, "Which one of you is the deputy? That Pelletier."

Jeb glared up at him, "I am, why?"

The man gave a cocky grin, "Got a message for you from Alex Cassidy."

"Then spit it out."

"He says you put out the word that you're huntin' him. Well, he's ready and waitin' for yuh at Pruitt's."

"I'm busy; tell him I'll be along when I'm good and ready."

The dirty man chuckled, "He said you'd turn yella and tuck yer tail."

With a quick move Jeb took a step and grabbed the man by his shirt front and jerked him out of the saddle. Next to where they stood was a horse trough filled with water. As Jeb pulled the startled man through the air he slammed him head first into the trough splashing water over him and out for four feet in all directions.

Jeb held the man's head under water as he flailed his arms and legs trying desperately to get free of the strong hands that were drowning him. The harder he struggled the more pressure Jeb put down on him.

People stopped on the boardwalk watching in horror. Those who knew the Pelletiers laughed and kept on walking. A man watching began to protest, "Say here, what are you doing to that man?"

Clint glared at the man, "Move along and mind your own business or you'll get the next bath."

The man gasped, "I'm getting the sheriff."

"He's already here," Paul spoke out.

The man and several others who had gathered were incensed that Paul was allowing this. "How can you condone this behavior?" the man said in a shaken voice.

"Because he asked for it. Now, move along like you were told."

"I'll be talking to the Commissioners about this," the man said as he scurried away.

Jeb finally jerked the outlaw back out of the water and flung him backwards. He landed flat on his back in the street gasping for breath and whimpering. "That's called a bath," Jeb said in a calm voice. "You should try one every year or so 'cause you smell like a gut wagon."

Breathing hard and gasping for air the man stared at Jeb with wild terrified eyes. He began to push himself across the dirt street getting closer to his horse.

"I said to tell that coyote Cassidy that I'd be along in my own good time. I'm busy right now. So, get along like a good little toady and tell him."

The man got to his feet shaking with fear and the exertion expended trying to free himself from drowning. With water dripping off his clothes and greasy hair he mounted his horse and rode away without looking back.

The newcomers were horrified at the violent scene that had played out in front of them. The old timers laughed knowing the man was one of the Pruitt trash. You didn't talk like that to a Pelletier and expect to walk away in one piece.

Jeb looked at Clint, "Guess, I'll go pay Cassidy a call."

"Not now." Clint held up his hand.

"He's a cheat when it comes to a gunfight, he won't play it square at all. He likes a hideaway gun; he gets you focused on talk or his right hand over his hip gun and then comes out with a smaller gun in his left. He sometimes uses a second who stands back and shoots you down while you're concentrating on him.

"Don't play into his game. You go now and I guarantee he will have a setup for you. You won't have a chance. You go in when he's least expecting you and take the fight right to him. He won't be set up and he'll have to fight straight."

"Can I take him?"

Clint nodded, "Oh, yeah, you're better 'n he is, just don't give him a hair of wiggle room."

Andrew protested, "Jeb's not a gunfighter."

Clint flicked his eyes over to Andrew, "Yes, he is." He read Andrew's questioning expression. "He's been my student for the past year. He can take Cassidy."

The Pelletiers parted company with Paul and Clint at the wagon and headed back up the canyon. Clint walked beside Paul toward his office, "You're likely to get an earful about that drowning business."

Paul shrugged, "Don't much care anymore."

"I didn't say you cared, just that you'd hear about it."

"It won't be the first time. Ben's been getting a bunch of complaints about me from the newcomers. He ignores them."

Clint grinned, "Sounds like Ben. You figure like me that Jeb will be back tonight for Cassidy?"

"Uh-huh."

"Guess I'll stick around town then. He might need someone watching his back. I know how Cassidy operates."

"If he sees us he won't want us to go along."

"Then, we can't let him see us."

Paul looked up and down the street. "He has to pass his old house to reach Pruitt's, it might be a good place to watch from. Meet me there just after dark."

"I'll be there."

Andrew pulled the wagon into the barn and began to unhitch the horses leaving the wagon loaded since Jeb and Jenny would be borrowing it for Wyoming in a few days. They tended to the horses and went into Andrew's house to the smell of supper cooking.

Jenny crossed the room from the kitchen and wrapped her arms around Jeb. He hugged her in return and gave her a kiss.

"Did everything go alright today?" she asked.

"Just fine. No problems."

They sat down to supper with all of them conversing on various topics. Tom kept glancing at Jeb thinking about how he had dealt with the dirty man in town. He marveled at how Jeb had handled him and how coolly he responded to the threat of Cassidy's challenge. He also considered what Clint had said about how Jeb should fight him. He had heard that Clint Rush was a gunfighter from Montana. If Jeb, being only six years older than him, could handle himself like that there was no reason he couldn't be that tough too.

After supper Jenny came into the sitting room where Andrew sat reading a book. "Pa, have you seen Jeb?"

Andrew put the book down, "No, I assumed you two were together."

"I haven't seen him since supper."

"Maybe he took a walk to think things over."

"He would have asked me to walk with him."

Tom overheard and went outside. He returned several minutes later. "Pa, Jeb's horse is gone."

Andrew cussed silently under his breath as he rose from his chair. Jenny looked at Tom, "Why would his horse be gone?"

Tom looked at Andrew uncertain if he should answer Jenny.

Jenny caught the look and began to get scared, "Pa, tell me."

Andrew met her eyes, "Cassidy is in town, he called Jeb out today."

Jenny sat down, her eyes reflecting the fear she felt, "I had hoped he would never come back. I knew Jeb would do this."

Andrew was up and moving. He grabbed his gun from the door peg and buckled it on. Putting on his hat and coat he hurried out the door.

Sarah walked up staring at the door. She looked over at Jenny sitting in the chair. "Where is Andrew going?"

Jenny only stared blankly into the room.

Tom answered, "Cassidy called Jeb out today and now he's gone.

Pa's going after him."

"Oh, no," Sarah's expression turned worried.

Tom put his hand on Jenny's head, "Don't worry sis, it's Jeb and Pa, and probably Paul will be there too. Jeb will be okay."

Jenny looked up at Tom, "You don't understand Tom, Cassidy is a professional killer, a gunfighter."

"So is Jeb."

Jenny gave Tom a curious look, "What do you mean?"

"Don't you know? Jeb's been working with Clint Rush for the last year learning to gunfight."

Jenny gaped at Tom, "He never told me."

Tom realized he might have said too much, but she needed reassurance that Jeb could handle this. Jeb was tough.

Sarah sat down next to Jenny and released a nervous sigh. "You know how our men are. You saw it in Denver. They will never back down when their wives and daughters are in danger. Yes, it is frightening, and we worry about them, but we can't change them . . . and, I don't think I want to. If they were not like they are, you and I and Rebecca would be dead by now or wishing we were. "

Jenny nodded, "I know, but I almost lost him once."

"What Jeb learned from Clint will keep him alive against someone like Cassidy."

"That's right," Tom put in. "Clint said Jeb could take him."

Jenny buried her face in her hands, "I just want this nightmare to end."

CHAPTER NINE

Every sound in the wooded mountainside surrounding the cabin made Marty Taggard jump. He knew that any minute the riders from the Ruiz ranch would pour down on them and shoot them to pieces. The ones that weren't shot dead would be hung. He knew that Mexican outfit was poison to rile and they had gone way past riling by killing the old man himself. It was like drawing the attention of a very big, very mean dog directly on you with a beef steak tied around your neck. The old man was too stupid and arrogant to see what a hornet's nest he had poked a stick into.

His brothers didn't care, they were just like the old man. Billy was at least dead, and he was the worst of the lot. He took satisfaction in knowing the brother that had bullied him and beat on him ever since he was little had his neck stretched. In secret he laughed to see Billy's blue face and snapped neck when their horses wandered back into the pasture carrying their grisly cargo.

Witnessing the shooting of the old Mexican boss and the other man scared him into the shakes. His old man had ordered them to go with him to kill the old Mexican. They all shot into the two men, but he couldn't do it. Instead he had shot over their heads, but fired enough shots so no one could say he didn't shoot too. He was scared of his brothers and the old man; if they thought he didn't shoot the men too they'd beat him half to death.

Now he had the Ruiz riders to fear. His life was made up of nothing but fear. He hated his life and wondered why fate had placed him in such a devilish existence.

Milo Taggard had been feeling pretty flush since the day they killed old Sebastian Ruiz. He drank whiskey non-stop and bragged about the shots he had made and then repeatedly made the boys account for each of their shots on the two men. They all boasted on how many times they had hit the greasers. Marty lied about where his shots struck.

Taggard took a pull from the bottle and chuckled, "I tell you what boys, it was pure-dee lucky comin' on them two pepperguts like that. Even the old cock of the walk hisself. Yes, sir-ee, pure-dee lucky. Showed them greasers to mess with Milo Taggard." He took a long drink and laughed.

Marty wondered if the bodies had been found yet. It was up on the mountain trail so it was possible they had not been found. It was also possible they would never figure out it was them who killed the two men. Marty shivered inside and thought that it was just as possible for cows to fly and his old man to be sober for five minutes.

He didn't hear any of the exchange between his brothers and the Ruiz men, but knowing what a big mouth Billy had he probably bragged about who they were. Billy was as stupid as he was mean. The more he thought about it the more he was convinced Billy had done just that. The best he could hope for was they would never find this place. He hoped a lot, but in reality had given up on hope many years ago.

Marty ventured a question to the old man using the same vernacular as the rest of them so they would not think he was of a different mind than them. "Do you think they found the old peppergut yet?"

Taggard's head swayed slightly from side-to-side as he tried to fix a glare on his youngest, and who he considered weakest, son. "Why, scared or something?"

"No, just wondering if they know yet what it cost 'em to kill my brothers."

The old man laughed, "I like that, 'what it cost 'em.' It cost 'em plenty that's for sure." He took another drink, finishing the bottle. He stared at the empty bottle and cursed throwing the bottle across the room where it bounced off the log wall with a hollow clunk.

He yelled out, "Jack, get me another bottle."

Jack, who was one up the line from Marty, ran for the shelf where the old man stored his whiskey. He cringed when he saw the shelf was devoid of bottles. He frantically searched for another. When the old man went without his liquor he got uglier and meaner.

Taggard cursed at Jack, "Well, what'd you do, take a Sunday stroll clear down to 'lizbethtown for it?"

"They ain't no more, Pa."

"*What!*" Taggard roared as he jumped from his chair and ran into the filthy, cluttered table lurching it three feet into the room spilling the covering of cans and trash onto the floor. Jack ducked out of the way as the old man stormed into the storage area. "You drank it up *Jack!*" he cursed the boy and tried to chase him. Jack stayed out of his reach.

Exhausted Taggard gave up chasing his son and flopped down on his bed. "Well, I need more," he shouted. "Who's got money?"

The boys all shook their heads.

"*No one's got money!*" he shouted louder. "Then, we need to stick someone up. Come on, you Ned. . . and Porky, you're comin' with me to rob some fool of his money and bangles and buy more whiskey."

He pointed with a wavering finger, "You, Booger and Jack, stay here and guard the cattle."

Baxter and Jack looked at each other and shook their heads. The old man always called them Booger and Jack whom they guessed was as close as his liquor soaked brain could get to Baxter's name.

Taggard stood up and half turned trying to find Marty. He pointed his finger at Marty, "You, lily liver, go back up the mountain and see if them greasers found the old buzzard yet. Now, you got me a-wonderin' 'bout it you little snot. Go on, get, and don't come back until you see for sure."

Taggard stumbled toward the door and shouted drunkenly, "We'll be at the snake pit." He banged into the side of the half opened door. Letting out a curse he slammed the door back and out of his way as he staggered out into the yard. "Saddle the horses, you little worm bellied maggots," he shouted at Ned and Porky.

Baxter looked at Marty and laughed, "Lily liver."

"I wouldn't talk, *Booger.*"

Baxter picked up a chunk of firewood and charged at Marty, "I'll teach you to smart mouth me."

Marty grabbed up an empty bottle from the floor and threw it at his unsuspecting brother hitting him squarely in the forehead. Baxter dropped the wood and cursed violently as he crumpled to the floor holding his hands over his forehead. Marty ran out the door to the sound of Jack howling with laughter behind him.

He quickly made his way to the dilapidated corral and his horse before Baxter got his senses back and came after him with a sixgun. The old man encouraged them to fight, but not to kill each other as he needed them to be the gang. Still, Baxter was a little off in the head and if angry enough might shoot him. Marty threw the blanket and saddle on his horse and pulled the cinch up tight. Hurriedly he jammed the bit in the horse's mouth and jumped into the saddle and kicked the horse into a gallop.

Once into the woods he slowed the horse down to a walk. His life was so miserable he wanted to cry, but that had been beat out of him years ago. It was at least a two hour ride to where they had ambushed the Mexicans. He would be free of his family for several hours at least. He thought about riding on forever, but wasn't sure where to go or what to do.

Old man Taggard slowly sobered as he rode toward the stage road between Elizabethtown and Cimarron. As the effects of the liquor left him he began to shake and shiver. Every once in a while he would swat at some non-existent creature in front of his face. He slunk down in the saddle growing surlier by the minute.

Ned and Porky glanced at each other knowing that as the liquor left the old man he'd start getting loco and seeing things. He'd been known to throw shots at his imaginary creatures. They hung back and watched him carefully.

The stage from Elizabethtown to Taos that took a dog leg course to Cimarron first, rattled down the road at them. The four horses were being held at a steady quick step. The stage carried two passengers and a strongbox containing several small sacks of gold dust from the Elizabethtown assayer to his bank in Taos.

Taggard stopped his horse at the side of the road, pulled his gun, and shot the driver. The driver fell from the steadily moving stage bouncing hard in the road. The shotgun guard was too busy grabbing for the reins to shoot. Ned shot the guard as the stage passed him causing the team to break into a gallop dragging the reins as they raced out of control.

Taggard watched with mounting rage as the stage tore down the road away from them. He rode over to Ned and punched him in the head knocking him out of the saddle. Ned hit the packed road with a cry of pain. "You stupid idiot," Taggard shouted at him. "We needed him to stop that stage, not send it into Texas."

In his defense Ned shouted back at him, "He wasn't going to stop. He'd just keep whuppin' them horses running away."

"It's gotta wreck, Pa," Porky said. "Let's follow it."

Taggard and Porky kicked their horses into a gallop after the stage leaving Ned in the road. Ned got to his feet rubbing his bruised shoulder and the knot growing on his head. He stepped back into the saddle and quickly followed them.

Another mile and they found the coach off the road and turned over. It lay on its side with wheels spinning in the air. The team was still running, dragging the broken shaft with them. Taggard stepped off his horse to look in the coach at the passengers. He threw the side door back and looked down into the coach. One appeared to be dead, the second was bloodied. The man lifted his hand toward Taggard, "Please help me."

Taggard drew his revolver and shot him. He yelled at Porky, "Get your lazy self over here and help me drag these dudes out."

Porky jumped down into the coach and hoisted the dead men up one at a time. Taggard pulled from the top while Porky pushed. Throwing the dead men down on the ground they quickly rifled through their pockets taking their money. Porky yanked a watch from the pocket of one of the men and held it up looking at it.

"What you gonna do with that?" Taggard growled at him.

"I like it, it's kinda purdy."

"You can't tell time anyway."

"Well, I want it," Porky insisted as he stuffed the watch into his pocket.

Ned had caught up and was searching around the wreck when he found the shotgun guard lying dead off the road. He searched his body and plucked his wallet. He was leaving the dead man when he found the iron box with a padlock on it. "Pa, over here."

Taggard walked over and looked at the strong box with a gleam in his eyes. "That's a money box. Get up on the road and watch for anybody comin' by. If you see somebody, kill 'em."

Taggard shot the lock off the box and threw back the heavy lid. "Whooeee!" he shouted, "there's a bunch a sacks in here." He grabbed one out and untied the string. Sticking his hand in the bag he pulled out a handful of fine gold mixed with small nuggets. "Pure gold!" he shouted.

He quickly grabbed the bags and shoved them in his saddlebags. He jumped on his horse and yelled at the boys, "Let's get drunk." He kicked the horse into a gallop with the boys following behind him.

———

Pablo led his party toward the place they had found the bodies of his father and Juan. Henry rode beside him while Jean, Cruz, and the two vaqueros who had been at the hanging rode in a scattered pattern in case there was another ambush on the trail. They began the ascent up the trail that led to Elizabethtown.

Before reaching the ambush site Pablo suddenly reined his horse to a stop and held up his hand. The party stopped and watched him as well as the country around them. Pablo and Henry were on a slight rise that allowed a view of the place they had found the bodies. Pablo leaned forward in the saddle peering intently ahead of him. "There's a rider down there," he whispered to Henry.

Henry turned in the saddle making gestures to those behind him that they were watching a man. The men slowly broke off to the right and left to surround the unknown man. Pablo and Henry nudged their horses off the rise and down toward the ambush site.

Marty Taggard was staring at the ground where he had last seen the bodies of the dead Mexicans. There were horse tracks and the twin lines of wagon wheels, the Ruiz outfit had found their dead leader. He needed to get out of there.

The sound of an iron horseshoe striking rock froze him in place. He was mounted and only needed to kick his horse to flee, but his fear wouldn't let him move. Then, he heard the unmistakable sound of brush scraping leather. Panic foamed up in his throat. He saw the first rider and then the next. The first one was a Mexican, the second a white man.

In an action, more of muscle response to danger than conscious thought, he jerked the reins around and kicked the horse. The horse jumped into a gallop.

Pablo dug his spurs into his horse's belly and yanked his reata free as the horse jumped into a gallop after the fleeing rider. Henry followed as the others broke from the brush and gave pursuit. The rider swerved in and out of the pines to try and lose his pursuer, yet Pablo stayed on him. As the rider broke into a clearing Pablo closed the gap to forty feet, spun a loop in the reata and sent forty of the sixty feet of braided rawhide toward the rider. The loop dropped over the man's head. Jerking back the slack he dallied the reata around the saddle horn and slammed the horse into a skidding stop.

The reata snapped tight suspending the shocked rider momentarily in the air as his horse continued to run out from under him. He crashed hard into the ground and bounced once.

Pablo coiled the reata as he rode toward the unconscious rider. He stepped out of the saddle and pulled the loop off the man. The others formed a circle around him while remaining horseback. Pablo rolled the limp man over on his back.

"He's just a kid," Henry remarked.

Cruz studied the face, "He looks like the ones we hung, same family."

Pablo looked at the face, "That would make him a Taggard. We will hang him."

"Wait," Jean called down to Pablo. "Maybe he can tell us where to find the others. Let him come to and we'll question him."

Pablo nodded, "Good idea."

Henry dismounted and hunkered down putting his hand on the kid's chest. "He's breathing. I have to wonder why he was over here." Henry removed the revolver from the kid's holster.

"Yes, that is odd," Pablo agreed.

Marty suddenly drew in a sharp breath that made him cry out in pain. He opened his eyes and stared up at the sky, he was having trouble comprehending where he was. As his shocked senses slowly returned, his eyes widened as he took in the unsmiling stern faces looking down at him.

"I see you are awake," Pablo said.

Panic filled Marty's eyes, "Please don't kill me, I didn't shoot no one, it was them."

"Them who?" Pablo asked.

"The old man and my brothers. They shot the old Mexican man and the other one. I didn't want to shoot 'em."

Henry helped Marty sit up, "You alright?"

Marty winced, "I hurt somethin' fierce."

"You took a pretty hard fall."

Marty stared up at Pablo's hard face, "Are you gonna hang me?"

"I am thinking about it. It depends."

Marty swallowed hard and coughed. "On what?"

"Are you a Taggard?"

"Yeah, I'm Marty."

"Your father Milo Taggard?"

"Uh-huh."

"I will tell you what Marty, you tell me everything I want to know about the death of my father and my friend and we will see whether we should hang you or not."

Henry handed Marty a canteen. Marty took a long drink and handed it back to him, his eyes reflecting confusion as to why this man was being nice to him. "I'll tell you whatever you want."

Pablo smiled, "Good. We might not hang you . . . yet."

"My old man told us that we had to kill your pa because of what your men did to Billy and the others."

"They were caught stealing my cattle," Pablo pointed out. "We hang people for that."

Marty nodded, "I know. I told him it was a bad idea to rustle from you folks. He just hit me and called me a coward. He's mean, just flat mean. He made us go and steal from you. My brothers didn't care; they're as bad as he is. I didn't want to do it.

"Then, after the hangin' he made us go with him to kill your pa. We rode over here to find him and found them comin' up the trail. We got off in the brush and they cut loose on 'em. I shot in the air. I never shot into 'em, I swear."

"Why did you do that?" Henry asked.

Marty looked up at Henry and shrugged, "It seemed wrong, and I was scared that when you found out what we'd done you'd come a-huntin' us. If I didn't shoot 'em maybe when you found us you wouldn't kill me too."

Pablo stared down on him, "Why should we believe that? You could be lying to save yourself."

Marty eyes still held fear as he stared into Pablo's cold expression. "I can't prove it, but I swear I didn't shoot, I didn't."

Jean asked, "Can you lead us to their cabin or hideout, whatever they have?"

"Yeah, I can. I can take you right there. Baxter and Jack are there now. Pa and Ned and Porky went down the road to rob someone 'cause Pa was out of whiskey and money."

Pablo snorted, "A charming family."

"They're scum," Marty said back.

Pablo looked surprised at the comment, "And you're not?"

"I don't want to be. I want out of there."

Pablo reached his hand down to Marty. Marty took it and Pablo pulled him up. "You help us and we will see what we do with you then."

"Sure, I'll do whatever you want."

"I want the cabin first. You will have to walk until we catch up to your horse." Pablo leaned closer into Marty's face, "If you try to run there are enough of us here to catch you and then I will just shoot you no questions asked, *comprendes*?"

Marty involuntarily pulled his head back from Pablo's fierce eyes. "Sure, I won't run."

Henry mounted back up and reached a hand down to Marty, "We won't make any time if you walk. Ride with me until we find your horse."

Marty reached up his hand, stepped into the stirrup Henry's foot had vacated for the purpose, and swung up behind him. "Why are you being so nice to me?" Marty asked.

"Because, I don't think you're as bad as the others. If you prove me wrong I'll shoot you fast enough, you can bank on that."

"I'm not."

"Well, you have a chance to prove it. Which way?"

"Just follow the trail, I'll tell you when to cut off."

Henry led the way as the others scattered out behind him, not trusting Marty very much or wanting to be easy targets should it be a trap.

Henry spoke back to Marty, "You do realize we intend to kill your brothers when we get to the cabin."

"I know. I don't care."

"I take it you don't like your family."

"Would you if you had a family like that?"

Henry shook his head. "Let's hope my original impression of you is right."

"It is. I don't want to hang for what they did."

CHAPTER TEN

Two hours passed before Marty pointed at a hair's width of a trail forking off into the pines and aspen. It could have easily been mistaken for a game trail. Henry pulled up with Marty still riding double. The others gathered in behind him.

Marty looked at them, "About a mile up this trail."

"Is this where you have been keeping my stolen cattle?" Pablo asked.

"Yeah, we bring them in from over there," Marty pointed to the west.

Henry spoke back to Marty, "Let me know before we get there so I don't ride right into their guns."

"I will."

They rode on for another half hour before Marty whispered to Henry, "It's close now, best stop here."

Marty slipped off the horse and looked up at the other men who still eyed him with untrusting suspicion. "It's up the trail a bit more, they can't see you from here."

"You said there were two in the cabin?" Jean asked.

"There was when I left earlier today. I doubt the old man and the other two will be back until tomorrow anyway."

Pablo looked at Marty, "Did these two in the cabin help kill my father?"

"They all did, except me."

Pablo stepped off his horse, "We are going to leave you here. I still do not trust you all that much."

Marty nodded, "Sure, I'll stay put."

"Yes, you will because I am going to tie you to that tree and gag you."

Marty shifted nervously, "You won't leave me like that will you?"

"No, we will come back for you. If you have lied we will hang you from this tree."

"I ain't lyin', I swear."

Marty sat down against the tree and willingly allowed himself to be tied to it. Pablo tied him and then pulled Marty's bandana over his mouth. They mounted and rode along the trail.

It took ten minutes to come in sight of the cabin set in a clearing. True to Marty's word it was as he had said. They took in the dilapidated corral, trash in the yard, and overall outlaw appearance of the place. Marty's saddled horse grazed in the grass dragging its reins.

"It certainly looks like an outlaw hideout," Henry remarked, "what a pile of trash."

"They will not expect us," Pablo said to the group. "If the look of this place is any indication they will be laying in there lazing about. We will surround the place. Should they run out the back go ahead and shoot them." Pablo gestured to Henry, "You and I will rush the door and kick it in."

The men nodded in agreement as they rode out to surround the cabin. Pablo and Henry waited until they could see the men in position around the cabin yard. Dismounting, Pablo and Henry made a silent run across the open yard stepping around bottles and cans. They stopped at the door for a second and listened for sounds from the interior. Hearing nothing Pablo cocked back his leg and slammed his boot against the weather cracked door sending it flying in pieces into the cabin. With guns drawn they rushed in the open doorway.

The two Taggard men were lying in their beds covered with dirty blankets. They both jumped up at the sound of crashing wood. Before they could react Henry had grabbed one by the shirt and Pablo had the other by his hair. Both Taggards shouted and cursed as they were drug out of their beds and slammed hard to the floor.

Cruz and Jean ran in the door while the last two vaqueros stayed outside and watched the yard. Jean grabbed the one Henry was holding and Cruz assisted Pablo. They roughly dragged the two young men out into the yard. The brothers were terrified and begging although they had no idea who had them. They were thrown down on the ground and surrounded by all the men who were now on foot.

Panic stricken, the brothers cast their eyes over the men above them. Realizing all but two were Mexicans, they knew it was the Ruiz outfit. Marty's warning about the danger of attacking this outfit that had earned him a fist to the head rushed back to them.

Pablo glared down at them. "You murdered my father and my friend."

"No, no, not us," Baxter lied. "The old man did it."

"Your old man can shoot twenty times with one gun? It must be some gun."

The two vaqueros broke from the group walking quickly to the corral where two horses stood with their heads down. One haltered the horses while the second found a coil of rope in the broken down tack shed. Pulling his knife he cut the rope in two equal lengths and deftly threw a noose onto the end of each.

The Taggard's hands were tied behind their backs. Then they were dragged, kicking and screaming to a dead tree with protruding dry branches that stood adjacent to the corral. They could see one man with ropes and the other with the horses.

Throwing ropes over the lowest tree limb, the vaquero tied the ends off to the top corral rail. The Taggards were shoved up on horses and nooses were fitted over their heads. Once in place Pablo did not hesitate as he slapped the horses hard across their rumps. Ropes snapped tight as the horses ran off into the woods.

Pablo turned to Cruz, "Go bring the boy up here."

Cruz immediately stepped into the saddle and rode back for Marty.

Turning their backs on the swinging corpses the men walked to the cabin to wait for Cruz. It was a short wait before Cruz rode back with Marty walking in front of his horse. Marty's eyes were drawn to the hanging tree although he felt no sorrow for his brothers. Baxter had tried to beat him with a chunk of firewood only a few hours before. The sooner they were all dead the sooner he could have his own life.

Pablo searched Marty's face and saw nothing that indicated anger or sorrow. "Do you have anything in the cabin you wish to keep?"

Marty nodded, "Yeah, a few things."

"Go in and get them."

Marty hurried in and returned shortly with some clothes wrapped in a rough bundle and a rifle. Cruz quickly drew his revolver and pointed it at Marty. Marty instantly dropped everything he was holding and threw up his hands. "I ain't doin' nothin', it's just that's my rifle. I want to keep it."

Pablo nodded toward Cruz that it was alright. "Go ahead Marty, take your things."

Marty hesitantly picked up his clothes and made sure he picked up the rifle butt forward so the muzzle pointed behind him. He looked nervously at Pablo, "What are you gonna do with me now?"

"Where are the others?"

"Likely Elizabethtown, the old man said they was goin' to the snake pit."

Pablo raised an eyebrow, "The snake pit?"

"It's a saloon and cathouse called 'Busters,' he keeps some rattlers in a glass case for people to look at, that's how it got called the snake pit."

"You are free to go," Pablo told him. "Take your horse and ride."

Marty began to walk backwards toward his grazing horse, "You're gonna let me go for real?"

"You gave me the information I wanted. You did not shoot my father and I believe you now. I am a man of my word. Go, make something worthwhile of your life and leave this behind."

"Sure, I will . . . thanks."

Marty caught up his horse and tied his bundle behind the saddle. Henry walked up to him and handed him his pistol. "Here's your gun back, don't use it except in self-defense hear?"

Marty took the gun from him, "Yes sir. I never wanted to be an outlaw in the first place." Marty stepped into the saddle and rode away through the trees.

Pablo turned to Cruz, "Burn it."

Cruz and the vaqueros quickly stacked dead wood against the wall of the bone dry cabin and lit it. The flames leaped up engulfing the wall as the men mounted up.

Pablo dug a tally book and a pencil out of his saddlebag. On a blank page he wrote, *cattle thieves and murderers.* He rode up to the hanging corpses and buttoned the note to the chest of one.

"We go to the snake pit," Pablo announced as they rode on toward Elizabethtown. The sound of crackling flames and the smell of smoke followed them as they left the scene behind.

They rode on through the hills until the buildings and smoking stove pipes of Elizabethtown could be seen below them in the valley. The grass was still green on the valley floor rolling up into the surrounding hills where it mingled with the darker green of the pines. Across the hills could be seen mine entrances and tailing piles next to shacks made of weathered brown boards.

The town was typical of a mining boom town. Stores and a variety of shops offering everything from tobacco and liquor to clothes were thrown up quickly to take advantage of the influx of prospectors chasing the lure of gold. The businesses, and the inevitable array of saloons, took in far more profit than the majority of prospectors ever realized. Days were spent in the mines and nights in the saloons drinking, gambling, and seeking entertainment.

In the midst of the rough board buildings and hanging on the fringes like winter wolves, were the highwaymen, card cheats, thieves of every stripe, and those like the Taggard family. Too lazy to work they preyed on the labors of others. Murder was nothing to them in their pursuit of ill-gotten gain; it was merely a step in the process. When thwarted in their pursuits they took it as a personal affront and sought revenge against any who would try to stop them.

It wasn't often that vaqueros rode into Elizabethtown and less often to see the likes of Pablo Ruiz leading them, his high bred persona emanating from him. The Mexicans tended to stay to the south, Taos, Santa Fe, or Las Vegas. The group drew stares and attention as the stern faced men rode casually down the center of the street. Well armed, well mounted, it was obvious to all that this was a fighting outfit from one of the Mexican ranches to the west or south.

Drawing further attention were the two white men riding with them who looked every bit as tough as the Mexicans. It was clear they were part of the company. The old man had a face like chiseled flint, hard and unrelenting, a man who had seen the world change around him and fought to keep his place in it. The younger man, casual and confident, bore a face resembling the old man's.

The men who watched the riders go by knew instinctively that this was an outfit best not crossed. They were on the hunt and each man watching mentally examined his back trail and past deeds to make sure he hadn't done anything to bring these men down on him. At the same time curiosity was aroused as to who they were hunting. It could make for interesting entertainment providing the subject of the hunt was someone else.

As the group moved along Jean asked a miner standing on the side of the street where they could find Busters.

"Oh, you mean the snake pit?"

Jean nodded, "We've heard it called that."

"Keep on like you are an' you'll see it, a couple of buildings are after it. Buster's got his name on the front. Say, did you fellas happen to come in from Cimarron?"

"No, we came across from the west. Why?"

"A freighter brought in four bodies from down Cimarron way," said the stage had overturned."

"Run away?"

"Nope, three of 'em was shot. They all had their pockets turned out and wallets thrown aside. The strong box had the lock shot off and was empty. The assayer said he had bags o' gold dust on that stage."

The group had stopped to listen to the miner's account of the killings and thefts.

"Any idea who did it?"

The miner shrugged, "Might a' been anybody, ain't no shortage of outlaws 'round here. A lot of men think it was that Taggard outfit, had their sign all over it. Can't prove that though."

Pablo moved his horse closer to the miner, "We have interest in the Taggards, have you seen them?"

Now the miner knew who they were hunting. "I haven't, but that don't mean they ain't in town." The man grinned slightly, "I take it you ain't friends of theirs."

"They murdered Don Sebastian Ruiz," Henry answered him. "We've come for them."

The miner let out a low whistle, "Heard of him, big bull of the woods out to the west. So, they killed him, huh. I'm not surprised by anything that outfit does though. You boys worked for Ruiz did yuh?"

"He was my father," Pablo answered with a bitter tone.

"Guess they're as good as dead then. So, you figure them to be holed up at Busters?"

"We were told they would be there today."

"Could be, ain't been there myself in a couple of days. I have seen old man Taggard and his boys there before though. If you do kill 'em I'm sure that assayer would like to look 'em over for his gold."

Pablo reined his horse back to his original direction. "Tell him to come when he hears the gunshots."

Pablo moved his horse along with the others following. The miner headed straight for the assayers office to tell him that the Taggards were about to get their tickets punched and he might want to follow along.

Reaching the building with 'Busters' hand written on a board tacked to the front wall Cruz pointed out a pair of horses tied to the rail in front of it. "Look, *patron*, those horses. Look at the brands."

"Those are my horses," Pablo said as he dismounted and walked up to the two horses tied next to each other. "I know my horses when I see them." Pablo examined the brands. "My brand has been run over . . . badly."

"We have lost some horses along with the cattle," Cruz added.

"You know the Taggards stole the cattle and run the brands," Henry said. "Stands to reason they would do the same with your horses."

Jean stepped out of the saddle, "I'd say Marty's information was good."

Pablo nodded, "Yes, it would seem so. Their laziness extends to being too lazy to run a brand decently. It is them."

Pablo looked at the two vaqueros, "You two stay out here and watch our backs that no one comes in behind us."

Both men nodded their understanding and dismounted. Each took a stand at opposite sides of the saloon door. Pablo marched with determination toward the door. Cruz was beside him, Jean and Henry directly behind them. Opening the door they stepped inside the room.

The room was longer than it was wide with oil lamps hanging from the ceiling casting off a dull light in the windowless room. A rickety narrow stairway led up to a second level, where it went beyond, that was lost in darkness. A glass case holding a pair of the namesake rattlesnakes was on the end of the bar nearest the door.

The appearance of the four men drew the attention of all in the room. Gamblers sitting at poker and faro tables along with three women working among the men stopped to look at them. Cards momentarily hung suspended in the fingers set to toss them down.

Rough, armed men were nothing new to the town, yet these men were more than that, they were wolves smelling blood. They moved into the room looking the occupants over. A woman wearing little more than her under garments sallied up to Henry. His burning glare caused her to swerve away without speaking.

"There are two sorrel horses out front," Pablo called out into the room. "Who do they belong to?"

Ned and Porky sat with Milo surrounding a table at the end of the room where the light was dimmest. The brothers exchanged glances and slunk down in their chairs to avoid notice. They could see that the two men in the front were Mexicans. They were riding two stolen Ruiz horses; it wasn't hard to figure out who was doing the asking.

The room went silent, no one moved or answered. Milo Taggard had drunk enough to loosen his tongue and bring out the meanness and stupidity in his nature. He growled out, "I ride a sorrel, what's it to a greaser?"

Pablo and Cruz walked slowly toward the table where the Taggards sat. They closed the distance and studied Milo Taggard who sat with a belligerent sneer on his face. He was bobbing his head back and forth part from arrogance, part from the liquor making his neck unsteady. The two young men with him had slunk lower in their chairs making Pablo wonder if they were holding guns in their hidden hands.

"Your horses carry the brand of the Ruiz hacienda. You did a poor job of running over my brand, however, I would expect everything you do to be of no value."

The silence in the room deepened and the confrontation was now of more interest than the cards or the women. A fight was brewing. Horse stealing was serious business and the name of Ruiz was at least known. Some who had been to Taos knew that old man Ruiz had been killed by rustlers. It looked like the Ruiz riders had tracked down their horse thieves if not the actual murderers of old Ruiz.

"You must have ate a bad chili, peppergut," Taggard chuckled, "you're imagining all sorts of things."

Pablo held a deadly stare on the man, yet his tone remained cool, "I take it I am talking to Milo Taggard."

Taggard puffed out his chest, "That's me, bigger'n life and twice as mean. You best get your little brown fanny for home and tell yer mama to give you a tamale before you get yourself hurt."

"I am Pablo Ruiz, you and your worthless sons murdered my father. Shot him to pieces from ambush like the yellow, sniveling coyotes you are."

Pablo noticed, even in the dim light, that the faces of the two young men at the table blanched to a deathly pallor and fear ruled their eyes. They began to fidget nervously. He knew then that these were the remaining Taggards Marty had told them were with Milo. Pablo watched their movements, but at the same time he kept his eyes on Taggard whose hands that had been above the table were now under it.

Jean and Henry stayed back watching the rest of the room. Pablo and Cruz were enough to fill the narrow end of the saloon trapping the three Taggards at their table against the wall. Four men at the table closest to the Taggards held their hands out to show they were empty, and slipped out of their chairs and got under the table.

Taggard's liquor soaked brain processed information slowly. Finally he growled, "What's this, you trying to box us in?"

Pablo held his cool tone, "We hung the two you left up at your shack. Then, we burned it to the ground."

Taggard jumped up roaring in rage. As he clumsily made his feet he lifted the gun he had held under the table. Pablo's lightning hand drew his revolver in one fluid motion. His shot took Milo Taggard in the forehead. He dropped straight down dead as he fell.

In a panic Ned and Porky jumped up, wildly driving shots at Pablo and Cruz as they tried to move out from behind the confining table. The bullets slammed into the walls and tables of the room causing all the occupants to simultaneously hit the floor. Pablo and Cruz immediately returned fire hitting the two Taggards multiple times. The last wayward shot from a Taggard gun broke the rattlesnake case.

As quickly as it had turned riotous with gunfire it turned silent. The thick black powder smoke hung in the breezeless room stinging eyes and making those who breathed it in cough. In the ensuing seconds, those who had taken to the floor stayed in place watching the four men.

Pablo walked up to the Taggards and pushed the bodies with his boot toe while the other men kept their guns out watching the crowd. Satisfied that the three were dead Pablo turned and walked back across the room. One of the rattlers from the case was coiled in an angry pose buzzing loudly in the doorway. Pablo shot it as he pushed open the door and went out followed by the other men.

Buster ran out from behind the bar and propped the door open to let in some air. He cursed when he saw the dead snake. The second one had been hit by the stray bullet and was spinning wildly in the broken glass on the bar. Men got up off the floor and made their way over to look at the dead men.

"So, that's the Taggards," a gambler commented. "Thought they was just one of those phantoms folks blamed for everything."

Another man snorted, "You ain't from around here are you? Everyone around here knew they were a bunch of no account outlaws."

"I was down in Taos," said a third, "when a Ruiz rider came in saying that old man Ruiz had been murdered."

The gambler pointed at the dead men, "They did it?"

"Appears that way."

The gambler laughed, "*Appears* it was a bad choice on their part. Kind of a scary looking outfit, weren't they?"

A dealer dressed in a suit and string tie resetting his table commented, "Those Ruiz vaqueros cut their teeth fighting Apaches. I knew Pablo Ruiz when he was a wild young buck, he's got a fast gun and a slow burn. The Taggards were nothing more to them than a nuisance to be eliminated."

The miner Jean and Pablo had spoken with on the way in, along with another man, ran up the street to see how the gunfight had ended. Seeing the four men he recognized walk out of the saloon answered the question as to who won. "Was it the Taggards?" the miner asked breathless from his run.

Jean looked at him and the man next to him, "*Was* is the word."

"You get 'em then."

"That was the last of the family; there won't be any more stage robberies or murders from them."

Pablo and Cruz were checking the saddlebags and stripping the saddles off the stolen sorrel horses. "Are you the assayer?" Pablo asked the man with the miner.

"Yes, I am an assayer."

The miner broke in, "He's the one I told you lost the gold in that robbery."

Pablo tossed a small, but heavy cloth sack toward the assayer, "This must be yours." He found the three other bags and gave those to the assayer as well.

The man was beside himself with excitement, "Thank you. I thought it was gone for good. I paid out a small fortune for this and if I couldn't resell it I'd be ruined."

Men and boys were running in from all directions as word of the shooting spread. They were clustered at the door to peer in and hear firsthand what had happened. One man wandering up looked at Pablo and Cruz throwing the saddles down on the ground and leading the horses away from the hitchrail. "Say there," he shouted. "What do you men think you are doing with those horses?"

"Taking back my property," Pablo snapped at him. "Do you wish to contest my ownership?"

"Well, no, but . . . "

Jean cut him off, "I'd just mind my own business if I were you, my friend is not in a good mood right now."

The man stared at Jean's hard features and realized that the shooting was connected to them and the horses. He had already said too much and hurried along his way without another word.

The men mounted up with Pablo and Cruz each leading a horse. Without looking back Pablo said, "We have dealt with one problem, now we must go back to the hacienda and deal with a much bigger one."

CHAPTER ELEVEN

Jeb rode the Palouse gelding his father had given him when he moved away. The horse had a lot of bottom and if allowed even a minimum of rest, food, and water could go indefinitely. He had already made one trip on him up into the canyon today and was now returning. He would be making the ride back up tonight as well. The gelding was also the most surefooted night horse he had ever ridden. It was still light, however, by the time he got out of the canyon night would have fallen.

He had no worries about arriving too late to catch Cassidy at Pruitt's as the place stayed busy until the late hours. By now Cassidy surely thought he had tucked tail and run. He'd be hanging around bragging about how he ran Pelletier off. Being that his family was hated by much of the Pruitt crowd he would have an attentive audience. Cassidy would also figure he could do what he wanted with Jenny as her husband was too scared to protect her, he'd be bragging on that too. It was unlikely he knew that Jenny had moved out of town.

Jeb knew the simple layout of Pruitt's hole as he had been in it a number of times. It was basically a one story house or storage building with logs cut and set upright to support the roof and ceiling. He considered where Cassidy was likely to sit and how to best get the jump on him. Clint had said to take him by surprise before he had a chance to set up anything underhanded. No wiggle room Clint had said. He didn't intend to give Cassidy enough to so much as move his little finger.

There was a quarter moon hanging in the clear starlit sky when Jeb entered the main street of Fort Collins. Pruitt's was on the opposite end of town. He rode through the town he watched grow up and change, he didn't care that he no longer belonged here. One last bit of business to tie off and then he'd be gone for good.

The shops were closed for the night. Lights shone out of the windows of George Mason's saloon and a few other places where people were working late. As he rode past his house, now dark and lonely, it seemed odd not to be going home to it. They had all pitched in to build the place, it had been home, built by friends and family. One day he would look back on it fondly as he and

Jenny's first home and there had been happiness and laughter there. One didn't forget things like that. Right now it was simply a structure in the town he was leaving with ill feelings.

'Shifting trails' Ian called it. When you think your life is headed in a certain direction only to have it changed by choice or circumstances. Ian's life had unexpectedly shifted for the better when he met Anne; it had been his choice to take that trail. On the other hand his and Jenny's trail had been shifted by circumstances that were no fault of their own, but they would turn it into something good.

He left the house behind as he closed the distance to Pruitt's. His thoughts returned to the business set before him and pushed all else out.

Clint was watching out the window of the dark house when Jeb rode by. "Paul, there he goes."

Paul stepped up to the window and looked out to see Jeb's back fading into the darkness. "He's going to Pruitt's."

"You think he wouldn't?"

Paul shook his head, "A Pelletier run from a fight? I was hoping Cassidy would just leave town, but when I did my check at Pruitt's this evening the man you described to me was there sitting in a card game."

"At least he won't be set."

"He's a dirty player, huh?"

"Dirty as they come. When you're not all that fast and make your living killing people you have to create an edge for yourself. Cassidy uses hideaway guns, distractions, and sometimes a paid accomplice."

"What was your run-in with him?"

Clint laughed under his breath. "It was in a low-life place on Denver's rougher end. I wasn't always a respectable rancher you know." He grinned.

Paul huffed a short laugh remembering his first encounter with Clint after he had gunned down Dally Oden in George Mason's saloon.

Clint continued on, "Cassidy was working for several loan sharks and establishments roughing people up or killing when hired to do so. He was pushing his weight around and made the mistake of trying to push it into me because I was newly in Denver and he didn't know me. I invited him to play and he backed down."

"You caught him by surprise with no time to set anything up."

"Exactly. Had he had time to set up he would have been braver. He still would have been dead, but a braver dead. I hung around Denver for a while and learned all about Cassidy."

"Jeb could still be in trouble if Cassidy has an accomplice in the place. Let's go. I want to make sure no one back-shoots him."

"Just don't let him know we're there, he doesn't need the distraction."

They went out the back door where their horses were tied. Mounting they headed for Pruitt's by a different way from Jeb's direct line.

The windows in Pruitt's had once held glass, but were one-by-one broken out and boarded over which helped to hold the rank smell inside. It wasn't a place for a man with a weak stomach. Tonight the front door was open spreading a shaft of dim light out into the dirt alley that ran in front of it.

To either side of Pruitt's there were old buildings, storage sheds and the like. No legitimate businesses were left in this corner of the town. The buildings, once in use and oiled for protection against the weather, were now only bone dry boards streaked black and brown with dried oil, they were a fire waiting to happen.

Jeb stepped off the gelding and tied him down the alley from Pruitt's in front of an abandoned storage building. He lifted the Remington from his holster and loaded a paper cartridge in the sixth chamber of the cylinder and pushed a cap into the rear end. He tied the holster against his leg and began his walk to the open doorway.

While outside he could hear the murmur of voices, clinking glass and an occasional rough laugh. Pruitt's was strictly a hangout for derelicts, drunks and outlaws. There was no brass rail in front of a polished hardwood bar like in Mason's saloon. No piano or music, no faro or roulette tables, nothing but drinking and poker.

He stepped into the room and gave it a quick scan. Pruitt was in his usual place behind the bar. He spotted Jeb at the same moment Jeb saw the man who matched the description Clint had given him of Alex Cassidy. He was sitting at a table playing cards with two other men, his right side to the door, his back to the bar.

Jeb moved quickly across the floor reaching Cassidy at the same moment Pruitt tried shouting a warning to him. Cassidy glanced up from his cards and took Jeb's rock hard right fist dead center in the face. The punch knocked Cassidy and his chair over backwards, his legs hitting the table hard enough to send the coins and discarded cards sliding into the laps of the men sitting across from him. His head smacked with a resounding thunk on the board floor.

There was no one in the room that did not know Jeb Pelletier, the reputation of the family, and what Cassidy had been saying about the school teacher. He had boasted that Pelletier was afraid of him and run off to hide. Most had wondered at that since they had never heard of a Pelletier passing up a fight. It was not unexpected that Jeb would show up, the only question was when. It was only Cassidy, a newcomer, who didn't understand the nature of the family.

Jeb stepped back from the table so Cassidy couldn't shove it into him. He was facing the bar as Cassidy untangled himself from the chair and lurched to his feet cursing wildly. He grabbed for his gun. Jeb's practiced hand flew to the Remington bringing it up and level in the blink of an eye. In that instant Jeb saw Cassidy's eyes flair open, his gun barely out of his holster. Jeb's first shot broke Cassidy's second rib on the right side spinning him a bit to that side. The second and third shoots tore into his heart.

A flicker of movement across the room in front of him caught Jeb's eye. Shifting his eyes to the movement, he saw Pruitt bringing the twin bores of a sawed off shotgun to bear on him. Without conscious thought Jeb thumbed back the hammer and fired at Pruitt. The heavy .44 caliber ball drove into Pruitt between the collar bones. He choked and gagged as the shotgun clattered to the bar top. Jeb shot him again, the bullet hitting three inches below the first. Pruitt disappeared behind the bar.

Jeb kept his boots planted and turned to look around him. He was glad he had put the sixth load in. The last thing he wanted was to have an empty gun in the middle of this place. No one moved from where they sat or stood. All eyes were trained on Jeb noting the lack of a star on his shirt. His flashing draw burned an impression in their minds. Cassidy was a reputed gunfighter and his gun lay impotent by his side.

Jeb's searching eyes stopped on the open doorway. He wasn't surprised to see Paul and Clint standing just inside the room with their guns drawn. The two men looked the room over drawing the occupant's attention from Jeb to them. Seeing no one moving or acting in a dangerous fashion, Paul holstered his gun and made his way toward Jeb while Clint held his position at the doorway. Gun in hand Jeb faced Paul not knowing what his actions would be. He was still the sheriff, but Jeb had no intention of being arrested.

"Where's Pruitt?" Paul directed his question to Jeb.

Jeb jerked his head toward the bar, "Back there."

Clint turned his eyes toward the bar to see the shotgun laying on top of it. "Was he trying to use that?" he called across the room to Jeb.

"He tried," Jeb answered, his tone glacial.

Paul walked past Jeb and looked down at Cassidy. There was a gun on the floor next to him. "He pull that gun on you Jeb?"

"Yeah, but he wasn't much good at it." Jeb remained guarded as to Paul's intent.

Clint walked to the bar and leaned over it, "Pruitt looks pretty dead back here," he called to Paul.

"Looks like a matter of self-defense all around," Paul announced. He then looked into Jeb's eyes reading the willingness to fight him too if need be. "Go home, Jeb. I'll deal with this."

Jeb stared at Paul for several seconds and then walked across the room and out the door. He walked quickly to his horse and took a deep shaky breath. The adrenalin surge he had experienced was wearing off leaving him feeling weak. He leaned against his horse and got himself gathered back together. He then reloaded the Remington.

Paul faced the room. "By order of the sheriff this establishment is closed as of right now. Everyone get out."

The men began to grumble and holler protests regarding the eviction. Paul shouted over them, "You have five minutes to vacate or I start making arrests. Any who resist will be shot. Pruitt's hole is permanently closed."

The men gathered up their poker money, downed their drinks, and angrily shuffled out the door. They cast killing glares at Paul who gave them right back. The men knew Clint Rush and diverted their eyes from him. No one wanted to challenge the Montana gunfighter.

Jeb stood by his horse in the dark watching the men file out and disappear in various directions. He walked back to the saloon and stepped inside. Paul and Clint turned to look at him.

"It was a fair shooting," Jeb said to Paul.

"There's no doubts in my mind Jeb. I'm shutting this place down."

Jeb looked at Clint, "I never gave him a chance to get set."

Clint gestured with his head toward the bar, "He still had an ace in the hole with Pruitt. You handled it right. Go on home. I'm sure Jenny is worried sick."

Jeb nodded and went back out the door. They could hear his horse walking away in the silent night.

Paul looked at Clint, "Want to give me a hand dragging these two out?"

"Sure. What are you going to do with this place?"

"I'd like to burn it down, but it would probably take the whole town with it."

Clint examined the half-dozen eight inch diameter logs that had been cut and placed upright throughout the room to shore up the roof. He slapped one, "You know, if you jerked these supports out I bet this whole thing would come crashing down."

Paul looked up and down the support logs. "You know, you're right. These are all that hold this place up. The walls and floor are full of dry rot."

"In the morning we'll get Reed over here with a team and some chain and drop this sorry mess to the ground."

"We'll do that. Let's get these bodies outside."

Together they dragged Cassidy's body across the floor dumping it unceremoniously in the dirt. It took some work to get Pruitt out from behind his bar, but they managed it and tossed him alongside Cassidy.

"I'll wake up the undertaker," Paul said. "Watch to make sure no one goes back in there." Paul mounted his horse and rode off.

Clint was leaning against the building when he heard a horse coming toward him. He watched as Andrew rode slowly down the alley coming to a stop next to the bodies.

Clint, not thinking it wise to surprise a Pelletier in the dark, stepped away from the building. "Evening Andrew."

Andrew's head snapped around and locked a stare on him. He recognized and acknowledged him. "Clint." He pointed at the bodies, "Jeb's work?"

"Uh-huh. You come looking for little brother?"

"Yeah, he rode away without saying anything. I knew where he was going though."

"You must have hauled pretty fast down that mountain."

"I took a short cut over the top of the canyon. A trail Pa found forty years or so ago. I take it that's Cassidy."

"And Larry Pruitt."

Andrew's face flashed a fleeting look of surprise. "How did that happen?"

"While Jeb was busy with Cassidy Pruitt figured to bushwhack him."

"Jeb's not that foolish to turn his back on the likes of him."

"He didn't, two slugs here and here," Clint pointed at the two spots on himself where Pruitt had been shot."

"Good riddance to him. Hear tell Jeb's been working with you on his gun fighting skills."

"That's right, he asked me to teach him. It likely saved his life; Cassidy was a known gun fighter."

"Where is Jeb now?"

"We told him to go home. Funny you didn't pass him."

"I came through town, knowing Jeb he likely skirted it. Is Paul around?"

"He went for the undertaker. Paul closed this outhouse permanently and ran everyone out. They didn't like it too much, but they went. In the morning we're going to pull it down and the trash will have to drift to some other town."

"Well, that won't be any loss."

The two men turned silent for a few minutes before Andrew turned his horse, "Best get back home and make sure everything is alright with Jeb. See you around."

Clint waved at him and leaned back against the building to wait for Paul and the undertaker.

————————

In the morning Reed Hall drove a team of draft stock freight horses toward Pruitt's. The wagon they pulled was loaded with chains and thick ropes. Paul and Clint rode alongside him as a crowd of the curious followed them. Word had spread first thing in the morning that there had been a shootout in Pruitt's where Jeb Pelletier killed the man who had maligned his wife and killed Larry Pruitt besides.

The old timers figured it was bound to come, there was no way a Pelletier would stand such talk and not make the one responsible pay in blood. Killing Larry Pruitt, the scum of the county, was a bonus. No one would miss him or his outlaw hangout. The newcomers, ignorant of Pruitt's history, clucked their tongues and said it only proved that the Pelletier's were savages.

The word also had it that Sheriff Lander had shut down Pruitt's and it was to be razed that morning. A lot of people wanted to see that happen. By the time Reed drove up the alley and stopped in front of Pruitt's a crowd of men and boys had gathered.

Reed unhitched the team from the wagon and positioned them so their rear ends faced the doorway of the building. Reed and Clint dragged chains in through the door while Paul made sure the curious stayed a safe distance back.

Reed and Clint wrapped the chains around the bases of four of the support posts and ran the chain back out the door. Reed then wrapped and knotted the end of a heavy rope around the ends of the chains and tied the rope to the heel chains running off the rear of the harness. Reed picked up the reins and standing to the side of the horses shouted out to Paul, "Keep 'em all back, here we go."

Paul ordered the excited crowd to stay back.

Reed smacked the horses with the reins and told them to get up. The horses snapped the chain and rope tight and momentarily jerked to a stop. Reed slapped the reins again encouraging the horses to pull. The heavy work horses leaned into the harness, dug their giant hooves into the dirt, and drove forward. A loud crash and the sound of wood wrenching and tearing resounded from inside the building as the horses continued to drive forward pulling the four twelve foot long logs through the doorway taking half the flimsy wall out with them.

Reed stopped the team and looked back. The crowd held their collective breath waiting for the finale. A slow creaking began to emanate from the rotten building and suddenly the roof caved in toward the center and the whole structure fell with a crash and a huge plume of dust that spread in all directions.

The crowd cheered and then delivered three hearty 'hip-hip-hoo-rays.' Paul smiled as did Reed as he backed the horses to release the pressure on the rope and chains.

Paul opened the tool box on the wagon and removed a piece of chalk. Picking up a broken board from the heap he wrote in large letters 'CLOSED PERMANENTLY.' He dropped the board back down on what had been the door to Pruitt's hole.

CHAPTER TWELVE

A week had passed since the funerals of Sebastian and Juan. Samuel Beckett had yet to return to the hacienda with the information regarding the disposition of the Grant. Work went on as usual with the stock and around the house as they all waited in nervous anticipation for Beckett's information.

Pablo had not informed his workers about the precarious situation of the Grant, waiting until he knew the actual situation and not a surmised idea, however they knew. Servants and workers had a grapevine that most patrons could only wonder at as to how they so accurately knew about information kept from them. The workers were worried, yet trusted to their patron to make it right.

Angelina was not one to sit idle while those around her worked. She did not think of herself as *la señora de la casa*, the ranking lady of the household who sat around while people waited on her. She was familiar with wealthy Spanish families who conducted themselves as such, but that was never in her raising.

Though her father had his policies as to what was servant's and vaquero's work, he would never allow her or Pablo to lie idly about doing nothing. He expected them to do something worthwhile as he detested the idle rich who lazed about fulfilling no useful purpose. These were people he often said were nothing but lazy toads who could not feed themselves and could barely go to the outhouse without assistance. He could have easily sat around giving orders; he was as wealthy as most others in his class, but Sebastian was a worker and expected his children to be workers as well.

Angelina wandered into the kitchen where Teresa had her sleeves rolled up and was up to her wrists in kneading bread dough. The gray haired cook looked over at Angelina and smiled, "*Bueno dias, señora.*"

Angelina returned the smile, "Good morning, Teresa. How are you today?"

"I am good, *Gracias señora.*"

Angelina let her eyes rove over the neat and orderly kitchen. "What can I help you with today Teresa?"

Teresa's mouth dropped open in shock, "No, no, you are *la seño-*

ra de la casa. It is not for you to do servant's work in the kitchen."

Angelina scowled, "Teresa, I have my home and my children, and I cook and make bread and clean after them. I am a mother and wife, not a doll to sit around in fine clothes being useless."

Teresa had stopped kneading leaving her hands in the dough as she blinked her eyes staring at Angelina. "But, *señora* it is not done. You are too good to work in the kitchen of the *patron's casa grande*."

"Oh, posh!" Angelina snapped. "It is done in my home, and this used to be my home, so it is done here as well, *si?*"

Teresa began to slowly resume kneading, "*Si señora*. It is truly your home and you can do as you wish."

"That is right, and I don't want to ever hear again that the work here is beneath me. You are not beneath me Teresa."

Teresa's gaping expression turned into a smile and then a light laugh. "How often I remember you as a little *nina* that would come in the kitchen and talk with me."

"And snitch your sweetbreads."

Teresa laughed, "And snitch, *si*. Now, you are a beautiful grown woman with your own fine family."

Angelina put her arm around the old woman's shoulders, "And you are my friend Teresa."

"*Gracias.*"

Angelina picked up a sweetbread from the table, "And I still snitch."

Teresa laughed, "And you still snitch."

Teresa's smile faded as her face turned worried, "*Señora*, will the *patron* lose the hacienda?"

"Not if we can help it. There are some things we can do to save it. Do not lose hope."

Teresa nodded, "I have known no other home but with Don Sebastian. My mother was cook to the Don's father, and I was born here."

Angelina did not take the old woman's fears lightly. "This hacienda has been in our family for one hundred years, we will not let it go so easily. There is also my husband's family as well who can do much to help."

With a nod Teresa continued with her bread dough. "It will be well then?"

"It will be well. Now, what will you allow me to do to help you?"

Teresa glanced at Angelina, hesitant to answer.

"It is done," Angelina reminded her sternly.

"*Si,* the meat needs to be put in the oven."

Angelina feigned ignorance, "Meat, hmm, what does it look like?"

Teresa cast a worried eye at Angelina.

Angelina caught the look and laughed, "Got you Teresa."

Comprehension dawned on Teresa and she laughed. "It looks like a cow only with no hide."

Angelina pointed at the quarter of a beef hanging from a hook. "That must be it there."

The two women laughed and joked as they worked together through the morning.

Pablo rode with Jean and Henry surveying the hacienda, checking on the cattle and horses. Along the way they met with vaqueros who gave them reports regarding the quality of the grazing and condition of the stock. Water was not an issue yet since the spring snow thaw had filled the river along with the streams and ponds.

The story of their killing the Taggards had spread among the vaqueros. Their approving looks of admiration for Pablo said more than words. Sebastian was highly thought of among his men and the killing of his killers set well with them. It lifted Pablo to an even higher estimation in their eyes.

Pablo's friends and family were included in the high regard they paid their new patron. Henry they knew as being the husband of Angelina, a woman they all admired and more than a few had secretly fallen in love with. Jean, they knew as a friend of Sebastian's and Pablo's. He was an *hombre* and they admired that.

Looking over a herd of mixed age cattle Pablo asked Jean, "Have you ever considered raising cattle?"

"Not really, we've got the Palouse horses."

"Yes, and very fine horses they are too, but what if the market for horses fails?"

Jean gave Pablo a questioning look, "How do you mean, fails?"

"What if men no longer ride horses?"

"What are they going to ride, elephants?"

"How much change have you seen in your life? When you first came into this country was there such a thing as a stagecoach or a train? Was there even a road?"

Jean frowned, "Well, no."

"Now, there are roads everywhere filled with stagecoaches. Trains are running many miles an hour on tracks. There is much talk that in a few years trains will be running through to Santa Fe."

"Okay, but what has that got to do with horses?"

"Men invented the train, no? What if one day men invent a conveyance that they can ride in, like trains, and they no longer ride horses?"

Jean looked at Pablo, "What kind of conveyance?"

Pablo shrugged, "Who knows, but if men can invent a train what else can they invent that runs on its own power?"

Henry caught the drift of Pablo's meaning. "You have a point there. We shouldn't count on only one source of income, things can change very quickly."

"I can't see that though," Jean argued. "Men riding in conveyances instead of riding horses? It'll never happen."

Henry argued, "What happened to the beaver market, Pa? Beaver were selling for huge sums. How many men grew rich off the fur trade? Then, the fashion trend of beaver hats changed and beaver were worthless. Many of the men who built their fortunes on beaver hats lost everything."

Jean pondered on that. It was true the beaver market had suddenly crumbled and all because of a fashion change. "So, you think that could happen with horses?"

"Maybe not tomorrow or next year, but putting all your eggs in one basket might not be such a good idea."

Jean looked back at Pablo, "Why cattle? Won't they go out of fashion as well?"

"People will always eat beef. Leather will always be used for boots and shoes and other things. The price per head will go up and down like all markets do, but there will always be a need for cattle. There might not always be a need for horses."

Jean scowled as he tossed around in his mind what Pablo and Henry had said. As much as he didn't want to accept it he knew there was truth to it. How much change had he seen? A bleak prairie on the Cache la Poudre River in 1825 was now filled with towns, homes, farms, and ranches. The mountain man was history replaced by easterners pouring in with their odd ideas.

"There might be something to that," Jean relented. "I'll have to do some thinking on it."

Henry pointed out, "Cattle use less graze than horses. We could put a couple hundred head of young heifers and cows, and a few bulls on the land we have in the canyon. Cattle would return a regular income. The horses can remain the primary product and cattle the secondary. Then, if something ever does happen to the horse market we have the cattle."

Jean was not a man stuck in his own ways. He could be stubborn, but was never bullheaded to the point of being too stupid to see the wisdom of others. He was willing to make changes. "I'll talk it over with Catherine; she always has a good head for such things. You might be right."

Pablo looked out over the grazing cattle, "I have around five-thousand head on fifty-thousand acres. I am not overgrazing and the vaqueros keep the cattle on the move to new graze. There are also two-hundred horses. We are doing well with both and need both." He suddenly stopped and frowned.

"What's wrong?" Henry asked him.

"I just realized that if the government takes the land they will take the cattle and horses on it as well. I will have nothing."

"How can they do that?" Jean asked. "You own the stock."

"Would the stock not be considered part of the Grant? I do not know. I will have to ask Mr. Beckett."

"I hadn't thought of that," Henry put in. "You've got me wondering now."

"Maybe I should quickly sell off a good number of cattle and horses so I will have the money anyway."

"I wouldn't rush into anything if I were you until you hear from Beckett," Henry advised.

Pablo stared off as he thought aloud, "I know many businessmen who take on partners and move their assets among them. I should consider partners whose ranchos I can move the cattle and horses to before I lose them."

"You would have to make sure they were men you personally knew and trusted. Maybe we should ride down to Taos and talk to Beckett about that to see if it's a wise idea or not."

Pablo nodded, "Yes, hopefully he can tell me something so I can begin to make the necessary moves to either save the hacienda or at least move the stock."

"Does your mail go to Taos?" Jean asked.

Pablo nodded.

"How often does it get collected?"

"Whenever one of my people makes a trip down they know to return with any mail and wires that have come for us. The last time was over a week ago."

"There might be an official letter from the government waiting for you telling you what they want."

Pablo scowled, "Yes, that is possible. Telling me how they intend to steal my family's land."

"Well, don't throw up the white flag yet, we just started to fight back."

Pablo laughed in spite of his anger, "I do not even own a white flag."

That evening after dinner Jean called Catherine to their room and closed the door. Catherine sat down in a chair while Jean paced a few steps. Catherine watched him for several seconds before saying, "You look like a man chewing on a problem."

"Not a problem, a decision."

"Okay, a decision then. Jean, you always do better when you just come right out with it."

"Pablo and Henry brought up some points today that I hadn't considered. They think we should go into cattle."

Catherine raised an eyebrow, "That is the dilemma you are wrestling with? Whether or not to raise cattle?"

Jean shook his head, "Not entirely. They thought the horse market might fall out one day and we would be holding nothing of value. If they're right we could find ourselves in dire straits. I am also upset thinking that all our work with the Palouse strain would come to nothing."

"So, they think we should diversify out into cattle as well."

"Yes."

"I think it is a wise move. There are quite a few of us now depending on the horses for an income and it won't be long before that is not enough. In this rapidly changing country a person should not depend on one sole item to provide their living. We have the land for it and there are several cattle ranches out east of us now."

"It would take most of our savings to buy the stock."

"It is an investment for the future."

"You think we should do it then?"

"Most definitely. I would not worry about the work with the horses going to naught. Saving a breed as fine as the Palouse horses will never be for nothing. They will always be of value, but I don't think we should depend on them solely."

Jean looked at her, "So, you think keeping the breed going is worthwhile."

"Yes, don't stop your work with the horses."

Jean smiled and nodded, "Alright, I'll start on finding a cattle breeder when we get back and buy some stock."

Jean's smile faded. He slid the curtain covering the window aside and gazed out to the hills with the moon shining down on the land.

"What else?" Catherine asked.

Jean turned to face her. "Pablo is concerned that if the government seizes the grant they will seize the cattle and horses as well."

"Yes, if it is all connected, they very well could."

"He wants to get the cattle off before that happens; sell them all or take on partners and move the cattle to the partner ranches. He doesn't know who he would want to do that with though. I'd hate to see him take on bad partners and get cheated out of what he's trying to save. I wish I could give him some advice, but I have no idea what to tell him."

"I don't know a tremendous amount about cattle, but is it possible to move cattle across the country? Say, for hundreds of miles?"

"A cattle drive you mean?"

Catherine shrugged, "I suppose that is the proper term."

Jean nodded, "That is how men moved cattle from Texas north to Kansas since the war to sell them. Drove them in herds of thousands. It takes a lot of men to do it from what I've heard."

"Has it ever been done in this part of the country?"

"Actually yes. A Texas man named Goodnight didn't want to pay Dick Wooten's toll for a big herd he was driving to Cheyenne. It was the first time cattle had been brought up into the northern territories. He made his own trail that went up past Bent's Fort and Denver up to Cheyenne. The last time he did it was a year or so ago from what I was told."

"So, it can be done."

"Yes, but what has that to do with Pablo moving *his* cattle off this grant?"

Catherine gave him a slight smile, "Don't we have a son struggling to rebuild a cattle ranch? Isn't Clint Rush trying to make something of the widow Webster's ranch? Couldn't they be Pablo's partners? You certainly know you can trust them."

Jean's face lit up with excitement as he grasped the full meaning of Catherine's ideas. "Yes, it's the perfect solution. We could drive the cattle due east until we struck Goodnight's old trail and then north to Clint's place and then on to Sweetwater County to Ian's. I'll discuss it with Pablo and Henry."

Catherine laughed with good nature, "Now, aren't you glad you brought me along?"

Jean smiled, "Someone has to be the brains of the outfit. I sure don't have them. We'd be lost if not for your good sense."

"We could never have survived without your strength, Jean. You are as smart as I am only in different ways. Actually, if not for you I would be dead now."

Jean's eyes narrowed, "Dead?"

"You don't remember that handsome young mountain man who saved the damsel in distress from the Blackfeet?"

Jean smiled, "That was a long time ago wasn't it?"

Catherine stood up, "We have always been good for each other, Jean."

"Yes, we have."

Catherine took Jean's hands and looked deeply into his eyes, "I know you like I know myself Jean, there is more still troubling you."

Jean nodded as his countenance fell into an expression of sadness. "I miss Sebastian. We were good friends. I wish I had made the trip down here more often to see him. I know how it is out here, a friend can be snuffed out like a candle in seconds and then you regret all you didn't say or do."

"There are three hundred miles between us and this ranch, Jean. It is not a quick trip and you were a busy man raising a family, turning six rough boys into men, building a horse ranch, time slips away."

"That's the problem, it slips away too darn fast and easy and we miss opportunities."

"Life is filled with lost opportunities, it happens to everyone."

"Without a moment's hesitation Sebastian rode out with his men to take back Rebecca from the kidnappers. He was there for us and I feel that I failed him as a friend."

"And you would have done the same for him wouldn't you?"

"Of course, in a second."

"Then, life has given you another chance, an opportunity to do just that for him."

Jean looked at Catherine confused, "How is that?"

"You help his son save his inheritance."

Jean held his wife's eyes for several seconds and then he slowly nodded his head. "And if it takes all I have, I will."

CHAPTER THIRTEEN

At breakfast Jean discussed with Pablo and Henry Catherine's idea of making Ian and Clint Pablo's partners. Pablo readily accepted the idea. Ian was a man he knew and could trust, and if Jean said Clint Rush was an honest man that was enough for him. The talk turned to using the Goodnight Trail.

"Yes, I am familiar with the Goodnight Trail," Pablo said.

"It can be done then?" Jean asked.

"I do not see any reason why not. We could pick up the Santa Fe Trail north of Cimarron and follow it east to the Goodnight Trail. There are no longer the long lines of freighters on the Santa Fe Trail, only stagecoaches and travelers. There is enough open land on each side of the trail, however, that the cattle would not have to be kept on the trail, only use it as a guide.

"I want to move out at least twelve to fourteen hundred head and some horses for the drovers. It will take several men. I can have some of my vaqueros help with the herd, but I cannot have them gone for the weeks it would take to move the herd to Wyoming. I will need them here for the cattle that are left and anything else we might need to do."

"That's understandable," Jean agreed. "My boys could come down and meet them, say at Bent's Fort, and take the herd the rest of the way up. How many would it take?"

"Eight or ten."

"If I could get at least six of my boys and family to meet them could you spare a few of your men the extra time?"

"Yes, I could do that and the rest of the vaqueros could come back here."

Jean looked at Henry, "After we see Beckett and find out where Pablo stands I'll send a wire to Jeb at the sheriff's office to tell Clint. I'll send one up to South Pass City for Ian, but have Jeb pass along the information to Ian or Will and Pete in case Ian doesn't get the South Pass wire."

Henry agreed, "We'd need to get them started down as quick as possible."

Pablo stood up, "We need to go to Taos and see Mr. Beckett; it might give us some idea of what time we have to work with."

Samuel Beckett was working in his office when the three men walked in. He greeted them heartily and invited them to sit.

"I am sorry Mr. Ruiz, that I have not made it up to see you yet. I seem to be buried in work lately that has kept me nailed to my desk. I have not found any information regarding your property so far. Checking with my government sources I found that there has been no official investigation begun into your father's death or to the Grant. That information has not made it to the General Land Office in Washington, nor is there a record of it in the local land office in Santa Fe."

Pablo looked hopeful, "If there is no investigation, could it be there is no problem with my ownership?"

"There will be eventually. The lack of a will and the Government's drive to gobble up the old grants almost guarantee someone will come nosing around at some point."

Pablo slumped a bit in his chair, "So, we have to wait and see?"

"For the moment. I am staying on top of it, as soon as I hear something I will know where to start. In my inquiries I have identified myself as your attorney and that all correspondence should come to me. I hope you don't mind my taking that initiative without speaking to you first, but I felt time was crucial to you on this matter."

Pablo waved his hand, "No, that is perfectly acceptable and I appreciate your concern on my behalf."

"I will act as promptly as possible on anything I receive."

"If the government takes the land and their purpose is to sell it, is there a chance I can buy back the hacienda?

"I don't know yet. I wish I did so I could advise you."

Pablo nodded his understanding, "Yes, you cannot act if you do not know what to act on. If the property is taken by the government will the livestock go with it or do the animals belong to me?"

"Unfortunately the livestock is part of the estate, a package deal so to speak."

Pablo frowned at the news. "Mr. Beckett, here is what we have been discussing. Perhaps it is illegal, but I am not going to give up all that my family has worked so hard for and owned for over one hundred years, without a fight. I want to take on partners in Colorado and Wyoming and move most of my cattle off the hacienda and onto those properties."

Beckett's expression remained neutral and did not reflect his approval or disapproval of the idea. "*Technically*, it is illegal because the estate is no longer in your hands, however, on the opposite side of the coin you have had no official notification that the government is seizing the estate have you?"

Pablo shook his head, "None at all."

"So, *technically*, moving your cattle off the property is not in violation of the law because you have not been told that you cannot."

"Then, I will do it. What do you think of my taking on partners?"

"Partnerships and divided property is often a sound business pursuit, providing of course those you partner with are reputable. Partnering with dishonest persons can ruin you very quickly."

"The proposed partners are Mr. Pelletier's son who is the brother to my sister's husband, and a friend of their family, both reputable men."

"In that case I would say to do it and as quickly as possible before any actions are taken against the estate."

The door to Beckett's office opened and a woman stepped in holding a handful of papers and envelopes. She stopped, "Oh, I'm sorry Samuel. I did not know you were in a meeting."

"That is fine, May. Gentlemen, my wife, May. She is my secretary and assistant, and keeps my distracted mind on track."

The men all greeted her politely. She nodded in return.

"I was at the post office and thought to bring the mail." She handed it to Beckett. "I will leave you alone to finish your meeting." She quickly left the office closing the door behind her.

Becket gave the mail a cursory glance. His eyes falling on an official envelope, he cut it open and read the enclosed letter. "Here it is, Mr. Ruiz. Official notification that you have two months to vacate the property."

Pablo's face fell showing his distress.

Beckett continued to intensely study the letter. "There is a contact address here for further information on the disposition of the property. Funny though," he mused as he read the contents. "This is the oddest official letter I have ever seen. It is written on official Washington General Land Office letterhead, however, though the wording is intelligent, it is quite basic, not overburdened with government bureaucratese as my experience would expect. In addition to that, it was sent from Albuquerque. This should have been sent from the Land Office in Santa Fe."

Pablo gave him a questioning look, "What does that mean?"

"I'm not sure, however, my inquiries must have reached this person or how would he know to send this to me. I will contact the address and find out who is on the other end of this. This could be a government party within the government with their own interests. Such as when a senator and his cronies bought up the Maxwell grant and resold it."

"How will this affect me and the hacienda?"

"This may be a similar group looking to sell the property unofficially, under the table if you will. If that is the case we may be able to strike a deal with them for you to purchase the property back."

"So, I might be able to buy the hacienda from this person?"

"Maybe. I have to check into it."

Jean narrowed his eyes and scowled at the paper in Beckett's hand. "Mr. Beckett, don't you find it a little odd that someone has learned of Sebastian's death and lack of a will, but the proper offices know nothing of it?"

Beckett's eyes reflected his agreement to Jean's thought. "Yes, indeed I do. I also wonder how they learned of it so fast. I should have been the only one outside of the family that knew there was no will."

"And from Albuquerque? How would that kind of information end up in a place totally removed from any of Sebastian's business?"

"Or an official land office," Beckett added.

"A spy," Henry said.

Beckett looked from Jean to Henry, "Someone in Taos you think?"

"How else would someone in Albuquerque find out about Sebastian's death?" Henry answered. "Someone is keeping track of local news, someone who also has access to private documents or connected to someone who does."

"A spy with inside connections," Jean agreed.

Beckett leaned back in his chair and stared at the top of his desk. "Yes. There has been so much activity in buying up the old grants of late that it only stands to reason that there would be those watching out for any opening to the grants. There is probably a spy in every town in New Mexico."

Pablo considered the implications of having unseen eyes on him and his private affairs. He didn't like it. He pointed to the letter, "That means no matter what I do this spy will report it to his friends."

"Yes, very possible," Beckett agreed.

Jean looked at Pablo, "Which could work to our advantage if we need to feed this group information."

Beckett slowly smiled, "Yes, indeed it could Mr. Pelletier."

Beckett turned his eyes to Pablo, "You know, Mr. Ruiz one of the problems with the mail delivery in the frontier is how unreliable it is. Mail gets lost as often as it gets through. Chances are I might never have received this letter today."

Beckett opened a drawer in his desk and dropped the letter in it. "Mr. Ruiz you have two months to set up your partnerships and get your cattle off the hacienda."

Pablo understood that Beckett was stalling for time and he needed to use that time for all it was worth. He stood up along with Jean and Henry. "Thank you Mr. Beckett, I will be in touch."

Beckett shook hands with all of them, "As will I, but let us keep it face-to-face from here on out."

Pablo's expression was one of concerned determination as they left the office and stepped outside. "Come, let me buy lunch while we discuss this further." Jean and Henry followed him to a cantina.

They walked into the small adobe room with tables and chairs filling the space. "It does not look like much, but Teresa's sister and husband run the place. It's the best food in all of Taos."

A woman, looking remarkably like Teresa, walked briskly from the kitchen area to their table. She smiled at Pablo, "Señor Ruiz, so good to see you. Thank you for honoring the cantina of my husband and myself."

Pablo smiled, "It is I who am honored by your excellent food. These are my friends, Jean Pelletier and Angelina's husband, Henry."

The woman smiled at them all and took their order. As she disappeared back into the kitchen Henry looked at Pablo, "At least we now know where we stand."

Pablo nodded, "Yes. I am undecided though. Should I wait to see if I can buy back the entire hacienda or create the partnerships anyway and move off a good number of the cattle and horses?"

"Partnerships, definitely," Henry quickly answered. "You still have no idea what is involved in getting the hacienda back, if you can at all. Beckett is stalling to give you that two month window to act. If you wait and find out you can't get the place back you lose all the way around. Besides, partnering is smart business."

"Yes, I can greatly expand my herds without fear of losing them."

"And at the same time help Ian and Clint build up. You all come out winners."

Pablo smiled and grew more cheerful the longer he thought about it. "And if I do lose the hacienda I will still be in business."

Pablo's cheerfulness suddenly faded, "But what of my people if I lose the hacienda. Where will Ignacio and Teresa go? Lucia and her children? Juan put his whole life, and the lives of his family, in Ruiz hands trusting us to always care for them. What of all of them?"

"You're not going to lose the place," Jean responded in a hard voice. "Even if you can only save the part your home is on, that is still thousands of acres. A man can do well with that and these people will still have a home. On top of that you will have the partnerships."

Pablo nodded, "That is what my father would have said. He never gave up and he always found a way to win out."

"Remember, you said you didn't even own a white flag."

Pablo smiled with chagrin, "Thank you for reminding me. I always looked to my father for answers and wisdom and he always had both. I miss him greatly, especially in this time of trouble. He would have known exactly what to do."

"I think you're doing fine," Jean said. "Sebastian would be very proud of his son right now."

"I hope so."

"You sound like him Pablo. Concerned about your people, taking responsibility, and taking action. Yes, Sebastian would be very proud."

Pablo smiled, "Thank you. Perhaps I can draw on your wisdom when I am not sure what to do."

"Pablo, you've got the whole Pelletier family behind you and we're going to back you and help you until you win this thing."

"I am humbled by your friendship Mr. Pelletier."

"There's only one way to wade into a fight, Pablo."

"And that's to win it," Henry broke in. He grinned at Jean, "My father taught me that."

"My father as well," Pablo smiled.

Jean moved the subject along, "Okay, let's get down to business."

"Moving cattle," Henry said. "What do you want to do Pablo?"

"Do Ian and Clint have the land for an extra five or six hundred head and extra horses?"

"I'm not sure," Jean said. "I haven't seen Ian's place, but from what I remember about that country the grazing is not bad. Plenty of grass and water. Clint's is drier and less grass. That whole eastern Colorado country is like that. I don't know, they might not."

"Is the land expensive in either area?"

"Not really, especially in that sparse Colorado country. Dollar an acre maybe."

"Since these men are to be my partners it is only right that I should expand their holdings to accommodate the extra cattle and the calves they will throw next year. I need to arrange for them to buy more land, with my money of course."

Jean thought for a second, "We would have to get the money to them fast."

"I could wire the money to their banks."

"I don't know how well that would work. The bank in Fort Collins is fine and could handle it, but I'm not even sure if there is a bank in South Pass City."

"And there is the matter of the spy," Henry reminded them. "He seems to have access to information that he shouldn't."

Jean agreed, "That's right, we have to keep that in mind in everything we do. We don't want to tip our hand that you are moving the stock off."

Henry leaned over the table. Jean and Pablo instinctively leaned in toward him. "This is kind of a complex matter, a lot more than can be told in a brief wire, and I don't think something like this should go over a wire anyway. Telegraphers are supposed to be discreet about what they send, but some can run their mouth as bad as a gossipy woman. A lot needs to be explained about the situation here, the partnerships and cattle, a drive, and land purchases."

"Okay," Jean acknowledge him. "I agree there is a lot more than can be covered in a wire and our business shouldn't be announced to anyone, especially since we aren't even supposed to be doing this. What is your solution?"

Henry lowered his voice, "With two horses I can be home in three days. Give me the money. I'll get it to Ian and Clint so they can buy the land, and get them headed back this way. I can fill them in on all of it."

Jean stared at Henry for several seconds. He glanced at Pablo, "What do you think?"

"I think it is risky riding with all that money, but I agree it is the surest way to accomplish this."

"And the fastest," Henry added. "Who knows how long it would take for them to even get the wires, let alone do everything else and get down here in time. All the while still not knowing what's really going on, just responding because we need them to."

"And the spy could cause our efforts to be stopped," Pablo added.

Jean nodded, "Okay. It's the best way."

Henry turned his attention to Pablo. "Can you draw the money from the bank here?"

"I can get enough for land. Our main account is in Santa Fe. While you are gone I will have it sent up here ready to buy the hacienda if I can get it. Should the spy learn of the money transfer he would have no idea of its purpose."

"Good. I think it would be better if I brought the boys all the way to the hacienda and we head out from here rather than wasting time trying to connect in the desert not knowing the others timing. I'm sure we can be back within three weeks; that still leaves five weeks before anything happens. The cattle will be in Colorado and Wyoming by then."

Pablo thought on Henry's plan for a minute before answering. "Yes, that will work. I will have my vaqueros cut out and hold the right breeding stock for the drive. When you get back here you can head them out right away."

CHAPTER FOURTEEN

The big Scotsman looked over the land and then back to Ian Pelletier who sat on a good square built Palouse gelding. "I hate to leave it," Duncan McKenzie declared in his deep rolling brogue.

Ian studied his neighbor, "It's a hard thing leaving your land."

"Aye, it is that, but my wife's health is worth more to me than land."

"Is she any better?"

Duncan shook his head, "No. We left Scotland for the coast of Maine and should have stayed there. I was told this Rocky Mountain air would be better for her than the damp seacoast, but it seems those who said that were wrong. She did better on the coast. I'll be taking her back to it as soon as I can sell the place, for I need the money."

"This is a good piece of land, water, trees, graze, it has it all. I'd buy it myself if I had the cash."

"And I'd make you a square deal on it too."

"I know you would. You've been a good neighbor Duncan. I hate to see you leave."

"And I hate to leave, but we can't always control the choices we must make."

Duncan and Ian sat on their horses for several minutes of silence before Duncan spoke again. "You have done well here, Ian." Then he broke into a smile, "But, then of course you *are* half Scot."

Ian grinned, "Come from tough stock on both sides."

"I still regret that I didn't know of Anne's plight against that Babcock or I'd of done something. I didn't know her husband all that well, he wasn't a neighborin' sort, if you know what I mean."

Ian nodded his understanding. Anne's husband, who it was accepted had been murdered by Vern Babcock, had been a hardworking man, but not a social one. "Anne kept it all under her hat, she has a lot of pride like that. My brothers and I actually pushed ourselves into the fight. She didn't want us involved."

Duncan scowled, "I still should of known, all the same."

"There are a couple thousand acres between your house and

ours, not exactly like you could look out your window and see what was going on. The problem is long resolved, so don't beat yourself up over it."

"Aye. Talk of Babcock's little empire going up in smoke and fire made the rounds for a hundred miles in every direction. Men were asking who those Pelletier boys were and when it got around that you were the Colorado Pelletiers folks knew to leave you alone."

"Except for the ones who stole three of my horses two days back. Owl is out looking for them right now trying to pick up a track."

"We are on the so-called 'outlaw trail' here and that will happen."

"It won't happen again if I catch them and make an example of them."

Duncan chuckled deep and hearty, "That would be worth the seein'."

Ian gathered his relaxed reins, "Thanks for pushing my strays back over to my side, I'd been looking for that bunch all day."

"What are neighbors for if not to help?"

"I hate to see you go, Duncan."

Duncan nodded looking sad. "You have a good day now, Ian."

The two men rode off in opposite directions.

Ian wished he could buy Duncan McKenzie's three thousand acres and join it to their two thousand; then they would have the makings of a good spread. They could then generate enough money to buy up other land parcels.

Ian thought of the mine. He might be able to get enough out of it to buy the McKenzie property. He had scraped enough of the gold from the little vein to buy two hundred head of breeding cattle, but the thought of going back down into that pitch dark suffocating hole terrified him. He would never admit, even to Anne, that the mine pit scared him to death. No one alive was to know that Ian Pelletier had a fear of something, especially a deep heart stopping fear like he had of that black hole. The very thought made him shiver. He would have to find the money another way or just suck in his fear and go back down. The thought knotted his stomach and made him sweat.

Ian rode back into his yard and dismounted. The day was waning as he stripped the gear off the gelding and turned him loose in the corral with a feed of meadow hay. He headed for the house.

Pushing the door open the first thing he saw was Anne stirring a pot over the stove with one hand and holding the baby on her hip with the other. The little six month old girl stared out into the world. Anne turned and smiled at Ian.

Ian hung his gunbelt on a peg by the door and walked up to Anne. They exchanged a kiss. He took the baby and held her. He smiled into his daughter's face, "And how is little Kate today?"

The baby smiled back at him.

"I'll bet Papa smells like a cow, doesn't he?"

The baby laughed.

"You know," Ian said to Anne, "I'm not sure if she's laughing at me or happy to see me!"

"Probably the second one, I know I'm happy to see you."

Ian smiled at her. It had been a good year and a half.

"I ran into Duncan McKenzie today, he pushed some of our strays back over. His wife is doing poorly and he's going to sell out."

"That's too bad, on both counts," Anne replied.

"Yeah, he's a good neighbor. I wish we could buy his place and add it to ours. That would give us five thousand acres. We could do a lot with that."

"How much does he want for it?"

"He never flat out said, but a few things he did say leads me to believe he wants about four thousand."

"That's not bad for three thousand acres of good land."

"Yeah, it's pretty much the going rate for government land, except it's about three thousand nine hundred more than we have."

Anne continued to work over the stove as Ian sat down and played with the baby. "I could go back down in the mine and see if I can't dig out enough gold. I got that much before."

Anne knew how much the black hole terrified her husband. He had never said it, and never would admit it, but she knew his fear of the mine. Even now his face took on a dark expression and sweat popped out on his forehead at the thought of it.

She looked over her should at him, "I don't want you going back into that old mine again, Ian. It's dangerous and there's not enough gold in there that I would risk losing you to a cave-in. No."

Ian was relieved for a way out of the decision. Anne saw his face lighten from it.

"It was pretty rumbly that last time I went down. The timbers looked rotten. I think they used old timbers to shore it up in the first place. There was more wood dust on the ground than dirt."

"I want you to seal the mouth of that hole Ian. I don't want anyone, especially you, going in there."

"I'll get to it as soon as I can." He was glad to be able to seal his fear permanently in that black pit.

Anne wanted to change the subject to something away from Ian's fear. "Any luck figuring out who took the horses?"

"Owl set out first thing this morning trying to track them from where they were taken."

"It's been days, can he still find a trail?"

Ian grinned, "Owl? Owl could track a lizard across dry rock in August. I don't know how he does it. I'm a fair to middlin' tracker, but I can't read sign like he can."

Anne nodded remembering how Owl had protected her during Babcock's attack and kept her hopes alive during their captivity in his jail. He never lost faith in his cousins and they proved worthy of his trust. "Yeah, I don't know what we would do without his help."

"Will and Pete were a huge help, but they had responsibilities at the canyon ranch." Ian snorted and laughed, "Did I actually use the word 'responsibilities' when referring to my crazy brothers?"

Anne grinned, "Yes you did."

"Either I'm softening up or they're actually calming down."

"Maybe a little of both. They do make me laugh though."

"That's what Jenny says, they make her laugh. There's been times I've wanted to wring their necks," Ian smiled with genuine warmth, "but, after that Babcock affair I gained a whole new respect for those two."

"Well, I hope they never get *too* calmed down, I'd miss their joking around."

Ian huffed a laugh, "I guess I would too."

The door opened and Owl walked in. He had lost little of his stoic expression that was natural to his race, yet he had opened up more and talked freely. He leaned his rifle against the wall and closed the door behind him.

Anne greeted him, "Hello Owl, supper's almost ready."

Owl smiled at Anne, "Good, I am hungry."

"Get anywhere with the tracking?" Ian asked.

Owl poured a cup of coffee and sat down. "I did find their trail headed south. Two horses with riders and our three without riders. They rode up to the three horses and herded them away."

"We'll ride down that way tomorrow. Probably went to Bitter Creek."

Owl nodded, "To sell them."

"We'd better find them before they do. It's not easy to replace those Palouse horses especially that stud and one of those mares was with foal."

The combination of squeaking wagon wheels, rattling harness chain, and horse's hooves striking hard ground sounded from outside. They all looked at each other. Ian stood up and handed the baby back to Anne. Crossing the room he pulled his revolver from the hanging holster and opened the door. Owl was behind him with his rifle.

Ian was surprised into momentary silence to see Jeb driving the wagon, Jenny beside him, and the bed filled with their belongings. Jeb pulled the team to a halt and looked at his brother. "Is the offer to come up and help you still in force?"

Ian stared for another second before answering, "Sure, yeah. I just never expected to see you take me up on it. What happened to the lawman?"

"Bit of a long story."

Ian smiled at Jenny, "Hey, pretty girl."

Jenny smiled back at Ian, "I hope we aren't going to be a problem inviting ourselves up like this."

"You're not inviting yourselves, Anne and I both told you to come up anytime."

Anne stepped out the door carrying the baby. She smiled at Jenny and exclaimed with a laugh, "Oh good, another woman to talk to. You can't ever leave."

Jenny looked relieved, "Thank you. Oh, the baby, she is so pretty."

Ian walked to the side of the wagon and helped Jenny down. She hugged him and then made her way quickly to Anne and embraced her. Her face lit up as she looked into Kate's smiling face. "May I?"

Anne handed the baby to Jenny. "Come in, I was making supper. I'll put some more on."

Jeb stepped down from the wagon and stretched his legs. He shook hands with Ian and then with Owl.

Ian looked over the wagon load, "Coming to stay?"

"If you don't mind."

"No, I welcome the help. Owl and I can't keep up with all the work. You can stay in our extra room until we build you a house."

"Thanks, I appreciate that."

"What's the story?"

Jeb went into detail about Cassidy and how the town turned on Jenny. As he spoke Ian's eyes narrowed and his face and neck turned red with anger. Jeb told how he quit the job and took Jenny up to Andrew's until they could get everything together to come here.

"Did everyone turn on Jenny?" Ian snarled.

"The old timers didn't. Ben and Alice didn't. Alice really lit into them about it. Mrs. Kelly defended her too. Reed, Clint, Paul and a few others were on our side, but the newcomers have taken control of the town. Paul's about had it too."

"So, what about this Cassidy?"

"He's dead. I called him out in Pruitt's and killed him."

Ian nodded his approval. "If you hadn't I would have."

"You think I wouldn't?"

"Not for a minute."

"Larry Pruitt tried to bushwhack me at the same time. He's dead too."

"That puts an end to him, and good riddance it is. What about his place?"

"I heard that Paul, Clint, and Reed pulled it down."

"Pulled it down?"

"Yeah, hooked a team to those support poles he had in there and jerked 'em out. The place is flatter'n a pancake."

"Good. Why don't we get your wagon under cover and the team cared for and then go in and eat."

"Sounds good."

Jeb climbed back up on the seat and drove the wagon into the barn. He got down and began unbuckling the harnesses. Ian and Owl helped him.

"Pete and Will were here for a while, but went back home last week," Ian told him.

"I saw them for a day or so before I left. They said they'd make it a point to go into town and give the pilgrims a hard time to make up for what they did to Jenny."

"Owl and I are going hunting a couple of horse thieves tomorrow, care to come along?"

"Like I wouldn't?"

Ian looked at Jeb and grinned, "You're sounding more like me every time I see you."

Jeb let out a heavy sigh, "There's been a lot happening the last couple of years that's hardened me I guess. I'm still angry over that town business too."

"It happens. Just don't let it get so controlling that you turn mean and dug down inside yourself. Something like that can kill your marriage."

Jeb grinned, "Sounds like a husband and daddy talking."

Ian laughed. "When Pete and Will told me I was hard to get along with, was surly and nasty, and a cross between a badger and prickly pear I had to stop and take an honest look at myself. I figured it was time to ease up a bit. Having Anne and Kate makes that a little easier to do."

Jeb grinned at Owl, "Has he eased up?"

Owl laughed, "In some ways. I would still ride into battle with him though. He has not eased up in that way."

"That's good to hear. If he gets any nicer he'll be turning into a Sunday school teacher."

Ian glanced at Jeb, "I could teach you what it's like to have this heel chain wrapped around your neck and what happens when I pull it real hard."

"Ah, that's the Ian I love."

They finished with the horses and headed to the house. Stopping under the extension of roof that projected past the front door they took turns washing in the basin. Once clean they went inside.

Jenny was cooing at the baby looking happier than Jeb had seen her since their trouble began. Her expression alone made him happy they had made the move. He couldn't help but smile as well.

Anne looked up from the stove when the men walked in. "Jeb, Jenny told me what happened to her. I'm glad you chose to move up here with us."

"Thank you Anne. It looks like the baby made a new friend."

Jenny was all laughs and smiles, "Oh, she's such a beautiful little girl."

"She is a cute one alright," Jeb agreed.

Ian had learned that the best way to help Anne in the kitchen was to stay out of the way. The kitchen was her kingdom and where she spent a good amount of her time since the baby was born. She had done a good deal of the ranch work prior to that, but the baby was her first priority now.

The three men sat down surrounding the table. "I'm going to build an extension on the side over there for a sitting room," Ian said, then added, "When I have the time."

"With two of us to help you now you might get the chance," Jeb answered.

"We have a lot of plans, but it takes money and that will take some time to raise. More land, more cattle and it'll grow quick enough."

Jeb nodded, "It takes time and money to build anything worth-while. Speaking of cattle, did you hear about Don Sebastian?"

Ian narrowed his eyes with concern, "No, what about him?"

"He was murdered by outlaws a few weeks back."

"The *Don*?"

"Yeah, I got the wire in Fort Collins before I left and got it to Pa and Ma. They headed south along with Henry and his family the next day."

"Wow, that's hard to believe. Have you heard anything else since then?"

"No. I have no idea what's going on down there right now."

Ian pondered the idea of Sebastian being dead. "I wonder if they need us to help find his killers."

"Between Pablo, Pa, Henry, and two dozen vaqueros I figure they've already taken care of that."

"No doubt. That was probably the first thing they did."

Anne spoke up from the corner of the room where she was work-ing. "Who was Don Sebastian?"

Ian explained, "Don Sebastian Ruiz, he's Angelina's father. He has a big land grant down around Taos that had been given to his grandfather by the King of Spain. They run thousands of cattle on the hacienda. Pa and Sebastian met back in the 50's, I guess it was, and started trading horses back and forth. Pa and the Don were cut from the same chunk of rawhide. When the women were taken by that Hornsworth crowd Sebastian took out after them and got Rebecca and Angelina back. Now, some outlaws murdered him."

"Oh, how awful. Who is running the hacienda now?"

"Likely Pablo." Ian chuckled, "It's hard to see Pablo as the patron. He was always a wild one."

Anne gave Ian a knowing look, "Certain events in one's life often make them change their priorities."

Jeb grinned, "That's right, it makes them *ease up*."

Ian turned a stern eye on his brother, "Keep it up."

Jenny cast a glance at the two brothers, "Have you two been at it already?"

"No," Jeb answered innocently. "Just commenting on Ian's changes."

After having spent the lonely, fear wracked months following her first husband's murder and the forced siege under the Babcock threat, Anne appreciated Ian and any company they received. She laughed, "This is going to be fun."

———

The next morning the men were saddled and ready to follow the trail of the stolen horses. Jenny had awakened in the night worried about Jeb. She had hoped his walking into danger had ended with his turning in the badge. He had killed Cassidy, but did not talk of it to her.

During the morning she spoke to Anne about her concerns and fears regarding Jeb's safety. Anne understood her worry, however she patiently explained that in this country men would always face danger if they were men of any worth. They could not sit back while men threatened them or stole from them. She had seen what Ian and his brothers were capable of, and Owl as well. She wasn't worried about their safety.

Owl picked up the trail where he had left it the day before. The tracks were wearing down from the sun and dust. However to Owl, they were like the writing the whites read so easily but was such a mystery to him. They rode on into Bitter Creek where outlaws were known to frequent.

Sitting on their horses the three looked the street over. Jeb asked, "Do you have the Circle P brand on the horses?"

"Yeah," Ian answered. "Put it on the right hip first off. I use a smaller iron on the horses than the cattle, so the brand is about half the size you see on the cows."

Jeb nodded, "Got it. We should split up."

"Agreed. Owl knows what these horses look like so he should go with you. You two go east, I'll take the west."

Owl and Jeb reined their horses to the opposite direction of Ian and they rode away from each other. Owl explained the markings on the Palouse horses as they rode.

The town was small, typical of the prairie towns springing up around mines; in this case it was coal that drew in the workers, professional gamblers, and outlaws. Jeb and Owl reached the end of the main row of buildings and rode around to a second street where the big barn and corrals of a livery stood. In the first corral were the three horses.

"Them our horses," Owl said pointing at the horses.

"Go get Ian, I'll have a talk with the hostler."

Owl turned his horse and put him into a quick walk to where they had last seen Ian. Jeb dismounted and tied his horse to the lower corral rail. He climbed between the rails and up to the three horses. The stud opened his eyes wide showing more white than iris at Jeb's approach. Jeb spoke softly to him and watched his eyes settle back down to normal.

The hostler walked briskly out of the barn and slipped between the rails. "Can I help you?" His tone was brusque and surly.

Jeb glanced at him, "Where'd you get these horses?"

"You need to check in with me before handling my horses. You can't just waltz in here like you own the place and start messin' with my animals."

Jeb glared hard at the man, "You didn't answer my question."

Jeb could sense the man growing nervous as he stammered an answer. "Bought 'em off a couple of fellas yesterday. Why?"

"They happen to give you anything proving they owned them?"

The hostler licked his lips nervously, "I didn't ask."

"You should have."

"Why's that?"

Jeb clearly saw the man was becoming frightened. His tough front was quickly falling apart leaving raw fear behind.

Pointing at the brand on the stud's hip, Jeb slowly said, "Because that Circle P is my brother's brand. Same brand on the mares. These horses were stolen from his ranch up by South Pass three days ago."

The hostler began to sweat. He pulled a dirty red bandana from his pocket and wiped his face. "I don't buy stolen horses."

Jeb squared up to the man, "You just said you didn't ask or appear to care where the horses came from. How would you know if you were buying stolen stock or not? Then, again maybe you deal in stolen horses on a regular basis and you're just plain lying."

The hostler, finding himself boxed in reverted back to his brusque talk. He saw his accuser was young and hoped he could bully him into backing off and leaving. He hung his right thumb over the butt of the waist high pistol on his hip and scowled at Jeb. "If you're accusing me of being a horse thief you'd better be willing to back that up."

Jeb slipped the loop off the Remington's hammer as he met the man's bluffing eyes. "You're a horse thief," he said flatly.

The man hadn't counted on the young man calling his bluff so blatantly. He quickly took a step back, dropped his hands to his sides, and looked flustered. "Okay, maybe I was a little hasty here. Whose brand is that anyway?"

"Ian Pelletier's."

The hostler's Adam's apple bobbed a second before his jaw dropped open. "From South Pass you say?" Everyone had heard about the Pelletier fight with Babcock. Blowing up a town full of outlaws makes for a hot topic of conversation in saloons and barbershops. The name Pelletier traveled with it.

"That's the one. He'll be here in a couple of minutes and you can explain to him why his horses are in your corral."

A renewed flood of sweat broke out on the hostler's face, "I'm sure we can work this out."

"I'm sure we can. How much did you pay for these?"

"Fifty each."

"Who did you buy them from?"

With nervous movements of his hands and feet the man hesitated, "I don't want to say."

"I suggest you change your mind and *say* . . . before my brother gets here. A little cooperation on your part might ease his temper a bit."

The man licked his dry lips, "Okay. They were outlaws."

Jeb snapped back with sarcasm, "Around here? Tell me it ain't so!"

"Dick Norton and Ralph Todd, Norton's a gunfighter. He'll kill me if he knows I told you."

"So, you did know these horses were stolen."

"I . . . I suspected."

"You can work that out with my brother. Where can I find Norton and Todd?"

"Last I saw them they were . . ." he stopped mid-sentence and whimpered. "That's them comin' right now. Please don't tell them I told you."

Jeb ignored the frightened man and slipped back out between the rails. He walked toward the two men who were approaching the corral. They stopped when they realized his focus was on them.

Jeb stopped forty feet away from where the two men stood. Never get closer Clint had taught him. The closer you get the better chance you'll get hit. "Understand you men sold those horses yesterday."

The man to Jeb's right answered, "Might have, what's it to you?"

"Plenty, since they were stolen off my brother's ranch up north."

The man chuckled, "That's a mighty dangerous accusation, son."

"It's no accusation."

Both men glared at him without speaking.

"Which one of you is Norton?"

The man who had spoken replied, "That would be me. Got a problem with that?"

"Just want to know which of you to shoot first."

Both men laughed. Norton's hand dropped to his revolver and locked onto the butt. Jeb's hand flew down and up bringing the Remington level. He fired first shot. The bullet slammed into Norton's solar plexus as his gun was still coming up in front of him. He dropped to his knees.

Todd yanked his gun out as Jeb swung the revolver to the left and higher, shooting Todd in the face. Todd let out a scream, dropped his gun, and slapped his hands over his face trying to hold back the blood that seeped through his clenched fingers.

Norton brought his gun up while gripping his free hand over his wound. Jeb shifted his gun back to Norton and shot him two more times. Norton fell face first throwing up a small cloud of dust.

Jeb stood his ground and watched the two men for movement. There was none. The clamor of running feet and shouts were making their way to the scene of the gunfight. Jeb turned to see Ian and Owl watching him. Owl's face was stoic, yet his eyes reflected approval. Ian stared at him, transfixed at what he had just seen his brother do.

Jeb began reloading the Remington. He looked at Ian and jerked his head toward the corrals. "Man over there has your horses. He knew they were stolen and bought them anyway. You might want to have a little talk with him."

Ian pointed at the dead men now surrounded by a crowd of the curious. "Who were they?'

Jeb rammed a load into the Remington's cylinder. "Your horse thieves. They took exception to my questions."

Jeb walked back to the corral with Ian and Owl, ramming loads into the Remington's cylinder as he went. They slipped between the rails and up to the horses. The hostler stood staring in fear at the men. He held his open hands out in front of him, "I didn't know they were Pelletier horses. Here, take 'em back."

Ian locked eyes on the hostlers whose eyes were filled with fear, "I intend to. I'll let you slide this time, but if you ever see that Circle P again you get word up to Ian Pelletier real fast, understand?"

"Yes sir, I surely will do that."

Jeb gave the hostler a cold look causing the man's Adam's apple to jump again. "You might want to check their pockets, they might still have some of the money you paid them."

"Thank you, I'll do that. Sorry for the misunderstanding."

Jeb nodded at him and walked away.

The hostler looked at Ian, "Do you know who that man was your brother killed?"

Ian shook his head.

"Dick Norton."

Ian shrugged, "Gunfighter I heard."

"What's your brother's name so I know to tell people to fight shy of doing bad things to you boys."

"Jeb."

"Jeb Pelletier, got it."

CHAPTER FIFTEEN

Henry rode into the home yard of the Poudre Canyon ranch trail weary, dust coated, and hungry. He led the second horse with a ten foot lead rope. He had swapped his saddle from one to the other every few hours and kept riding, sleeping only when he was falling out of the saddle in the dark. He had made the three hundred mile ride in under three days. The horses were exhausted, yet holding up well.

Andre was with Pierre in the corral checking over a pregnant mare. They looked up at Henry with surprise. Leaving the mare, they walked up to Henry who remained mounted. Andre looked up at him, "Is there trouble?"

Henry nodded, "Yes."

Pierre stood at the horse's side and studied Henry's face. "You have ridden far, you should come down."

"I can't. My back is broke, my knees are locked, and I don't know where I am." He grinned at Pierre, obviously sleep deprived and punchy.

Pierre glanced at Andre whose eyes were reflecting amusement at Henry's words. "He is crazy with exhaustion Father."

"Yes, he is." Andre spoke in a loud voice to Henry, "You must tell us what the trouble is Henry."

Henry looked back at his uncle, "Help me off this horse."

Pierre and Andre both reached up and guided Henry down as he swung his leg over the saddle and slid to the ground. They held him upright as he winced in pain and put his full weight down on his legs."

Pierre took control of the two horses while Andre supported Henry until he could stand unassisted. Henry nodded his thanks.

"What happened?" Andre asked. "Where are the others?"

"Still back at the hacienda. There's trouble, I need to get everyone together to explain."

Having heard the voices, Will and Pete came out of the main house to see what was happening. They hurried to Henry's side. "What's going on?" Will asked.

Andre answered, "I am not sure, Henry is too tired to get much out of him."

"Trouble." Henry said, "We have to act as quick as possible."

"Let's get him in the house, we've got grub on the stove," Will told him.

"Wait," Henry stopped them from leading him away. He turned around and stumbled back to his horse and untied the saddlebags from his saddle.

Tom walked out of the barn with a shovel in his hands. Seeing Henry he ran to join the group. Henry looked at him as he gripped the saddlebags tight against his chest, "Go get your Pa, I need him up to the house."

Tom nodded and ran down the path to his house.

Pete and Pierre took Henry's horses into the corral and tended to them while Andre and Will helped Henry to the house. Going into the house Henry flopped down on the settee still clutching the saddlebags. "Man, it feels good to sit on something soft that doesn't move."

Will grinned at him, "Old age already Henry, or just going soft?"

Henry grinned back at him and slurred, "If I was Ian I'd have a smart come-back for that."

Will handed Henry a glass with two fingers of whiskey, "Here, this'll brace you up and make a man out of you again."

"Maybe enough to get up off this thing and kick your tail around the room a few times!"

"There you go...your old self already."

Will spooned out a plateful of stew from the pot on the stove. "Are you up to coming to the table or should I feed you while you pretend to be tired?"

"Put it on the table, I'd crawl before letting you feed me like a baby." He took a drink from the glass and stood up. His face winced at the stiffness and pain in his back and legs. He shuffled slowly to the table and sat down, tossing the saddlebags on the table.

"You in love with those saddlebags or something?" Will asked. "Ma'd kill you if she was here for throwing those dirty bags on her clean table."

"Yes, I am, and yes she would, but she would understand if she knew what was in them." Henry carelessly shoved his spoon through the stew spilling some over the plate and onto the table. He put the spoonful in his mouth and made a face, "Prairie dog again?"

"It's coyote, shut up and eat your stew."

Pete opened the door and walked in with Andre and Pierre. Pete looked at Henry, "Pretty good prairie dog, huh Henry?"

Henry looked up at him, "I knew it was prairie dog." He jerked a thumb at Will, "He said it was coyote, but I know the difference."

"No, coyote was last week."

Andre looked in the pot and spooned up a piece of meat and examined it. "Sure looks like elk to me."

"Shh," Will whispered, "it only looks like elk, that's the secret."

Andre laughed and dropped the meat and spoon back in the pot.

Andrew was next in with Tom, Sarah, and Rebecca. Jacque and Red Horse walked in seconds later completing the adults left at the ranch. "Okay, what's going on?" Andrew demanded his tone anxious.

Everyone took chairs around the table watching Henry eat the last of his stew. He finished and pushed the bowl away. "Good prairie dog boys."

Rebecca scrunched up her face, "You ate a prairie dog?"

"It might have been coyote," Henry replied.

Rebecca made another face.

"That's enough Rebecca," Andrew stopped her from saying more. "Why did you ride back alone Henry?"

Henry turned his whole head to look squarely at his elder brother. With his eyes dull and slow speech he explained what had happened to the Ruiz property due to Sebastian's failure to make a will and the eviction letter Pablo's attorney received. He continued on, "In hopes of keeping the hacienda Pablo's attorney is tracking down the people who sent the letter to see if he can buy the place back. Pablo is hedging his bet against losing the place and wants to take on partners and spread the cattle out to their ranches."

"Who are the partners he wants to take on?" Pete asked.

"Ian and Clint Rush." He slapped his hand down on the saddlebags, "Pablo sent ten thousand dollars with me, five for each of them to buy additional land for the cattle he wants to drive up here."

"I know Ian would welcome that," Pete agreed. "I can't see Clint turning down a deal like that either."

Andrew was slightly annoyed by Henry's slow and rambling explanation, but realized that his brother was exhausted. He nodded, "Okay that explains the hurry, to get the land secured before

Pablo is evicted."

"Yes. There is still hope that he can buy the land back from the government, but he's not banking on that."

"So, he wants to move his cattle up here," Andrew said as he comprehended Pablo's plan.

"At least a good portion of them."

"How many head is he talking about moving?" Will asked.

"Twelve to fifteen hundred head."

Will whistled, "That's a big drive."

Henry nodded, "We're going to use the Goodnight Trail past Bents Fort and up to Clint's place, then on to Cheyenne and west to Ian's."

"I take it you're riding on to Ian's with his half of the money," Andrew commented. "How about Clint's share?"

"I figure to ride to Fort Collins tomorrow and give Jeb the money for Clint and have him get started buying land while I ride to Ian's place."

"You haven't heard have you?" Andrew said. "Jeb and Jenny left Fort Collins and moved up to Ian's."

Henry gaped at Andrew, "What happened?"

"A man named Cassidy, who had been the enforcer at the house Jenny was held captive, found her in town and began making approaches to her. He wanted her to conduct business with him or he would spread the word all over town that she had been a Denver prostitute. Naturally she refused to cooperate with him and he made good on his threat and spread lies about her. The newcomers in town turned on her and she was fired from the school. Jeb got mad and quit his job and took her up to Ian's to get away from the talk."

Henry stared at Andrew as he listened to the story. "That's horrible. What about this Cassidy?"

Andrew glanced at Sarah and Rebecca hesitating a second before answering, "Jeb killed him."

"If he didn't one of us would have."

"I went after Jeb and got to town to find Paul and Clint at Pruitt's hole dealing with the aftermath of Jeb's visit. Jeb had killed Larry Pruitt at the same time. Seems Pruitt tried to backshoot him and didn't make it."

Henry snorted, "That's one worthless man best planted."

Pete grinned, "Paul, along with Reed Hall and Clint pulled the timbers out from under the roof and dropped Pruitt's shack flat. It's gone."

"Even better. So, Jeb has moved lock, stock, and barrel to Ian's ranch?"

Pete nodded, "Yeah. Ian had asked him to come up and help if he ever got tired of being a lawman."

Henry thought in silence for a minute trying to reorganize his plan through his foggy mind, but was unable to think clearly. "Okay, I'll have to rearrange the plan a bit."

"Will and I will ride with you to protect the money."

"Yeah, that would be good. One of the reasons I covered ground so fast was because I have it. Made me a little nervous."

"How long ago did you leave?" Andrew asked.

"Day before yesterday."

Andrew looked startled, "Good Lord, three hundred miles in two and a half days. No wonder you look so beat up."

Henry grinned, "Yeah, it was a ride."

Will grinned, "Now I feel guilty about picking on you."

Henry looked at him, "No you don't."

"Actually, I don't. It was a heck of a ride all the same."

Henry smiled and shook his head, "It's all kind of a blur right now."

Andrew broke in, "What can we do to help? Sebastian and Pablo rode for us and got Rebecca back from the kidnappers. I'll do anything to help him out."

"That goes for all of us," Pete added.

Henry yawned and then said, "Pablo needs us to drive the cattle up here. He can spare a couple of vaqueros, but in light of the situation he needs them there."

Andrew nodded, "So, we need to go to Taos and start the drive from there?"

"Yes, as many of us as can go."

"Well, I'm going," Andrew stated firmly.

"I want to go too, Pa," Tom urged.

Andrew looked at his son, "Okay, I think your mother can spare you."

Sarah agreed, "We owe the Ruiz family such a huge debt that you and Tom going to help is the least we can offer."

"That makes five of us," Pete said. "Ian and Jeb will ride too, and I'm betting on Clint as well. That makes eight."

"I want to help," Red Horse volunteered.

"Nine," Pete concluded.

Andre spoke up, "Several of the mares are ready to foal and will need help. Me and my sons will take care of the horses while you help our friend."

"Thanks, Uncle Andre," Andrew said. "We can't leave the mares unattended."

"Then, I guess we're squared away on the matter," Henry concluded. "We need to move fast. Andrew, can I get you to ride to Ian with his land money and get him started? I'll ride to Clint's place. Ian knows Pablo Ruiz and it will be easy for you to fill him in, Clint doesn't know him and I will have to explain it all to him."

Andrew answered without question, "I'll leave in the morning."

"Good. You take Pete and I'll have Will ride with me. We will head back to the hacienda as soon as we finish with Clint. Have Ian and Jeb meet you here when they have the land locked down. I'll tell Clint to expect all of you to swing down and pick him up."

"Sounds like a plan. What kind of a time window are we talking about?"

"You will need to be heading south within ten days. That should give Ian and Clint time to buy the property. They can always let Anne and Ida complete the details if there are any left when you need to leave."

Andrew looked at his brothers as they all nodded in agreement. "Alright," Andrew stated flatly, "ten days and we ride." He looked back at Henry, "I never did ask...did you find the men that murdered Sebastian?"

Henry nodded, "We found them. It was a family of thieves and murderers, a father and his no account pack of sons."

Pete glanced at Henry, "*Was* a family?"

Henry looked back at him, "*Was.*"

Nothing more needed to be said. Sebastian's murder had been made right.

Henry stood up gripping the edge of the table to keep from falling. "Right now though, I'm going back to my house and get some sleep . . . or not." He dropped back down in the chair, his head tipped forward and he started snoring.

Everyone laughed. "The folk's bed," Andrew said with a grin.

Along with Pete and Will they picked Henry up and dragged him to the bedroom. They pulled his boots and dirty pants and shirt off and threw a blanket over him. They walked out laughing.

"I think we should put him in one of Ma's nightgowns," Pete whispered with his eyes full of mischief.

Andrew walked out of the room raising his hands in the air. "I don't know anything about this."

Will and Pete exchanged glances and grabbed Catherine's nightgown off a peg behind the door. "I don't know," Will looked at the garment. "I think it's too small, if we rip it Ma'll have our scalps."

"The dressing robe," Pete pointed at it hanging next to where the dress had been. "It'll fit."

Will grinned, "You mean that lavender colored one with the lace around the collar?"

Pete nodded. They hung the nightdress back up and took the robe. Rolling Henry back and forth they got him into the robe. They wrapped packing string around Henry to hold the robe in place.

"Ribbons in his hair," Pete whispered

Will fished red ribbon out of Catherine's sewing box and tied three bows into Henry's snarled hair. They left the room laughing.

In the morning Pete and Will were awakened suddenly with the first light of day streaming through the windows. A furor of cussing and angry shouts emanated from the folks' bedroom. "What the heck was that?" Pete questioned sleepily.

Suddenly his eyes snapped open. "That was Henry and he's on the warpath." He burst out laughing.

Will stayed in his bed chuckling until an apparition appeared in the doorway. The dim light illuminated a man in his socks and long handles glaring daggers of rage at them. Wrapped around him in a tangle was the robe secured with knotted twine, the ends flaring out around him. He had yet to spot the ribbon bows in his tangled hair.

Pete sat up on the edge of his bed. "Henry, I don't think you should be wearing Ma's clothes. You look right pretty in it, but it's just not right."

Will lay with his face sticking out of his blankets. "You don't often see a man wearing women's clothes, but I did hear of this fella in St. Louis once."

"I like the hair ribbons," Pete stifled a laugh. "I never knew you had such female tendencies big brother."

Henry reached his hand up and felt the bows in his hair. He howled with indignation and yanked at the ribbons which only succeeded in painfully pulling his hair.

"*Get me out of this*," Henry roared. "*Now*, or I'll tear you both into dog meat."

Pete looked at Will, "Someone got up on the wrong side of the bed this morning."

Will grinned, "Old men get grouchy like that."

"You mean when they wear women's clothes to bed?"

"Yeah."

Henry clenched his fists and his jaw at the same time. He turned and stormed out of the room and promptly returned with a stick of firewood. He swung it at Pete who ducked the swing with a howl of laughter.

The door to the house opened and Andre walked in. "I heard a lot of shouting in here . . ." He stopped and stared at Henry who stared back at him, his face crimson with embarrassment and anger.

Andre smiled, "You fell asleep yesterday. You should never do that around these two. The dress is very nice on you though . . . and the bows."

Henry stood clutching the firewood and seething. Andre quickly left the house stifling a laugh.

Pete slipped on his pants and walked up to Henry, "Here let me help you out of this. Didn't anyone ever teach you to tie a bow instead of knots?" He pulled his Barlow pocketknife out of his pocket to cut the twine.

Will sat up and pointed at Henry's head, "Want to keep the ribbons in, they look mighty fetching."

Henry glared at him.

"I guess not," Will concluded.

Once released from his decorations Henry walked out of the room and began building a fire in the cook stove. He was angry until he was washed, shaved, and again dressed in his own clothes. The first cup of coffee brought forth a burst of laughter in seeing the humor in the trick his brothers had played on him. One day he would get even though.

Andrew met his brothers at the house where an awake and fully functional Henry gave him the paper wrapped five thousand dollar bundle inside an oilskin pouch to protect the bills in case it rained. He explained some further details about the partnership and intended cattle drive to Andrew for him to pass on to Ian. Saddling up they left the yard, Andrew and Pete heading north, Henry and Will going east.

Henry and Will skirted Fort Collins as Henry did not want to get involved in conversation with any of his friends or tear into one of those who had belittled Jenny. He wanted to stick strictly to business as time was of the essence.

Arriving at what had formerly been the Webster ranch, now operated by Clint with the widow Ida Webster; they were met in the yard by Ida. It took her a bit to recollect Jeb's brothers as she had not seen them but a time or two. Even so Clint spoke well of the entire family and she felt she knew them through him and Jeb.

Ida smiled up at them, "Good morning, gentlemen. I know you are the Pelletier boys, but you must forgive my ignorance, I don't know your first names."

They dismounted and stepped up to Ida each tipping his hat to her and introducing themselves. "Is Clint around?" Henry asked. "I have some important and time sensitive matters to discuss with both of you."

"He is out with Joe checking the cattle."

They remembered Joe. He had been twelve when his father had been murdered by the renegades. "How is Joe doing these days?"

"Like a new boy, actually a young man now. Clint has taken him under his wing and taught him so much and has kept him on the straight and narrow during a boy's difficult years."

Henry smiled, "That's good to hear, Clint's a good man."

"Indeed he is. He has helped us so much since that awful night. Perhaps you have heard that Clint and I have decided to wed."

"Well, that's wonderful. Congratulations." Henry said.

Will added his congratulations to her as well.

"If you will excuse us," Henry apologized, "we'll ride out and find Clint and have him come back here so we can talk."

"Very well. He said they would be in the north end."

"Thank you, we will be back with him."

The two rode out looking for Clint. A half hour later they saw two riders moving a dozen head toward a waterhole. They rode toward the riders.

Clint and Joe left the cattle at the waterhole and turned to face the oncoming men. Once Clint recognized who they were he spoke to Joe and they rode toward Henry and Will.

The men met and shook hands all around including with Joe, who was treated like any other adult.

"We have some business to discuss with you and Ida," Henry told Clint. "It needs to be tended to right away."

Clint waved his hand toward the house, "Okay, let's go back to the house."

Reaching the house they all dismounted. Henry fished the bundle out of his saddlebag and followed Clint into the house. They sat down at the table as Ida poured coffee all around for them and sat down next to Clint.

Henry smiled, "First off, congratulations on the upcoming wedding."

Clint smiled in return, "Thank you."

"Second off, are you in the market to expand your holdings and take on a profitable partnership?"

Clint lifted one eyebrow, "We're always interested in expanding, but I'm not so sure about a partnership. Who is it?"

"Pablo Ruiz, of the Ruiz hacienda out of Taos."

Clint shook his head slightly, "I heard Jeb make mention of a Ruiz, but sorry, I have no idea who that is."

"Our family has been close friends and doing business with Don Sebastian Ruiz for about thirty years. They have a fifty-thousand acre hacienda out of Taos that was a grant to Sebastian's father about a hundred years ago. My wife is his daughter.

"Conditions on the hacienda have suddenly taken an abrupt change. Sebastian was murdered by outlaws a couple weeks back and the hacienda has passed down to his son Pablo. A fine, upstanding man himself, Pablo has run into a problem. His father did not leave a will, believing as did his father, that the land would automatically pass down to Pablo in the event of his death. Now, the government has come along and wants to seize the property since there is no will. Pa is down there now and we are trying to help Pablo save the place.

"Pablo wants to move about twelve to fifteen hundred head off the place in case he loses it and wants to take on partners to spread his holdings out. We recommended you and Ian."

Henry unwrapped the money and laid it on the table. Clint and

Ida's eyes widened at the stack of bills.

"Five thousand dollars of Pablo's money to buy as much land as you can with it."

Clint whistled, "Wow. Land around here is government owned and going for just over a buck an acre."

"If you are willing to take on the partnership we need you to buy as much as you can, as fast as you can. Pablo has two months to get off or make some kind of deal to buy the land back, if that's even possible. He needs to move the cattle off quickly to his partners. He'll put six to seven hundred head of good breeding stock on your place."

Clint looked at Ida, "What do you think, Ida?"

"If Mr. Ruiz has been a friend of the Pelletiers for that many years, that is enough for me to vouch for his sincerity and honesty. I believe we should accept his offer."

"I do to. It almost sounds too good to be true."

Clint turned his attention back to Henry, "We'll do it."

"Good."

"How do I get to talk to Pablo to work out the details?"

"We need to ride down and drive the cattle back up here. You can talk to him face-to-face when we get there. If you come along that will make nine of us for the drive."

Clint looked at Ida, "Can you get along without me for a few weeks?"

"I can manage."

Joe turned his pleading eyes to Clint, "Can I go too? I'll work hard."

"You work as hard as two men no doubt about that, but your ma might need you here with me gone."

Joe turned his face to his mother, "Can I?"

Ida laughed, "Oh, those eyes! I'd have to be an ogre to say no to those eyes."

Joe's face lit up, "Does that mean I can go?"

"It's alright by me. Do you want him to go with you Clint?"

Clint studied Joe with a serious expression, "It will be hard work, long hours in the saddle, and eating light. No whining allowed."

"I'll do my share, Clint, I promise."

Henry broke in, "Andrew's sixteen year old son is going. We could have him and Joe handle the rumuda."

Clint nodded, "That would be a good job for them." He looked back at Joe, "Okay, you can go."

Joe smiled triumphantly.

"He and Tom will probably make good friends," Henry said.

"When do we head out?" Clint asked.

"Andrew is headed up to Ian's right now. I told them to meet at the canyon ranch in no more than ten days. They will swing down and pick the two of you up on the way south. Be ready to go about then."

Clint nodded, "Nine days about. We'll be ready. I'll ride to Fort Collins today and get the ball rolling on buying as much land as I can with that money."

Henry and Will stood up to leave. "We're heading back down now. See you in New Mexico."

CHAPTER SIXTEEN

Henry and Will rode across the patio in front of the adobe. Jesus rushed out of the stable to meet them. Henry dismounted handing his reins to the boy. He patted the boy on the back, "Thank you, Jesus."

Will stood on the ground and let Jesus take the reins to his horse. He smiled at the stable boy who smiled in return. He led the horses to the stable disappearing into its depths.

Henry looked at Will and gestured in the direction Jesus had gone, "Saving the place is about more than land and cattle. This is the only home a lot of these people have ever known."

Will understood. "Then we'd better make sure it stays that way."

"That's the idea."

Pablo walked briskly from the open doorway of the house with Jean slightly behind him. Pablo extended his hand to Will and then to Henry. His eyes were anxious, "Were you successful?"

"Yes. Clint has accepted the offer and went right out to see how much land he could buy. Most of what surrounds him is government and cheap. Andrew rode to Ian's to explain the offer. I can't imagine he would say no."

Pablo's strained and worried face showed a loosening of the tension that gripped him day and night. "That is good news. How many can come and when?"

"Looks like we can count on nine, including myself, for the drive. I told them to get together and be out of the canyon headed this way within ten days. They could be here in two weeks or even less if they can settle the land purchases early."

"Excellent. My vaqueros have already started separating the cattle for the drive. They will hold them ready to set out as soon as your family arrives."

Pablo looked Henry and Will over. "You need to eat and rest now." Pablo stepped into the house and instructed Ignacio to have Teresa bring them food.

Jean spoke briefly with his sons and walked back into the house with them and Pablo. They sat at the dining room table. Teresa brought a plate of meat and tortillas along with a pot of coffee and cups. Henry and Will thanked her as she left the room.

"Anything new at home?" Jean asked.

Henry nodded as he rolled meat into a tortilla and wolfed it down. Swallowing the last bite he followed it with half a cup of coffee. Jean waited patiently for him to finish. Catherine walked into the room and sat down as Henry and Will greeted her.

Henry poured his cup full again. "Jeb and Jenny are not in Fort Collins anymore. They've gone to Ian's."

Catherine leaned toward him, her expression filled with concern. Jean's eyebrows lifted, "Why?"

"What I understand of it, and I don't have all the details, is that a man named Cassidy, who was the enforcer for that house Jenny was trapped in, showed up in Fort Collins. He saw Jenny coming out of the schoolhouse and approached her and made certain demands of her. He said that if she didn't comply with his demands he would tell the town she had been a Denver prostitute before moving to Fort Collins."

Catherine gasped, "How wretched. Oh, that poor girl!"

Jean's face darkened as his anger slowly boiled up.

"Naturally she refused to comply and he made good by spreading lies all over town about her. All these newcomers turned on her like coyotes on a rabbit. The old timers and our friends defended her, but they are being buried under the easterners pouring in. The school board fired her for being an inappropriate person to teach children. I guess Alice Evans and Peter Anderson really let them have it with both barrels, but like I said, they're outnumbered. Mrs. Kelly laid into the gossips at church as well."

Will broke in, "I saw Jeb for a day before he left for Ian's place. Jeb said he lit into them at their meeting and the next day handed in his badge. He took Jenny back to Andrew's and then they moved to Ian's. That's where they are now."

Catherine sat stiff with indignation and fury. "When we get back home I intend to let some people have it myself."

Jean's whole countenance turned deadly, no one harmed his family, physically or verbally. "What about Cassidy?"

"Jeb called him in Pruitt's and killed him. Seems Larry Pruitt thought it was a good opportunity to bag himself a Pelletier and pulled a shotgun on Jeb. Jeb killed him too."

Jean nodded his approval. "Figured Pruitt would get shot or hung eventually."

Will broke in, "Paul didn't press any charges against Jeb. In fact he got together with Clint and Reed Hall and they razed Pruitt's saloon. Dropped it flat."

"Good," Catherine snarled. "From all I've heard of that wretched place flat is how it should be."

"I'm sure Jeb will be riding down with the crew and you can get the details from him."

"He's better off this way," Jean said. "Jeb was never cut out for town living."

"It's changed a lot since we first knew the town," Henry agreed.

Pablo waited patiently until the family had finished talking about Jeb. He then said, "I have had word from Mr. Beckett."

Henry turned his attention to Pablo, "What did he learn?"

"Ignacio was in Taos yesterday. I had asked him to check in with Mr. Beckett to see if there were any further developments. He has learned more and wishes to meet with us as soon as possible. I was hoping you would get back so the three of us could sit in the meeting with him."

"Did he tell Ignacio anything?"

Pablo shook his head, "Only that we needed to meet as soon as we could get to his office."

"It's a bit late today, how about first thing in the morning?"

"My thoughts exactly," Pablo agreed.

Pablo, along with Henry and Jean, arrived at Samuel Beckett's office the next morning. Beckett was happy to see them and guided them to chairs in his private office and closed the door. "I have learned some most interesting information about your grant, Mr. Ruiz."

Beckett sat down behind his desk and removed a sheet of paper from a bottom drawer. "The grant is for sale, however, not through the normal government channels. It seems a consortium or group of some sort has managed to get their hands on information pertaining to lands such as yours. This leads me to believe they are connected with the government in some way. I suspect their spies learn of lands opening up, tell this group, who then obtain the information about the land through various sources."

Beckett glanced over the paper in his hand. "The man I was led to contact is indeed in Albuquerque, a Colonel Merton Endicott, United States Army retired."

"How did you manage to track him down?" Jean asked. "Sounds like a hard man to find."

"I continued to send wires to contacts of mine who directed me to other contacts. Someone along that line must have passed the word to Endicott because *I* received a wire from *him*."

"Isn't that a little odd?" Henry asked.

"It is to be expected that there is a chain of information among these types of people."

"Someone had to have told Endicott about Sebastian's death in the first place and knew there was no will. How would anyone know that?"

"The news of his death was wide spread, but only I knew about the issue with the will," Beckett said.

"Endicott or this group got that information awful fast," Henry put in.

"Sounds like the telegrapher is the spy, or at least connected to him," Jean said.

"That would be my first guess," Beckett agreed. "We will have to be careful."

"What did this Colonel Endicott say?" Pablo asked.

"His wire said that he understood that I was representing the Ruiz Grant and wanted to discuss buying the property. I returned his wire saying that I was and asked the details of sale and where we could meet."

"What did he say?" Pablo was growing excited.

Beckett looked at Pablo obviously trying to say the right thing. "He said that we could discuss a sale, but . . . the land could not be sold to a Mexican. Any attempt to buy back the land for you would forfeit the deal."

Pablo sank in his chair with disappointment that was quickly replaced with anger. "Then, this Endicott will have to fight this *Mexican* and my men for the Grant. I will not roll over and give up to this coyote."

Henry snorted, "So, the land has been taken by this group to be sold under the table and Endicott is their face. We're dealing with a bunch of crooks in other words."

"That's about the size of it, yes."

"We need to figure out a way to buy the land through the legitimate agency."

"I believe it is too late for that as it is already in the hands of this group and I am certain the proper agencies will never see the information these people have. I have no idea how deep this group is or what government agencies they belong to, however, I am sure they are government affiliated."

"Is there no way we can get around them?" Henry asked.

Beckett shrugged, "I don't know, but I will keep trying."

Jean sat in deep thought staring at the desk top, "Would he sell it to a French Canadian?"

All eyes turned to Jean. Beckett looked at Jean as Jean lifted his head and met Beckett's eyes. "Please tell me what you are thinking, Mr. Pelletier."

"With the falling off of the fur trade the Hudson Bay Company went into land dealing. They sold millions of acres of Rupert's Land to the Canadian government that has now become part of Canada. Hudson Bay absorbed the Northwest Fur Company years ago leaving a lot of wealthy fur merchants that had been part of the Northwest Company broke. It would only be natural that some enterprising men displaced by Hudson Bay would want to challenge them in land deals.

"In my youth I encountered a man named Victor Lamoureux, a powerful fur merchant for the Northwest Fur Company. A man very proud of his position who enjoyed flaunting that power. I am sure it came as a great shock when he lost that power to Hudson Bay. He is no doubt dead by now, however, he would be one to try and fight back against the company that ruined him." Jean grinned, "I am sure his son, who would be about my age, would wish to carry on his father's revenge."

Beckett studied Jean, "I think I know where you are going with this, but please clarify for me."

"Victor Lamoureux the second, the son, is interested in acquiring American land cheap to further his company advancement against the hated Hudson Bay."

"You would pose as Victor Lamoureux's son?"

"Yes." Jean broke into a thick Montreal accent, "I wish to acquire American land. I can make Colonel Endicott a very wealthy man if he will deal well with me."

Beckett nodded, "Yes, I see. However, there is a catch to the idea, if the land is sold to the name Victor Lamoureux the second, and there is no such person, the land would revert back to Endicott."

Jean pointed at Henry as he resumed his normal voice, "Not if he was working behind front man, Henry Pelletier. The land would be bought in Henry's name, who is being represented by the Lamoureux Land Company. Henry would then be the legal owner of the land."

"I see. Henry would be the Lamoureux front just as Endicott is this group's front. Make Endicott believe that you are giving him the inside track to further land deals and wealth if he plays well with the Lamoureux Company. It could very well work."

Jean nodded, "Set up a meeting between us. Use the telegrapher and make it sound as if you are working your own deal under the table undermining Pablo and making a profit for yourself by sending Endicott these Canadian land buyers."

Beckett turned to Pablo, "What do you think of that idea Mr. Ruiz."

Pablo grinned, "Cheat the cheater, why not?"

"Very well then, I will set up the meeting."

Henry stopped him, "We need to bait him first." Henry turned to Jean, "Remember when I was a kid and I was trying to catch that black fox and he wouldn't come near the trap?"

"And I told you to set out a piece of meat every night for two weeks until the fox got accustomed to a free meal," Jean answered.

"On the last night I put meat in the trap and the fox walked right into it."

Jean smiled, "Good idea, very good."

Beckett gave Henry a look that asked for further explanation.

"If two wealthy Canadian land buyers suddenly appear out of nowhere offering him a too good to be true offer he will know it is. Cheaters think everyone is cheating them first. He'll be suspicious and bolt. Hint to him over the next week or two that you have a line on a Canadian company looking for land and that you are checking it out and will get back to him."

Jean added, "That way you can get him worked up for the meeting. Let it slip that you are looking out for your own interests as well and hope to make a profit yourself. He will expect that and it will make him think you really are setting up a deal."

Beckett grinned, "Yes, that is good. I will feed him bits of information through our friendly telegrapher. Drop bits of information to him that is not in the wire. He will run that back to Endicott as well."

"It will break down his suspicions, one cheat helping another for mutual profit. After a while he will be chomping at the bit for the meeting," Henry concluded.

Jean turned to Pablo, "I will work a deal to get the land as cheap as possible, but I will need a thousand dollars for bribe money and about thirty thousand in cash to take to the meeting. Seeing the actual bills will always turn a greedy crook faster than only the mention of money."

Pablo was intrigued with the plan. "I will have that for you. I did have some money transferred up here from Santa Fe, but if the spy or spies learn that I pulled out the money Endicott will smell a trap. I will give you a letter of authorization to withdraw my money from the Santa Fe bank and then no one but us will know."

"I will wait two days before I send the first wire suggesting I have a lead on the buyers," Beckett said. "I am sure our local spy knows you are here today."

"Yes," Pablo agreed. "He will think we all cooked up this idea if you wire him right after we leave."

Beckett leaned back in his chair with a satisfied smile, "Gentlemen, we are about to trap a fox."

CHAPTER SEVENTEEN

Colonel Endicott sat at his desk in the small office in his home, across from him sat Kendrick. He didn't like the man, but he was his only contact with the *League,* as the consortium referred to themselves. It was a regular meeting he was forced to hold with the man to keep the League happy. It was also their way of keeping an eye and thumb on him. The people behind the scenes were the nervous type ready to eliminate anyone who might cause them a problem or expose them in anyway.

A knock at the front door brought Endicott out of his seat to answer it. He was happy for the interruption, any excuse to get away from Kendrick. The man was sneaky and made his skin crawl. He was always relieved when their little meetings ended and Kendrick slithered back out the door.

A boy stood at the door holding two pieces of paper. "Telegrams for Colonel Merton Endicott," the boy announced.

Endicott took the telegrams and gave the boy two-bits. He closed the door as he read the telegrams. The first one was interesting while at the same time raising his suspicions. The second wire, from his informant, said what the first did not.

Kendrick overheard the boy's announcement and met Endicott in the front room. "What is so interesting in those telegrams?" Kendrick inquired. His smug look indicated that he already knew what was in the messages. He and the League had informants as well; in fact the same one Endicott had who was expected to send him all wires first.

Endicott lifted his eyes from the paper and focused on Kendrick, "Seems that Samuel Beckett, the Ruiz attorney, has a lead on a Canadian company that wants to buy land in the United States. He is looking into it. The second is from my man in Taos. He says that Beckett let it slip that this Canadian company does not mind dealing under the table and that he stands to make something on it as well if he can set up a meeting between us."

Kendrick's clean shaven face and perfectly trimmed mustache lifted with his smile, "Lawyers never let anything just *slip.*"

"Not generally, unless there is a purpose for it. I do know that land is moving fast in Canada right now so I prefer to remain interested."

"Almost as fast as it is in New Mexico. Grants are falling like dead leaves, something you need to stay abreast of."

Endicott frowned at Kendrick, irritated that the man insinuated that he was unaware of the events surrounding him. "Yes, I have noticed that as well, I'm not an imbecile."

"No, Colonel you're not. That's why you have this position. You know the country better than most. It's simply that the League doesn't want to lose because of a bad decision from this office."

Endicott stiffened, "I do not make *bad* decisions."

Kendrick brushed a bit of dust from the cuff of his expensive suit. "I will report the possibility of a deal to the League and be back in touch with you. Be careful and don't make any decisions without the League's approval."

"I know the policy."

Kendrick gave him an amused, oily smile, "Yes, I'm sure you do." He walked out the door.

Endicott stared at the front door Kendrick had gone through. He loathed the man, likening him to a Mississippi Riverboat bottom dealer or a water moccasin which he considered one in the same. He wanted out, but the League was known to assassinate those who tried to leave with too much knowledge. They limited that knowledge by using Kendrick, however, any knowledge not under their strict control was too much as far as they were concerned.

He had no idea who was in the League except that it involved some very powerful politicians and industrialists. There was a lot of money behind them and they wanted even more. He suspected they had seized on the grant idea the day Chaffee and his friends bought the Maxwell grant and sold it for double what they paid. Chaffee's deal was above the table, the League's rarely were.

The League members, who clearly had access to government resources, stole the information regarding the no heir or no will grants or properties before the General Land Office or local land offices could receive the information. They sold the properties and pocketed the money without the land office ever knowing the grants had opened up.

His last military command was at Fort Sumner before the army sold the fort to Lucien Maxwell. He chose retirement over a new post and bought this house in Albuquerque. He regretted the day

Kendrick showed up making him a lucrative offer to work for the League. It had been presented to him that his knowledge of the country would be beneficial in helping to locate abandoned properties that they could buy and resell. He was promised generous commissions and finder's fees. As it turned out, the commissions were not generous and he had yet to receive a finder's fee. There had been far more threats than commissions. It didn't take long to realize he was up to his ears in a corrupt system. Now he was trapped and needed a way out.

He read over the telegrams again. Maybe he could swing his own deal with these Canadians and leave the country. He could go to South America or some nondescript village on the Mediterranean Sea. He had no family to leave behind and it would be a simple matter to disappear. It was a thought he would hold in the back of his mind.

He hesitated to double-cross the League. With Kendrick and others watching him he had to be careful. Everything he did, every message, every word seemed to get back to Kendrick. He had no fear of the slimy crook, but he was no fool either. Cross the League, and you die. It was as simple as that. He would have to do what they told him, at least until he saw a way to get out with his skin.

Three days later Endicott received a second telegram from Beckett. He had the name of the Canadian, it was Victor Lamoureux II of the Lamoureux Land Company. He was working on contacting them. There was a name, his interest was peaking.

Without notice Kendrick strolled casually into the office. Endicott looked up at him, "Don't you believe in knocking?"

"I did, perhaps you didn't hear me."

Endicott scowled at him, "What do you want?"

Kendrick gave him the oily smile he so hated, "Victor Lamoureux, is it?"

Endicott knew he should be surprised that Kendrick already had the information, but he wasn't. It was obvious his informant was Kendrick's as well. He would keep that in mind. He had his spies out picking up every loose bit of information for him, it was only natural Kendrick would have men doing the same.

"According to this it is."

"I will make inquiries as to the company's legitimacy."

"If they operate under the table I doubt they leave business cards on silver trays."

"We have ways of finding out."

"Well, don't be surprised if you come up empty."

"If that is the case then it is better to forego any dealings with them."

Endicott wanted to meet with these men whether Kendrick approved or not. The League wanted the grant sold in two parts, splitting the two townships the grant encompassed. He was told that with the livestock each piece was priced at fifty-thousand dollars and when he found someone willing to pay it to contact them through Kendrick.

"I believe that decision belongs to the League, not you."

Kendrick's smile dropped off as he glared at Endicott.

"If the Canadians want to meet I should do so and see what they have to offer. It could be lucrative with future potential. Dealing with foreigners could have its advantages in leaving no tracks in our own yard. I don't think the League would pass up the sale if Lamoureux offered the cash. I will pass on to you what I find out." Endicott snorted, "Of course you have the information before I do anyway, don't you?"

Kendrick kept his glare on Endicott, "Make the contact then, but bear in mind we will be watching you."

The Colonel stood up and faced the man, "Do not threaten me."

"I never threaten or bluff."

Endicott flipped back the front of his suit jacket to reveal a shoulder holstered revolver. "Nor do I."

Kendrick nodded, "I see. We will be in touch."

"Make sure you knock next time and learn a few social skills before you barge into my home. I might think you are a thief and shoot first, look second."

"Now who is threatening?"

Endicott held a level stare on Kendrick, "I never threaten."

Kendrick bowed his head to Endicott and left the room without another word.

"I trumped him that time," Endicott whispered to the empty room, "next time I might have to shoot him."

At that moment he made the decision to play to his own advantage. He would meet the Canadians and if the deal looked bad he would throw it back on Kendrick. If it looked like money would cross his desk, he would make his own deal and leave the country.

Kendrick had given him the legal land transfer paperwork, but for only one township. The paperwork for the final township was held back from him in case he tried to sell both and keep the money. He could sell one at least and take what he could get for it.

He sat down and wrote a letter to Samuel Beckett telling him he was interested in meeting the Canadians. He added that if those he represented were not interested, he might be. He added that Beckett could expect to receive secret letters with the factual details and obvious general wires as he was being watched and his private affairs monitored. That should be sufficient to tip off Beckett that he was willing to sidestep his group. He slipped the letter into an envelope and stamped it.

Leaving the office he went to his front room and peered out the windows from behind the half drawn drapes. He did not see anyone watching the house, yet he was hesitant to walk to the post office. He withdrew back into the house pondering how to mail the letter.

Outside, from the rear of the house, he heard children shouting in Spanish and playing. Walking through the house he opened the back door and looked out. Several Mexican children were playing in the open lot behind the house. He called out in Spanish to one of the boys asking him to come to the door.

With hesitation the boy approached him as he stood back in the open doorway. Endicott handed the boy a silver dollar and the letter instructing him to go immediately to the post office and mail the letter. The boy's eyes flared wide at the gleaming dollar.

Endicott told him that if he hurried back proving he had mailed the letter he would give him another dollar. Should anyone ask where he was going with the letter he was to say he was mailing it for his *patron.* The boy ran off gripping the letter.

Closing and locking the back door, Endicott crossed back to the front door and went out. He made an obvious show of walking down the street for the benefit of any watchers. He continued on to the telegraph office and sent a wire to Beckett stating that he wished to set up a meeting with the Canadians. He watched the telegrapher send the message and returned home.

The next day he checked the telegraph office to find a wire from Beckett stating he was expecting the Lamoureux people to arrive any day. He added that it should prove to be profitable all around. Smiling, he folded the paper and slipped it into his pocket. It would take several days for his letter to arrive in Taos and again as many to receive a reply. He would make a show of going to the post office every day to pick up what mail he had so when the letter from Beckett arrived there would be no suspicion regarding why he was receiving a letter.

———————

Excitement swept through Ian and Anne's house at Andrew's explanation of Pablo's proposition. They both instantly agreed to the partnership. Anne did not know Pablo Ruiz, however, that was unnecessary since her husband and family did.

Ian took the money and rode directly to Duncan McKenzie's house. Stepping off his horse he knocked on the front door. Mrs. McKenzie answered the door. Ian was momentarily taken aback by her appearance, it was clear she had been ill.

Ian pulled off his hat, "Mrs. McKenzie, I'm Ian Pelletier."

"Oh, yes, Duncan has spoken of you."

"Is he to home?"

"No, he is out on the east range."

Ian smiled, "Almost at my doorstep. Thank you, I will go find him."

Ian mounted and headed east. After crossing the range he spotted Duncan with Booker Rose, his sole remaining ranch hand. Duncan had sold off most of his cattle to pay his wife's medical bills and trips to Cheyenne where the closet decent doctor was located. The two men were moving several of the few head left. They stopped as Ian rode up to them.

Duncan extended his hand, "Afternoon, Ian."

They shook hands, and then Ian and Booker shook hands in greeting.

Ian grinned, "I've got some good news for you, Duncan."

Duncan sighed, "I can use some good news."

"Still interested in moving back to Maine?"

Duncan eyed him suspiciously, "You found me a buyer?"

Ian jabbed a thumb into his chest. "A friend of our family, Pablo Ruiz, a big cattleman in New Mexico, wants to go into a partnership with Anne and me. He wants me to buy extra land so we can drive about seven hundred head up here. How much do you want for the place, land, stock, and buildings?"

"Would you be able to do four thousand? I think that's a fair price seeing how most of the cattle are gone. I'll throw in the few that's left."

Ian put out his hand, "Call it good. Let's go back to your house and put it on paper."

Duncan's smile filled his face. "Then, what are we sittin' around here talkin' for? I've got a bottle of scotch up to the house to seal the bargain."

Booker asked Ian, "How do you plan on bringing the cattle up from New Mexico?"

"From what I was told, by way of the Goodnight Trail, through Bent's Fort."

"I made that drive twice with Mr. Goodnight. First in '66 into New Mexico and again in '70 up to Denver. Seems I'll be needing a new job. Could you use a hand that knows the Trail?"

"With these new cattle, and it only being my cousin, brother and me, yes we sure could."

"He's a top hand," Duncan broke in. "Stuck by me through it all. You'll not find a better man in Wyoming."

Ian nodded, "Wages 'll be slow at first until we can start marketing some beeves."

"Figure you'll catch me up. Pelletiers are good for it."

"You know my family?"

Booker chuckled, "Who doesn't?"

Ian smiled, "I guess we do get noticed."

"You could say that. So, you're moving seven hundred head up the Trail?"

"Close to fifteen hundred at the start. Pablo has also taken on a second partner, a good friend of mine, down in Larimer County. Half will be left off with him and the rest trailed up here. You might have heard his name around, Clint Rush?"

Booker burst out laughing. "Yeah, I've heard of him. Clint and me came up from Texas together on that '66 drive. We were pals down around the Panhandle country. We hung around this country for a while before he headed up Montana way. Kind of lost track of each other after a while."

"Well, he'll be on the drive along with my brothers. We figure to have nine or ten for the drive."

Booker nodded, "That should be enough."

"Pack up your gear. You can ride back with me when Duncan and I finish our business. We'll be heading out first light to join the others around Fort Collins."

"Fort Collins, huh. The gunfighter Jeb Pelletier...is he one of your kin?"

Ian stared at Booker, "That's my little brother, he just moved up with us. What's the word on him?"

"That he outdrew and killed Alex Cassidy in Fort Collins. Knew Cassidy in Texas, fast hand with a gun, but a black hearted coyote he was. I hated his guts. Heard too Jeb gunned down Dick Norton and his partner down in Bitter Creek, but I don't know if that's true or just talk."

"It's true. Norton and his friend stole three of my horses."

Booker nodded his acceptance of Ian's word. "Here tell he's something else with a six-gun. Sounds like Clint."

Ian frowned as he considered what Booker had said. Jeb had changed alright, he was colder, harder. Now, he had a gunfighter rep and that was never good. He looked at Booker, "Do me a favor Booker, don't mention anything like that in front of Jeb's wife."

"She won't hear it from me boss."

Ian walked into the house waving the deed to the McKenzie Ranch. Booker Rose stepped inside the door and waited, hat in hand. "We've got it," Ian announced.

Anne smiled, "Things are truly looking up for us." She looked past Ian to where Booker stood.

Ian gestured for Booker to come in further. "Booker was working for Duncan and now he's working for us. Booker Rose, my wife Anne."

Booker bowed his head slightly, "Mrs. Pelletier, it's a pleasure."

"Welcome Booker," Anne replied.

Ian continued his introductions, "This is my brother Jeb's wife, Jenny."

Booker bowed his head to her, "Ma'am."

Jenny nodded back at him.

"You'll meet Jeb and our cousin Owl when they get in."

"Owl? Is that a nickname?"

"No, short for Eyes of the Owl, he's Crow. You don't have a problem working with an Indian do you?"

Booker shook his head, "Not Crows. Got a grudge against Comanche and Sioux though, seeing how they've both tried to kill me."

"You and Owl have that in common, he hates the Sioux."

"I'm sure him and me 'll get along just fine."

A shuffling of boots came in the open door behind them and they turned to see Jeb walking in. "Here's Jeb now. Jeb, Booker Rose, he's going to be working for us."

Jeb and Booker shook hands.

Ian added, "Booker knows the Goodnight Trail, in fact he's an old saddle pal of Clint's, they were drovers together."

Jeb smiled, "Clint's a good friend of mine."

Booker nodded, "Mine too, ain't seen him in years though. Sounds like he settled in a bit, rancher now is he?"

"Yeah, he's got a decent place he's building up."

"That's good to hear. I was a little worried about his direction there when we chose to take different trails."

"You don't have to worry about that anymore," Ian said.

"Sounds like it. Guess I ought to get settled in, where should I throw my roll?"

"Tack room in the barn is about it for right now. We converted a shed to a living place for Owl."

"That's fine, we're going to be on the drive anyway. I'll go get myself squared away in the barn then."

"Wish we could offer you better housing," Anne apologized.

"Oh, barn's fine ma'am, my bones 'd likely go into shock if I was to sleep in a house."

"We'll be building a bunkhouse before winter," Ian commented.

"We will have supper in an hour Booker," Anne said, "Be sure and come back in."

"Yes ma'am, I will." He turned and walked out the door.

Ian handed Anne the final thousand dollars. "While we're gone see if you can pick up some more land."

Anne took the money from him, "I'll see what I can do. Is Owl going to stay here to help out with the stock?"

"I'd rather he did. I'll talk to him when he gets in. I'm sure he won't mind staying. He's kind of gotten in the habit of protecting you ever since that Babcock business."

"Yes, he has. I'd feel better if someone was here with Jenny and me and the baby."

"Owl will do it."

Ian turned to Jeb, "Why don't you and me take a walk?"

Jeb was headed for the coffee pot but stopped at Ian's comment. He knew better than to argue with his hard-nosed brother when he took that tone. It was the same one he used when threatening to knock his head off for being such a problem to Jenny before they were married. "Can't have a cup of coffee first?"

"Later."

Jeb nodded and followed Ian outside.

Jenny looked at Anne, "What's that all about?"

Anne shrugged, "Brother to brother business I suppose."

Jenny looked at the closed door, "Ian can be pretty tough on his brothers."

"Yes, he can, but it's because he cares about them."

Jenny nodded, "He acts so rough toward them, but he truly does love them."

Jeb stopped by the corral. "Okay, can you tell me what you want to say without us strolling all over the country?"

Ian faced him, "Probably. Booker asked me if the gunfighter Jeb Pelletier was my kin. The word is out about Cassidy and Norton. You're getting a reputation you don't want."

Jeb frowned, "I'm not trying to get one."

"No, but you are all the same. You've killed two known gunfighters. You need to rein it in a bit before you have every idiot who thinks he's fast looking you up."

Jeb snapped, "There's nothing to rein in, it's not my fault people talk."

"Then stop giving them something to talk about."

"I'm not going to stand around and get shot, if that's what you mean."

Ian snapped back at him, "Did I say that? Don't get smart."

Jeb held his tongue. You didn't smart off to Ian unless you wanted to be picking yourself up off the ground.

"I don't blame you for going after Cassidy. If you hadn't, I would have, but you dug up that fight with Norton and Todd. You could have waited for me and Owl and we would have taken them together."

Jeb knew he had sought out the fight and was probably lucky to win it, but his stubbornness had dug in its heels. "I did what I had to do."

"You did what you *wanted* to do. Clint would be the first one to tell you that too."

"He's the one who taught me."

"Did he tell you to dig up gunfights, or did he teach you how to finish them if they come to you?"

Jeb clenched his jaw and growled, "Fine, I get the point."

"Good, and get it in your head. You want to make your wife a widow, just keep it up."

"I said I get the point. Back off."

Ian stuck his face directly in Jeb's. "Don't tell me to back off, little brother. Being fast with a gun can save your life. It can get you killed just as quick when a faster gun comes along and there's always a faster gun, as Cassidy and Norton found out."

The two brothers glared at each other for several seconds neither blinking. Ian growled, "I don't want to be going to your funeral little brother. I need you alive to help me run this place."

Jeb broke eye contact and stepped back. "We're heading for the Canyon first thing in the morning, right?"

"Yes, we're up against the ten days Henry was adamant about."

"It'll be six days to Taos from here."

"Likely."

"Then, we'd better push it and make it in five. Pablo needs us." Jeb turned and walked back to the house.

Ian watched him walk away with his back stiff and his temper simmering under the surface. It reminded him of himself at that age. "I'm your big brother," Ian whispered. "It's my job to protect you even if you don't want it."

CHAPTER EIGHTEEN

Three days had passed since Kendrick's last visit. Endicott spent much of that time researching Canadian land issues and the companies involved. He was reading a paper on the Hudson Bay Company when a loud rapping resounded at his front door. He made his way to the door and opened it to find Kendrick facing him.

Kendrick smirked, "I am practicing my new social skills; I *knocked.*"

Endicott ignored the sarcastic remark. "Learn anything about Lamoureux?"

"May I come in? Isn't that how the social skills work on your end? I knock, you say 'come in?'"

"Only if I want you to come in."

Kendrick huffed, "Fine. There is, or at least was, a Victor Lamoureux back some thirty or forty years ago. He was an influential and wealthy fur merchant for the Northwest Fur Company. Northwest was taken over by the Hudson Bay Company and the story of Lamoureux ends there. He likely lost his shirt and committed suicide."

"Hudson Bay went into the land business in recent years, maybe Lamoureux formed his own land company to compete against the company that cost him his fortune."

"That would be difficult to do since he's dead or if alive, he is a hundred and twenty years old, which is unlikely. How do you figure he is in the land business aside from occupying a six-by-three hole?"

"He started the company and his son now runs it. Didn't you notice the double I's after Victor Lamoureux's name? That would indicate his son . . . the second. You should have, your sycophant spy sends you the same messages I get."

Kendrick bristled with anger and indignation. "Sarcasm will not serve you well with the League."

"I am not insulting the League. I am speaking directly to you."

"Then, you are insulting me personally."

Endicott shrugged, "However you wish to see it."

"You are quickly overstepping your bounds, Colonel Endicott."

"No, I am quickly growing tired of your company. Tell the League

I will successfully handle this deal like I have the others. Good day, Mr. Kendrick." He closed the door.

The next four days passed without another visit from Kendrick. This day there was a letter for him minus a return address on the envelope. He put the letter in his pocket and casually strolled back to his house whistling a tune. Once inside he bolted the doors and tore open the envelope.

The neat handwriting was brief and read: *I understand your situation. Victor Lamoureux II has arrived with his front man, Henry Pelletier. They wish to set up the meeting as soon as possible. They will need three days to make the trip to you. I have received a handsome finder's fee from them. I have learned that these men are wealthy, yet very shrewd. A word to the wise, you stand to make a nice profit for yourself if you do not attempt to push a hard sell or too high a price at them. They will prove to be worth a good deal to us for a long time if you do not run them off. A little less profit now for much more later. SB*

He pondered the wording, just like a lawyer to talk in circles. The line about his receiving a 'handsome finder's fee' struck him since he had never received the fees the League promised him. Then again, maybe it hinted at their willingness to bribe him to get the deal they wanted. He could live with that. "Very well, Mr. Lamoureux," he spoke aloud, "four days from today and we shall meet."

He walked to the telegraph office and found the expected cover wire from Beckett indicating that Lamoureux was in Taos, ready to meet, and asking for a day. There was no time for a letter to Taos and back so he had no alternative but to wire the answer. He sent back a simple numerical message indicating a meeting date in four days.

He returned to his house knowing the Taos telegrapher would relay the message back to Kendrick. The League man wasn't the brightest and it may take him a while to decipher the meaning of the numbers. Should Kendrick figure it out he might even try and sit in on the meeting. He would prevent that though.

Would he play for the League or for himself? That would depend on how the cards laid out on the table. He was keeping all his options open. Should Kendrick prove to be an interference, well, he hadn't fought in two wars without learning a thing or two about dealing with the enemy.

Beckett made the ride up to Pablo's house bearing the letter and wires from Endicott. Pablo and Henry met him on the patio as Jesus led his horse to the stable. Pablo was filled with hopeful anticipation, "Do you have news from Albuquerque?"

"That I do. It seems our fox is interested in the bait."

"Come inside, we will talk about it." Beckett followed Pablo and Henry to the office that had been Sebastian's and now was Pablo's. He could not find it in his heart to change anything from how his father had it.

Jean was talking with Catherine in the front room and as the men passed Pablo called him to join their meeting. The four men went into the office where Pablo and Beckett sat down. Henry and Jean stood and listened.

Beckett read the letter and wires to them. After reading he said, "I believe, from the tone of Endicott's writing that he is looking to make his own deal apart from the people he is fronting."

"We'll have to make sure we entice him into making that choice," Jean commented.

"That is where a good bribe will come in," Pablo grinned.

Jean agreed, "Make it worth his while to sell to us for less and pocket what he wants out of it."

"Yes, that is how I read it," Beckett said. "He wants a meeting in four days. Will that time frame work for you Mr. Ruiz?"

Pablo looked at Henry and then Jean, "Can you be ready in that time?"

"Yes, we can be there," Jean answered.

"You will need to go to Santa Fe first to get the money from the bank," Pablo reminded him.

Beckett broke in, "I would suggest arriving in Albuquerque on the stage though. Dressed in suits and fully acting the part to give Endicott the full impression of your positions."

Henry looked at Beckett, "But we don't want to be seen leaving Taos on the stage with Endicott's spies in town."

"Ride to Santa Fe from here," Pablo said. "I have a good friend, Emil Martinez, who operates a livery near the center plaza. Tell him you are helping me and he will keep your horses. Then, put on your suits and take the stage on into Albuquerque."

Jean nodded, "Good plan. We'll do that."

Pablo turned his attention back to Beckett, "Set the meeting, Mr. Beckett. Jean and Henry will be there in four days."

"I will instruct Endicott to meet them at the stage station."

Jean grinned at Henry, "Remember any of your French in case we use it?"

"*Un petit peu*, I think I've retained a little."

"*Bon.*"

Jean said to Beckett, "When Andrew and Henry were growing up I still spoke a good deal of French, they picked up on a lot of it. I eventually spoke only English, though I still write primarily in French and have difficulty reading English. Catherine has been tutoring me patiently for the last forty years."

Beckett smiled, "The perfect man for this task."

Jean grinned, "*Oui.*"

Beckett stood up, "I had better get right back to my office and send the wire. I also want to line up all the legal paperwork so when you come back with Endicott's version of the deed, which I have my doubts is totally legal, I can register the sale and make sure your ownership is solid and legal."

Pablo stood up with him and shook his hand. "Thank you, Mr. Beckett for all your help."

"Your father was not only my client, he was my good friend. His murder was almost too much to bear and the ruling on the Grant unfair. The least I can do is save his work and legacy for you."

"I appreciate that, thank you." Pablo escorted Beckett out to the patio where he called for Jesus to bring up his horse.

* * * * *

Two days ride from the hacienda Jean and Henry arrived in Santa Fe. They found the hotel Pablo had suggested and checked into a room. They dropped their bedrolls in the room and took the horses to the livery of Emil Martinez.

They found Emil in the livery sitting in the tack room repairing a bridle. He turned to them, "*Buenos dias señores.*"

"*Buenos dias,*" Henry returned the salutation. "I am the brother-in-law of Pablo Ruiz. My father and I are on a mission for Pablo. We have borrowed his horses. He said you would put them up while we are gone."

Emil showed excitement, "*Si,* for my good friend Pablo, anything. I will feed and care for his horses at no charge. How long will you be?"

"We are going on business to Albuquerque, maybe five days before we return."

"That is not a problem. Pablo's horses will be fat and rested when you return. Pablo has done me many favors. It is my honor to return favors to him."

Henry nodded his head toward Emil, "*Gracias, amigo.*"

They returned to the hotel and unrolled their suits out of the bedrolls. Jean frowned as he looked over the wrinkled and mashed clothes. "They look like they've been in a bedroll for two days."

Henry shook his jacket out, "We won't look very convincing in these. We can ask the desk clerk if there is anyone on the plaza who can make these a bit more presentable."

"A lot more presentable," Jean's frown deepened.

They carried the suits downstairs and asked the clerk behind the hotel desk where they could get their suits freshened up. He cheerfully directed them to a tailor shop where the clothes would be professionally tended to.

Thanking the clerk they made their way to the shop. The tailor was friendly, telling them that his father had been a tailor, and his father had been a tailor in Spain. "To the royal family no less!" the man proudly announced. He assured them if they returned that evening their suits would be ready.

Jean and Henry ate in a café, and then went to a shop to each purchase a small traveling bag. They returned to their room to discuss the plan for dealing with Colonel Endicott.

"We can't be in a big hurry," Jean explained. "Wealthy Montreal businessmen hold themselves above the common man and are patient and clever in getting what they want out of a deal. Our demeanor must be self-impressed and constantly manipulating the deal to our favor. Don't be anxious or show the least sign of resignation to what Endicott wants. It's our way or no way."

"What if he won't give us what we want?"

"We walk out."

Henry raised an eyebrow, "We walk out? Then what?"

"We already know he likes the taste of the bait. He won't give up, he'll want us to come back the next day and talk some more. If Beckett is right and Endicott is looking to double-cross the people he represents and take the money for himself, he won't want to lose us. We will hint at how unscrupulous we are and he, being the same, will feel safe in dealing under the table with us."

Henry considered what his father had said and agreed. "If he's dealing under the table he will take less than the asking price to get the money."

Jean nodded, "That's what they do."

Henry gave Jean a quizzical look, "How do you know so much about how these men operate?"

"From working for the fur merchants in Canada. The wealthy and important men involved in the fur trade dealt viciously with each other. We even saw that in this country, during the rendezvous days when one company backstabbed another to get the furs. In Canada it was a much bigger business, cutthroat between Hudson Bay and the Northwest Fur Company. The fact that the elite men of both companies thought us voyageurs were only ignorant 'canoe paddlers' as they like to call us, they would speak openly in front of us. I listened and learned how they operate."

"That makes sense. I will follow your lead."

"Remember, I am the big man representing the Lamoureux Land Company. You are the front man for us in America. You are my uncle's son and working hand in glove with us from your home in Denver. You called me in because you are watching for these land deals for us and you heard of this one and contacted Beckett."

"Got it."

"Now, let's get the money out of the bank before it closes."

―――――――――――――

The ten o'clock southbound stage left the station at ten-thirty. Jean and Henry wore their perfectly pressed and brushed suits. They each carried their newly acquired traveling bag containing their extra clothes and personal items. On the bottom of each bag were neat rows of bills, fifteen thousand dollars in each bag. In Henry's inside suit coat pocket he had a bound group of bills for the bribe if it was needed. It was a thousand dollars in smaller bills to look more impressive.

The next day the stage pulled into Albuquerque. Jean and Henry stepped off the stage with Jean acting angry over the dust that covered his clothes. Jean brushed at the clinging dust with his free hand feigning irritation. Henry, being the American from the frontier, merely made a token gesture of dusting himself off.

As a man who they took to be Colonel Endicott approached them Henry said aloud, "Mr. Lamoureux, you will have to get used to a little dust, after all this is the frontier."

Jean took the hint and without looking around slapped at the dust. In a thick Montreal accent Jean complained, "This is despicable, you would never find such roads in Montreal. Look at my suit, it is ruined."

The man who was approaching stopped beside them. "Mr. Lamoureux?"

Jean straightened and lifted his chin slightly to appear haughty, "You have me at a disadvantage, sir."

"I am Colonel Merton Endicott. I was to meet you here."

"Oh, yes, we were told you would meet us," Jean replied coolly. He extended his hand to Endicott making sure to squeeze lightly, as a merchant of Lamoureux's class would not have a firm handshake.

Jean gestured toward Henry, "My assistant Henry Pelletier."

The two men shook hands, with Henry applying a firm western handshake.

Endicott was sizing the two up as he spoke and shook hands. Lamoureux was a city dandy and Pelletier was more appropriate to the country.

Jean handed his bag to Henry and resumed vigorously slapping at the dust on his pants. "I apologize for my appearance Colonel Endicott. I had not expected to spend days on a coach consumed in a perpetual dust cloud. My appearance is always impeccable." He glared at Henry as if to blame him for the dust. Henry merely shrugged.

"Yes," Endicott agreed, "it is a dry, dusty country. After I drive you to your hotel I can recommend a shop where they can have your suit cleaned."

"Thank you, I will appreciate that."

Endicott gestured toward his waiting buggy, "Shall we?"

"Of course." Jean stopped slapping and followed Endicott. They climbed into the two seat buggy and sat down.

Endicott took the reins and flicked them over the horse's back. "I will leave you off at your hotel and come back around in say, two hours?"

Jean nodded, "That will be sufficient time for me to bathe and have my clothes brushed."

Endicott turned his head to look back at them, "It will be my honor to take you both to my favorite restaurant for dinner."

Jean nodded, "Thank you. The meals at the stage way stops left much to be desired."

Arriving at the hotel they climbed down from the seat. "We will meet you again in two hours," Jean said as he nodded a farewell.

Endicott drove off leaving Jean and Henry standing together. They entered the hotel and registered for separate rooms. As they walked up the stairs to their rooms Henry whispered to his father, "What a twit."

"Endicott?"

"No, you," Henry laughed.

Jean grinned, "Do you think he believed it?"

"Oh, yeah, he thinks you're a pompous weakling. I can see it in the way he looks at you."

"Good, that's what I was trying to be."

Henry chuckled, "You succeeded."

"We need to wash up and get these clothes cleaned. We need to keep these bags with us so don't leave it behind in your room."

"Consider it tied to my hand, Mr. Lamoureux."

Two hours later Jean and Henry were standing in front of the hotel, clean and refreshed. Jean whispered to Henry, "Remember to use the bribe after I walk out of the meeting unless I direct you otherwise."

"I remember."

Endicott pulled up precisely two hours from when he had left them off. He greeted them and drove to the restaurant.

Over dinner they made conversation about the two countries, the developing west, and how much money there was to be made in it. They did not specifically discuss the sale of the Grant; however, Jean and Henry were well aware of how Endicott was maneuvering the conversation around to get a feel for their ethics and business sense. They worked in that they were open to deals above or below the table.

At the end of the dinner Endicott asked, "I realize you have had a long and uncomfortable day, but are you interested in returning to my home where we can begin discussions on the sale of the Taos property?"

It was not lost on either Jean or Henry that he did not refer to the property as the Ruiz Grant. Jean gave him a slight smile, "Yes that would be fine. I have other pressing matters and do not wish to remain in this dust bowl any longer than necessary."

Endicott paid the bill and stood up, "Then let us not dally, gentlemen."

They left the restaurant and drove to Endicott's home. Jean and

Henry took in the modest house as they followed Endicott in. There were no servants or extravagances that would tie Endicott to the place. He lived like the soldier he had been, simple, and ready to move on short notice.

Endicott led the way to his office gesturing for them to take seats. He offered them a drink which they accepted. He sat down behind his desk facing the two men across from him.

Endicott began, "I represent a group of men who hold some degree of power and prestige in political circles. They are actively buying and selling land that they have found abandoned or taken over by the government. It is all perfectly legal so you need not worry about ramifications in that area."

Jean sipped the drink and smiled, "Yet, all matters need not be known by the authorities do they, Colonel Endicott?"

Endicott studied Jean, trying to decide if that was a casual statement or a declaration that all does not have to be legal. He smiled in return, "What they don't know doesn't necessarily hurt them."

"Indeed."

"The Taos property is comprised of slightly more than two townships or fifty thousand acres give or take a few. My group wishes to split the property in half and sell the southern twenty-five thousand acres separate from the north twenty-five."

Jean frowned, "It was my understanding that the entire property was for sale."

"It is, however, they feel it is more advantageous to sell it as two distinct properties."

"So they can profit more from two than the single, you mean," Jean commented dryly.

Endicott merely smiled at the statement.

"How much do they want for each half then?"

"Fifty thousand."

Jean chuckled lightly, "Of course not. The price is outrageous. For the entire property it is even too much, for half . . . ." he chuckled and shook his head.

Henry broke in, "Colonel Endicott, let us put this horse trading aside, what is the actual price your people will sell the property for?"

"That *is* the actual price, Mr. Pelletier."

"I have been up to the property," Henry spoke casually. "People are still living on it and it is filled with livestock."

"The cattle come with the property and are worth a good deal, thus the higher price."

"There is nothing on that property that warrants more than one dollar an acre."

Jean looked incensed as he glared at Henry, "You told me the property was merely land. Having it filled with people and cattle creates severe complications."

"The cattle . . . ." Endicott began.

"Are in the way," Jean tersely cut him off, "as are the people. I do not have the time to trade cattle. I want to develop this land immediately."

"You can sell the cattle off," Endicott urged.

"Shall I sell the people off as well?" Jean's tone was sarcastic.

Endicott shrugged, "Run them off."

Jean put his glass down hard on the table. "Attacking and killing people, risking prison or the gallows, does not further my company's interests." He glared at Henry, "I was misled. I have wasted my time."

Henry looked at him and scowled, "I *did not* mislead you, Mr. Lamoureux. I did not realize having cattle on the property would be an issue for you. I thought they could be sold."

"Well, it *is* an *issue* for me, Mr. Pelletier, and what of the people presently occupying it? Do you plan to sell them as well?"

"The land is still a good investment."

"At such an exorbitant *price*," Jean raised his already angry voice, "because I am expected to pay for livestock I do not want!"

"I can make it work for you, Mr. Lamoureux."

"I think otherwise. I traveled a great distance from Montreal on your word, Mr. Pelletier. I endured horrid coach rides, choked on dust, and ate disgusting food because I believed you had a prize for me here. Now, I find it is half the land for twice the price and filled with cattle and people. I cannot foil my family's enemy by spending double for half and wasting time trading cattle and relocating unwanted people."

Henry argued, "I did not know you would object, I apologize. Is beating the Hudson Bay Company your sole goal?"

Jean's voice raised in pitch, "*Profit* is my first goal, a lesson I learned from my father. Undermining Hudson Bay was his passion after they ruined him. So yes, I am interested in both."

Endicott took in the argument keying on the Hudson Bay refer-

ence. It was as he had expected, it was the original Victor Lamoureux who began the land company to compete against the company that had ruined him. His son was carrying on the revenge.

Endicott held up his hand, "Please, gentlemen, let us control our
tempers. There was merely a misunderstanding."

Jean glared at Endicott, "*Misunderstanding*! Colonel Endicott,
let us speak of misrepresentation which is far different from misunderstanding. I am not a fool to be played as a fool." He stood up.

Endicott's eyes flashed fear, he was losing the man and his money, and with it his chance to get out. "Please, Mr. Lamoureux, I am
sure we can come to an accord."

"I am returning to the hotel, the two of you may discuss your
misunderstanding if you wish. I have had enough of this."

Endicott stood up, "I will drive you."

"No thank you, the walk will allow me time to cool my temper
and plan my return home from this most fruitless folly."

Endicott forced the panic from his voice, "Perhaps tomorrow we
can speak further?"

Jean sniffed, refusing to look at him or acknowledge the plea, he
walked out.

Endicott stood in silence as he heard his front door close. He
looked at Henry who was still seated. "Did I offend him? I never
meant to."

Henry waved his hand, "My father's nephew has a hot temper."

"You two are related?"

"In a roundabout way, yes. I am originally from Canada, but
moved to Denver many years ago. I was contacted and recruited
by the Lamoureux Land Company to find land deals in the United
States, particularly in the reorganizing west. I have made some
excellent deals for them and profited nicely by it. This, however, is
the first time the head of the company, Mr. Lamoureux, has ventured down himself. He is a bit fussy."

Endicott thought the man well beyond fussy, but kept his
thoughts to himself. "I tried to find information on the Lamoureux
Company and found nothing."

Henry smiled, "And you won't. You see the Lamoureux Land
Company is intertwined within other companies and will never
show up as such."

"Why is that?"

"To be frank, because their methods are not always legal. Land is not always obtained through the proper agencies. They get what they want and are willing to recruit the right people to insure they *do* get what they want . . . no questions asked. You could stand to do well with them for future land deals, as I have."

Endicott rubbed his chin, "I see, however, there seems to be a problem with this Taos property."

"Yes, the cattle and people. I thought we could quickly deal with both, but it appears Lamoureux wants a very rapid turnaround on this. The western lands are a fast moving product right now, I suppose I can see his point and why this is an issue for him."

Endicott frowned, "I had hoped to do better with Mr. Lamoureux. It has been a poor first impression on my part."

Henry smiled, "Maybe you and I can come to an accord without the fussy old lady interfering and we both come out with money in our pockets." He chuckled, "After all isn't that what we both really want?"

Hope rebounded in Endicott's mind, "Yes, let you and I talk." Endicott held up the liquor bottle, which Henry refused. Refilling his glass Endicott asked, "What do I need to do to move him?"

"Give him what he wants and he will be back for more."

Endicott leaned back heavily in his chair. "I cannot circumvent the people I represent. I have to do as they wish. Therefore, I cannot lower the price."

Henry gave him a patronizing look, "Really Colonel? I find it hard to believe that a man of your importance, a former high ranking military officer accustomed to giving orders, would submit to anyone. It would seem a man like you would prefer to do business for himself, not bowing before lesser men."

Endicott stiffened in his chair, the comment had struck a raw nerve. He *had* been the man giving orders and now he was taking them and it was a sore irritation. He studied the man across the desk from him, he understood what Pelletier was leading into. "I have considered it."

Henry pulled the bundle of bills from his pocket. He saw Endicott's eyes track their movement. He had the man's attention. Henry lightly shook the bills in the air. "One thousand dollars Colonel, yours merely for giving him whatever price he wants. Your people never have to know about it."

Endicott smiled nervously, yet focused on the bills. "I only have the paperwork to sell twenty-five thousand acres of the property.

The group has retained the second half."

Henry tipped his head to the side, "We are willing to buy the south half, the better half, for now."

"What about the cattle and people on the land? He is adamant about not wanting that."

"Let me deal with that. All the old lady needs to know is that the land will be immediately cleared for his purposes. He will want a much lower price though."

"How do I explain to the people I represent why I sold the land for less? If I do as you wish I may well forfeit my life. These are desperate people."

"A soldier concerned about his life?" Henry made a tsking sound. "I cannot see you as a coward, Colonel Endicott."

Endicott bristled at the reproach. He made up his mind he wasn't taking orders from anyone again. He reached for the bills, "I will consider it."

Henry pulled the bills back. "We will meet tomorrow at noon. I will have the old lady with me. This will be yours if you accept his offer. Then, you can do wherever you wish with the money."

CHAPTER NINETEEN

Endicott dropped Henry off in front of the hotel with a promise to pick them up at noon. He drove back to his house with his mind alive with plans to give the pompous Frenchman what he wanted while still trying to get as much as he could out of him. He would take the money and leave the country.

Concentrating on these plans he knew being in the center of the country with no fast moving transportation created a problem for quick escape. Then again, his pursuers would have the same problem except he would have a jump on them. He had decided on Europe, less revolutionary problems there than in South America. Italy or Greece perhaps. He would head west and take a ship around the horn to Europe. The League would have no idea where he went. Should anyone catch up to him he would kill them and keep going. This was his chance and he wasn't about to lose it.

As Endicott was mulling over decisions for his future, Henry walked up the stairs and knocked on Jean's door. Jean opened the door and ushered him in. "How did it go?" Jean asked.

"Like luring that black fox in."

"He's ready?"

"Oh yeah, he's more than ready. When I flashed the bundle at him he all but jumped across the desk for it. He's picking us up at noon."

"Good. I will have calmed down by then," Jean laughed.

"He was scared he had run you off and lost his chance. I told him you had a hot temper and were a fussy old lady. I told him we both stood to make a lot if he gave you what you wanted."

"Fussy old lady?"

Henry grinned, "You acted like one. I used that to downplay your importance to what I wanted. It got him to come around to my way of thinking since we were both undermining our people."

"Can we get the whole thing, both halves?"

"He said he only had the paperwork for half. I told him we would take the southern half."

"With the houses and all, good! Half is better than none."

"I told him we would settle for that."

Jean nodded, "With the new partnerships and 25,000 acres Pablo will still do well."

"There is still the chance Beckett can do something later on to get the second half for Pablo."

"One thing at a time. First we meet again with Endicott and secure the south half."

―――――――

At noon the next day they met Endicott again in front of the hotel. All the money had been placed in the bag Jean carried. Jean feigned irritation, acting merely civil to their host. Endicott made pleasant small talk that Jean answered with monosyllable answers.

Arriving at the house, Endicott led them inside and to the office where they sat down as they had the previous day. Jean placed his bag containing the money on the floor beside them. Endicott offered them drinks which they refused.

Jean began the talks, "Mr. Pelletier informed me that you are willing to negotiate the sale."

"I would like to talk further, yes."

"At a more reasonable price, I would expect."

"I am, let us say, working as my own agent now."

Jean nodded and lightly smiled, "Very good, it makes matters easier."

Endicott glanced at Henry, "Mr. Pelletier indicated there would be compensation to me if I agree to a deal. I will want that."

Jean glanced at Henry as if in disapproval. In French he snapped, "Working our own side, Mr. Pelletier?"

Henry answered in French, "No, sir, merely smoothing the path to a successful agreement where we all benefit."

"Your money?"

"Of course. I am invested in the company."

Jean nodded, "Very well."

Endicott's eyes flicked back and forth as the men spoke in a language he did not understand. He looked at Henry, "Translation please."

"Mr. Lamoureux asked if I was working my own deal. I assured him it was my own money and it was to smooth the talks."

Endicott nodded, "On that note, before we go further . . . my compensation?"

Henry pulled the money from his pocket and laid it on the desk in front of him. He held his hand down on it. "Depends on the selling price."

Endicott's eyes momentarily held on the bundle of bills. He then turned his attention to Jean, "As I said before I am only able to sell half of the property, twenty-five thousand acres, at this time. Mr. Pelletier has requested the southern half. I can enter that on the paperwork as I can use it for either half."

Jean met his eyes, "How much?"

"Thirty thousand."

Jean did not blink or flinch, "Still too much. Lower your price to something more reasonable."

Endicott opened his mouth to speak when the sound of the front door hitting hard against the wall made him jerk forward, startled. He jumped up and quickly rushed to the front room. To his annoyance Kendrick stood in the room obviously upset.

"I told you to knock," Endicott snapped at him.

Kendrick ignored the command and shouted, "You met with the Canadians yesterday and did not tell me."

Endicott chuckled, "Your toadies are lagging behind in providing you information. Yes, I met with them. They wanted a ridiculously low price and left unsatisfied. I refused to undercut the League."

"Is that a fact? Why then are cattle being driven off the Ruiz Grant?"

"I don't know anything about it. Why should I?"

"You are the one in contact with that Mexican's attorney. I thought *you* were on top of *everything!*" The last comment was accusatory.

"No, that's *your* job Kendrick. *You* are the one who is supposed to keep everything in order and in line, including me. Don't try to shift the blame on me for your failures. Who told you this anyway?"

"The telegrapher who has been passing information to me. He saw several men driving a large herd of cattle past Taos headed east."

Endicott snorted. He had suspected that his Taos informant in the telegrapher's office was doing double duty. Spying on Ruiz and reporting any actions he was involved in to Kendrick first.

"If the Canadians didn't buy the property then that Mexican is illegally removing the cattle," Kendrick shouted. "They are part of the property. Didn't you make that clear with that attorney?"

"We didn't discuss cattle, only land."

"Well, they are stealing the cattle. I'll have the law on them."

Endicott grinned, "The law? Do you really think the League wants the law involved? You do that and you will come to a quick end. If you want those cattle back I would suggest you gather up some of your bully boys and stop them."

"Where are those Canadians now? Maybe they do have something to do with this!"

"I haven't seen them since yesterday and they did not want the cattle which was one of the reasons they refused to pay the price. I doubt they are stealing cattle they never wanted. It has to be that Mexican trying to hide his cattle before he loses the place."

Kendrick growled, "You had better do something about this."

"No, *you* do something about it." He grabbed Kendrick by the upper arm and forced him toward the door.

Kendrick shook his hand off, "Touch me again and I'll kill you."

Endicott pulled the revolver from his shoulder holster and pointed it at Kendrick's nose. "You broke into my house. I have every legal right to shoot you."

Kendrick stared at the gun's muzzle. "You will hear about this, you're finished. I'll see to that."

"You do that, right after you save your own hide by dealing with the cattle rustlers. Now, get out."

Kendrick turned on his heels and stormed out the still open door. Endicott closed the door behind him and locked it. He walked back to the office and sat down.

Jean was smiling at him, "So, all is legal, nothing to fear from the law. My, my, but it does sound like someone is, how do you American's say it, claim jumping?"

"Land jumping," Henry corrected.

"Oh, yes . . . land jumping, and now there are no more cattle to make the land *so* valuable."

Jean lifted his chin to Henry, who then moved the thousand dollars to Endicott's side of the desk and left it.

Jean removed fifteen thousand dollars from his bag and laid it on the table. "Sixteen thousand dollars, Colonel Endicott."

"Cash on the barrelhead," Henry added.

"Take it or leave it," Jean challenged. "Or the law may come asking to see your books."

Endicott stared at the money, he was fairly cornered and he knew it. This was as much as he was going to get. He had no choice now but to take the money and run, but that was what he planned to do all along anyway. He was hoping for more though.

Inwardly he cursed Kendrick for his big mouth. He might have gotten more out of the Frenchman; however, it was still a goodly sum, more than he ever made as a soldier. He could live quite well for a long time in a Mediterranean villa. If he didn't take the offer, Lamoureux or Pelletier would have the law on him. In addition, he would now have Kendrick reporting him and the League's thugs would be coming for him. It was move now or never. He reached into a drawer and removed a folder of papers.

"I accept, Mr. Lamoureux." He began writing on the papers.

"Place the property in the name of Henry Pelletier," Jean instructed.

Endicott nodded as he filled in the lines and finally signed the bottom. He handed the papers to Jean.

Jean looked the papers over as he allowed the ink to dry. Struggling with the English he handed the papers to Henry. "How do these look to you? I am not altogether familiar with American procedures."

Henry read the papers. They were general and he wondered if they were the official deed and bill of sale to the property. If it wasn't, it was enough for Beckett to secure the legal deed in Henry's name.

Henry smiled, "Very good, Colonel Endicott." He took the pen and signed his name below Endicott's. He blew gently on the ink to dry it and then touched it for dryness. Once dry, Henry handed the papers to Jean who returned the papers to the folder and placed the folder in his bag.

Henry glanced out the office door, "Sounds like you have a problem on your hands with cattle stealing."

"Not for long." He gave Henry a suspicious stare, "Do you know anything about the cattle being removed?"

"Me? Why should I know or care about the cattle? We don't want them."

"You should, you own them now."

"I'll check into it."

Endicott suspected the two of being more underhanded than he had given them credit for. He didn't care actually, he had what he wanted.

Jean and Henry stood up, "Thank you, Colonel," Jean said. "You have dealt well with me. I will keep you in mind for future transactions."

Endicott smiled knowing that he would be long gone before this pompous French crook ever called on him again. He got what he wanted and that's all he cared about.

He stood up, "I will drive you back to your hotel."

Jean nodded, "Thank you."

After dropping off the two men, Endicott returned to his house. He immediately began to pack his clothes and the few things he would need. He could buy the rest when he settled. He distributed the money between his two carpet bags and on his person.

Going out the back door he entered the little stable behind his house. Not wanting to be trapped in a stagecoach where he couldn't duck and hide if need be he planned to ride north to Cheyenne and pick up the Pacific Railroad to Sacramento. Setting his two bags down between the stall wall and the horse, he bridled his horse and reached for the saddle blanket.

A voice behind him spoke low and threatening, "Taking a trip are we?" It was Kendrick. He turned to look at the man he hated.

Kendrick gave him a satisfied, smug grin, "I thought you were up to no good. You made your own deal with the Canadians, didn't you? So, where are you running off to?"

Endicott had no intention of letting this weasel stop him, not when he had the money and was so close to escape. He pretended to be afraid.

"Please, Kendrick, don't tell the League."

Kendrick was obviously enjoying his position over Endicott. "Not so tough now are you? I've already sent wires to the League about your secret meeting and to my 'bully boys', as you put it. They will take care of the Mexican and the stolen cattle. Now, what am I to do about you?" he said with a sneering smile.

"I'll share the money with you Kendrick."

Greed lit up in Kendrick's eyes. "How much did you get?"

"Fifty thousand, I'll give you half."

"Well, since I have you over a barrel let's say, sixty-forty. Sixty for me."

"Okay," Endicott made his voice tremble. Turning his back to

Kendrick he bent over his bags in the narrow space between the wall and the horse and opened a bag.

Kendrick watched from outside the stall with avarice dancing wildly in his eyes.

Endicott reached in the bag and stood up. "Here's your sixty." He thumbed back the hammer on the small revolver as he turned and fired directly into Kendrick's chest.

Kendrick's eyes flew open wide with pain and surprise as the bullet tore into his lung. He fell to his knees grasping his chest, his breathing hoarse and ragged. He looked up, his eyes pleading for help as Endicott aimed and deliberately put a bullet into Kendrick's forehead. He fell forward into the dirt floor of the stable.

Endicott finished saddling his horse and led him out of the stall where he tied the bags to either side over the saddle's cantle. He dragged Kendrick's body into the stall and forked hay down over it. Mounting, he heeled the horse into a fast walk putting Albuquerque and the League behind him.

Henry and Jean made a quick trip to their rooms to change clothes. Jean packed the remaining money in his bag and carried it as they walked down the stairs bound for a small cafe and a late lunch.

Once out on the street Henry released a heavy sigh. Jean glanced at him, "Are you alright?"

"I was really nervous and now it's letting go and I feel like a dishrag."

"You did a good acting job for being so nervous."

"My brain was running two steps ahead of my mouth. I was trying not to ruin it by saying something wrong." He looked at his father, "Where did you learn to speak such highbrow? I never heard you talk like that at home."

Jean smiled, "Your mother's constant insistence that I speak better, and I grew up around it."

"I thought you grew up in a voyageur family with eleven brothers?"

"I did, but we dealt with wealthy merchants, remember. We took orders from them, and had to listen to them talk to each other. The way I spoke in there was exactly how Maurice LeSueur and Victor Lamoureux spoke. I only copied them."

"Not the nicest people were they?"

Jean thought back on the day he killed Claude LeSueur, now only a hazy memory. He remembered running with Andre ahead of Maurice's assassins, and the confrontation with the arrogant Lamoureux. "No, they were not."

Henry looked up and down the street, "What do you think Endicott will do now?"

"Run. He double-crossed his group, and if I picked up right on the argument he had with that other man they aren't the kind to let him get away with this."

"That's why he settled for our offer."

Jean nodded, "That's what I was counting on. What he got will take care of him for a long time."

"If he lives long enough to spend it."

They walked in silence to the cafe where they sat down and ordered from the black haired Mexican girl who greeted them at the table.

Henry scowled, "We could only get half though."

"Originally, when this first started, we didn't expect Pablo to get any. He was out all around. At least now he can keep his people working and in their homes, and him in his family home. Not to mention he can still raise a lot of cattle on twenty-five thousand acres."

"That's true, but if Endicott did run we won't be able to get the other half."

"I wouldn't count it out. I don't believe they have a legal hold on that land and I'm trusting that Beckett can get it wrested away from them and back into Pablo's hands one day."

Henry smiled, "Beckett is one smart lawyer, if anyone can do it he can."

"So, let's be happy for what we could get and let tomorrow take care of itself."

The food arrived at the table carried by the waitress. They paid her and began to eat. Between bites Henry paused, "Do you think that man who was arguing with Endicott will send people out to stop the drive?"

Jean grinned, "Against Ian and Clint?"

Henry chuckled, "Yeah, foolish question."

CHAPTER TWENTY

The Pelletier crew arrived at Pablo's adobe house the day after Jean and Henry left for Albuquerque. Pablo was pleased to see them and welcomed the larger than expected crew. He ordered a yearling steer be butchered and cooked for a feast for everyone.

It had been years since Ian had seen Pablo, but they easily renewed their old and trusted friendship. Andrew reiterated several times how much he appreciated what Pablo and his father had done to rescue Rebecca. Jeb had met Pablo once when he was a boy, yet they remembered each other.

Pablo and Clint became instant friends. They were men of equal qualities each seeing themselves in the other. Later Pablo would sit down with Clint and Ian and discuss their partnership.

Catherine was excited to see her sons again and hugged them each in turn. She hugged Jeb last and looked up into his face. "Can we talk about what happened?"

Jeb nodded, "Yes, you need to know." They went to Catherine's room and shut the door.

Catherine sat down on the edge of the bed. "Henry told us a bit, but he didn't have all the details except that a man from Jenny's past showed up in town and made threats against her. Then, he spread lies and the town turned on her."

"That's it in a nutshell." He then went on to tell in detail what had happened and how they ended up going to Ian's.

Catherine's eyes burned with outrage as Jeb revealed the details. When he finished she said, "I will be having words with a few women in that town."

"Mrs. Evans and Mrs. Kelly are on our side for sure." Jeb smiled, "The three of you could turn some things around in that town."

"I think we will before matters get too out of hand with these eastern immigrants." She studied Jeb's tired face, "How do you feel about not being Paul's deputy any longer? I know you wanted to be a lawman."

Jeb shrugged, "I don't really mind. I'm just not cut out for town living and was sick to death of dealing with sniveling, whining people. I had expected being a lawman to be exciting, chasing outlaws, keeping the peace, and all it amounted to was ninety-nine percent listening to people's complaints. One farmer wanted me to do something about the coyotes that killed his calf. Can you believe that?"

Catherine shook her head. "They do not understand the west at all."

"That's for sure and I don't miss it."

"How does Jenny like being up on the ranch?"

"She loves it." Jeb chuckled, "Her and Anne are such great pals and she dotes on little Kate."

Catherine smiled, "That's good. It is not how you planned for it to be, but it seems to have worked out."

Jeb nodded, "Shifting trails."

Catherine gave him a questioning look.

"It's something Ian said to me once. Life sometimes changes the circumstances of our direction and puts us onto a different trail than we had planned."

"Oh, I see, yes, shifting trails. Going from one trail to another."

Catherine stood up, "We should rejoin the others." She hugged Jeb, "I'm happy it's working out for you."

"It is," Jeb smiled at her. "Probably a lot better than it would have living in town.

The next day the men rode out with Pablo and his vaqueros to begin gathering in the cattle for the drive and getting them staged to move out.

Pablo was riding with Ian and Clint discussing the cattle he was sending on the drive, when they spotted two of Pablo's men riding toward them. Sandwiched between them was a man. The three men stopped their horses and watched the vaqueros coming with the third rider. Pablo soon recognized the man in the middle as Marty Taggard. He wondered what had happened now concerning the last remaining Taggard.

Stopping in front of Pablo one of the vaqueros said, "*Patron*, we caught this one driving several head of young cattle."

The second vaquero added, "Except it was strange *patron*, he was driving the cattle into those we had already separated. They do not have your brand."

Pablo looked at Marty, "Hello Marty. What is your story?"

The two riders were surprised that Pablo knew the young man.

"Mr. Ruiz," Marty started with a nervous quiver in his voice. "I was driving them back."

"Back?"

"These are the cattle my old man and brothers stole from you. They have run over brands, but they're yours. It took me a long time to find them and head them back to your property. I don't know that I got them all, though."

Clint and Ian had heard the story of the hunt for the Taggards and their ultimate demise. This was the young man Pablo had said helped them.

Pablo smiled, "Well, thank you Marty."

"It was the least I could do after all that happened. I ain't like them."

"I know you are not Marty, you are a good man."

Marty's countenance brightened at the compliment.

Pablo nodded toward his two men that it was okay and he would take it from here. The two vaqueros returned to the gathering.

Pablo asked, "What are your plans Marty?"

Marty shrugged, "Ain't got none. Not sure what to do. Around here my name is something men spit out with cuss words and I can't blame 'em none. I need a new country to start over in so I figured I'd drift. I just wanted to make things right before I left though."

Pablo nodded toward him, "It was an honorable thing to do."

Clint asked Pablo, "Is this the young man you said helped you out?"

"Yes, this is Marty Taggard, a fine young man with much promise."

Clint looked Marty over. "That took some doin' to bring in that bunch by yourself, you must be a pretty good hand."

Marty shrugged, "I know a little."

"You said you need a new country. Seems I need an extra hand up in Colorado. Looking for a job?"

"Yes, sir if one is to be had."

"Thirty a month and found. We're growing and you could grow right up with us."

Marty's face brightened, "Yes, sir, I'll work plenty hard too."

"I'm sure of that. Got a bedroll?"

"Back in the woods where I've been livin'."

"Get it. You're on my payroll as of today. We're driving this herd out in the morning."

"Yes, sir!" Marty spun his horse around and galloped away.

Pablo grinned at Clint, "I think I made a good choice in partners."

Ian chuckled, "Picking up strays again are we?" He slapped Clint on the back.

"If someone had done that for me when I was his age I might have avoided a lot of bad decisions and not done a lot of what haunts my dreams. I know all about needing a new country and a new start."

Clint's comment indicated he had a checkered history. Ian knew about some of it. To a man like Pablo histories were only that . . . histories. What a man did and said today was all that mattered and Clint Rush was a man worth riding the river with. He and Ian both knew it.

Pablo nudged his horse toward the gathered cattle. He waved his hand over the expanse of animals, "All young breed stock, heifers, cows that have successfully calved at least once, and a proper number of bulls. I will sell off the steers as soon as possible and only keep breeding stock since I have no idea what will become of the hacienda."

Pablo rode around the herd with Clint and Ian flanking his sides. "I have a remuda gathered as well, three horses per rider. Keep the horses on your ranchos to work the cattle with."

They rode further past the gathered herd to a cluster of young cattle held separate from the rest. He looked at Ian, "Those are the two hundred head I talked to you about."

Ian nodded noticing the yellow slashes on the sides of the animals. "Nice young stuff."

"The best of the herds, it is little enough. My men are marking them with yellow paint so when the time comes to separate them from our herds it will be easier."

Clint asked. "Will any of your men ride with us?"

"Yes, four vaqueros will be on the drive until you leave the cattle off in Colorado, then they will return. You will have more than enough men to finish the drive up into Wyoming with less than half the herd."

"How many head altogether?" Ian asked.

"Sixteen hundred head. It will be a big drive and perhaps draw unwanted attention."

"We'll be ready for that," Ian remarked. "Every man on the crew can shoot."

"Good. If the people trying to take my land catch wind of the drive someone may try to stop you."

Clint scanned the herd watching the vaqueros rope and paint the cattle. He casually said, "It'll be their funerals if they try."

"Just as long as it is not yours," Pablo replied. "Let us go back and we will prepare the supplies for your trip."

———————

That evening they all ate outside beside the spitted and roasting yearling. The men discussed the trip and met the four vaqueros who would be making the trip with them. Pablo looked over the crew that was about to drive the challenged herd north. The League claimed he did not own the cattle, he claimed that he did and these men were willing to stake their lives to back him. He felt the strong friendship that bonded them together for a common cause.

Clint was telling the group, "Booker and me made the first drive with Goodnight and Loving in '66, from Texas up to Fort Sumner. Loving was killed by Comanches on that drive. Booker and me drifted on up to Montana and rode together for a spell. Booker went back to Texas after a couple of years."

Booker glanced at Clint. They had parted company when Clint started hiring out his gun to people he considered scum. That was in the past and didn't count for anything now. He added to the story. "I went back up the trail with Goodnight again in '70. Goodnight carved a new trail over Trincheras Pass to Cheyenne. Between Clint and me, we know that route pretty good."

Eugenio, one of the four vaqueros, listened and then said, "Then the two of you should ride point on the drive. My *compañeros* and I have never driven cattle over that trail." His three friends agreed.

The boys, Tom Pelletier and Joe Webster, sat silently spellbound listening to the tales and adventures of the men they were to ride with. They knew their jobs were to keep the remuda together. It was an adventure in itself to be in the company of such men.

Marty had ridden in just before supper and was welcomed by the crew. He volunteered to handle the pack horses that would carry their food and other supplies. It was not a glamorous job as far as drovers were concerned, but essential to their survival. He also wanted to start off with his new friends and boss by taking a lower position and proving his worth rather than demanding a prestigious position on the drive.

It was voted on by the crew that the men would rotate positions on a regular basis. In this manner no one was stuck riding drag all the time or wearing themselves to a frazzle as swing riders chasing down and cutting back the herd quitters. The only exceptions were Booker and Clint who would remain at point and trade off as scouts. The remuda and pack-string would move parallel to the herd to avoid the dust and keep pace with the drive.

The morning drive started off slow, forcing sixteen hundred head of cattle to leave the comfortable range they had always known was a formidable task. It was two hours of solid riding and a change of horses to get the animals up and moving collectively.

Once they were on the move the swing riders had their hands full keeping the herd quitters in the line and not cutting back for home. It took another two hours to get the animals into a flow of movement, but the drive was underway. The line of cattle strung out for a quarter mile as an older cream colored bull took the lead like he was assigned to it and led the way behind Clint and Booker.

The drive would head south before turning east to come out of the mountains above Taos and then aim due east to intercept the Santa Fe Trail above Cimarron. As the Santa Fe wound to the east and north they would eventually tap into the Goodnight Trail and then north through Trincheras Pass.

The Ruiz drive, as it was called by the crew, drew attention along the way. Many of those who made their living between Elizabethtown and Taos knew of the situation between the Ruiz outfit and the Taggards. It was also rumored that the great hacienda of Sebastian Ruiz had been taken over by the government. The drive was considered a gutsy move by Ruiz to defy the United States government and their claims to his land and all that was on it. Many came out to watch what could well be the last great cattle drive in New Mexico.

The first day they made it to within five miles of Taos where they camped. The cattle were bunched and four men at a time rode four hour guard shifts circling the cattle through the night. The next day they passed through the mountains and camped in the canyon between Cimarron and Elizabethtown.

The second night the guards spotted several men on horseback surveying the herd. The local outlaws were coming out to look over the herd and study how best to pick off the animals. A pair of riders approached Jeb who was riding his guard shift before dark.

Jeb stopped his horse and watched the men as they approached him. One of the men smiled, "That sure is a lot of cows. Can't recall ever seeing that many in one spot."

Jeb eyed him coldly, "They won't be here for long."

"Drivin' 'em, are yuh?"

"It would seem that way."

The man glanced at his partner, "Seems it would be mighty hard to keep track of all of them, some might wander off."

"They know it would be a mistake to wander off."

The man grinned, "How would cows know that?"

Jeb locked his eyes on the man's, "I doubt they would wander off without help."

"Meaning?"

"Meaning we've got the guns and we won't waste time discussing points of law with cattle thieves. We'll just kill them and drive the herd over their bodies."

The man stiffened, the grin dropping from his face, "That almost sounds like it was directed at me."

"It was directed at whoever makes the cows wander off."

The man wasn't sure how to reply to that without implicating himself as a potential cattle thief. "Whose outfit is this anyway?"

"Ruiz, Pelletier, and Rush."

The man's eyes flickered back and forth as he thought about the names. What the Ruiz outfit had done to the Taggards was well talked up. He had heard of the others before, but not sure where. He looked at his partner, "You know them names?"

The second man answered, "Ruiz, yeah." He looked at Jeb, "Would that be the Poudre Canyon Pelletiers?"

"Part. There's Ian and Jeb Pelletier from South Pass and Clint Rush from Fort Collins area."

The two men exchanged looks. The second man asked, "Any truth to that business up in Wyoming where a Pelletier outfit blew up a town?"

"It's true. That would be Ian and my brothers."

"I recall now hearing of Clint Rush," the first man said in a low warning tone to his partner. "Gunhand."

The man grinned at Jeb, "Looks like a pretty well-heeled outfit. You shouldn't have any problems."

"That's how we see it. You might want to pass that along."

Both men turned and rode slowly away.

Eugenio stopped his horse next to Jeb as he made his circle of the herd. "What did they want?"

"They were curious if cows could wander off from such a large herd."

Eugenio grinned, flashing white teeth under a full mustache, "What did you tell them?"

"That we'd shoot cattle thieves and drive the herd over their bodies."

The vaquero laughed, "Straight and to the point. I like you *amigo*." He continued his circling ride around the herd.

The following day the drive reached the Santa Fe Trail above Cimarron. Here the land leveled out and better time could be made than pushing the cattle through the mountains. They moved the herd south of the Trail to avoid clogging the road that travelers and the stage used. The cattle were settled on the Canadian River grasslands for the night to graze and water.

As the men were circling the herd to stop them in their pace four riders approached the camp where Marty was unloading the packhorses with Jeb's help. Ian stood with Clint and Booker discussing the route. Marty called their attention to the riders. They stopped their discussion and watched the four ride boldly in.

The riders stopped short of the camp and looked them over. The rider in the middle called out, "Territorial Marshal Darby, I need to enter your camp."

"Come on in," Ian called back.

They watched the riders, not liking the looks of the three that rode with the marshal. Ian looked up at Darby as the men pulled their horses to a stop. "You have a badge to prove who you are?"

Darby pulled back the lapel of his light jacket to reveal the badge pinned to his shirt. Ian nodded his approval.

The marshal stayed mounted but two of the men with him began to dismount. Clint spoke in a calmly, yet no nonsense tone, "We said you could ride in. No one said anything about making yourself at home. Until we know your business I suggest you stay horseback."

The two men stopped in mid dismount and stared unbelievingly at Clint. A quick scan of the hard, unwelcoming faces and belted revolvers convinced them to heave themselves back up in the saddle, which they did. The marshal glanced back at the men with him and then focused his concentration on Clint. "You're a careful man."

"I'm still alive in this country," Clint remarked.

"What's your business marshal?" Ian asked.

Darby jerked his head in the direction of the men with him, "These men claim to be the new owners of the Ruiz ranch and you're stealing the cattle from it. I looked the cattle over and noticed the SR brand on them."

"First off," Ian began, "Pablo Ruiz is the owner of the Ruiz hacienda. I have no idea who these men are." He jerked a thumb at Clint, "Him and me are Ruiz' partners, and I guess we should know."

Darby's eyes flickered back and forth as he thought on that. "Do you have any paperwork to show you own these cattle?"

Pablo had given Ian and Clint signed authorizations and brand ownership documents for over the trail in case they were challenged. Ian walked to his horse and pulled an oilskin pouch out of the saddlebag. He removed the papers and walked back to the marshal handing the papers to him. He took them and read over them.

"My partner has the same papers," Ian said. He turned a hard stare on the three men behind the lawman, "Let's see their papers of ownership."

Darby handed the papers back to Ian and scowled with irritation, "I believe I have been used as a monkey, gentlemen, your documents are in order."

Darby glared back at the three men, "What kind of game are you playing here?"

One of the men snorted, "Game? Those rustlers are playin' the game. That property went up for grabs when old man Ruiz croaked. We got it all legal and the cattle come with it."

Ian put his hand on his gun butt, "Who are you calling a rustler?"

The man clamped his mouth shut as Jeb stepped forward and mirrored Ian's stance, as did Clint and Booker.

Darby glanced at the cattlemen and their positions. Turning his glare back on the talker he snapped, "You'd best shut your mouth right now. These men are holding authorized ownership papers. Let me see yours."

The man hesitated trying to think of an answer. "Well, I sure don't carry such around in my pocket."

Darby's scowl deepened, "If I had enough evidence I'd arrest you all for making a false accusation. If you thought to make me a party to your cattle rustling you were sadly mistaken. Now, if I were you boys, I'd ride far and fast before I get mad."

The talker set a hard look on Ian, "You haven't heard the last of this."

"Come back anytime," Ian grinned wickedly. "We'll be happy to make it the last."

The three men jerked their horses back and loped away down the river.

Darby turned his attention back to Ian. "Sorry about this. They came in all flustered about their cattle being stolen so I had no choice but to check it out."

"You're welcome to step down and take supper with us."

"Thanks, but I've had too much of my day wasted by them and had better get about some real business. By the way where are you headed?"

"Colorado with part of the herd and Wyoming with the rest."

"Mind if I ask your names?"

"I'm Ian Pelletier, this is my brother Jeb, and my partner is Clint Rush."

"Any relation to the Colorado Pelletiers?"

"Yes sir that would be us."

"My friend Nathan Stuart, U.S. Marshal in Denver, has mentioned you."

"Yeah, Nathan's a cousin to our mother."

"He said you were honest folks, good friends, but bad enemies. Guess if those boys come back looking for a fight they'll find it."

Ian grinned, "They'll find it alright."

Darby nodded, "I'll be off then."

"You might want to take a ride to Taos and see an attorney named Sam Beckett. He could tell you a lot about the underhanded doings of a bunch of land thieves."

"That could be interesting. Those men I rode in with part of that?"

"Likely. They sure have no claim on these cattle."

"They sure enough got on my bad side. Think I'll look Beckett up and see what we can do about all this." He turned his horse and rode back to the west.

Ian looked at Jeb and then Clint. "The only way those men could know that the land was in contention is if they were part of that outfit trying to get their hands on it."

"They were sent to stop us," Clint said. "They just wanted to try and get the law to do it first."

Ian agreed, "In that case they'll be back."

"With more men," Jeb added.

Ian looked back at the fire Marty had started. "We'd better get to eating, it might be a long night."

CHAPTER TWENTY-ONE

Jean and Henry had taken the stage out of Albuquerque bound for Santa Fe. After depositing the remaining money back into Pablo's bank account they picked up their horses and rode back to Taos. Their first stop was Samuel Beckett's office as Jean wanted to find out how authentic the bill of sale was they had received from Colonel Endicott.

Beckett welcomed them into his office and had them sit down. He asked anxiously, "How did it go?"

Henry frowned, "We could only buy half of the land."

Jean added, "Colonel Endicott claimed that the group he represented wanted to sell the grant in two twenty-five thousand acre sections. He had the forms and paperwork for one, but not the other. We bought the southern half."

Beckett nodded, "That's the half with the houses and buildings on it. If you could only get half that was the half to get."

Jean handed Beckett the papers, "Here is what he gave us. We need you to check them over and tell us how authentic they are or if you need to do something else to make the purchase ironclad."

Beckett carefully read the papers over. "Interesting," he murmured.

"What is?" Jean asked.

"These forms are actually from the General Land Office in Washington. They are authentic and the purchase is legal as it stands."

Henry looked at Beckett, "Can it be contested at all?"

"If it is I have a solid case to fight it in court. This is a legal land purchase from the General Land Office itself."

Henry and Jean both smiled showing satisfaction in having succeeded at least in part.

Beckett glanced at the paper again, "Did you really get twenty-five thousand acres for fifteen thousand dollars?"

Jean nodded, "And a thousand dollar bribe to get him to bite."

"How was he, this Endicott?"

"Anxious to sell. I'm certain he was double-crossing his group and running off with the money."

"Pretty much a crook then, I take it."

"An opportunist at least."

"What I'm wondering about," Henry interjected, "is how they by-passed the local land office? We have heard nothing from them."

"That could be simple enough with the right people in the right places. The local offices, as well as the General Office, are over-worked and underfunded. The agents are known to be open to bribes and selling lands before any of the proper offices even know the land is available."

Jean huffed, "Cutting out the government and pocketing the money themselves."

"Exactly."

Henry surmised, "In other words someone local knew of Sebastian's death, found out there was no will, and made a deal under the table with Endicott's group."

"They must have a man in the General Land Office then. That's how they have the proper forms to make the sale legal," Jean added.

Beckett nodded, "It seems to be a more common practice than I first realized. I have been digging a little deeper and the information regarding Sebastian's death never did make it to the local land office or the General Office. It was picked off before it became official that the land was open. That would lend credence to your thought Mr. Pelletier."

Henry frowned, "Then, the second half will be difficult to get if Endicott has run off."

"Possibly. This group still has their hands on that portion of the property and could end up selling it to anyone."

"Can you track it down?"

"Maybe." Beckett paused in thought and then said, "I will do one better and contact some people I know and begin an investigation into this group. If we can break their hold and the land does end up at the local office we could buy it then."

"But, that might never happen and the land will remain in lim-bo," Henry commented with a hint of discouragement.

"That is possible too. However, nothing ventured, nothing gained."

Henry nodded his agreement. "Do what you can then. We had better get back to the hacienda and tell Pablo what we have."

Jean and Henry stood up and shook hands with Beckett. They

exchanged farewells promising to stay in touch over the land issue.

———————

The hour was late and the land pitched in darkness when Jean
and Henry arrived at Pablo's house. The sound of the horse's
hooves roused Jesus who came staggering out from his room in
the stable rubbing the sleep from his eyes. Henry patted the boy on
the back, "Go on back to sleep Jesus, we can care for our horses."

The boy nodded and yawned, "*Gracias*." He stumbled back to his
room.

While they unsaddled the horses Pablo walked into the barn. "I
thought I heard horses."

Jean and Henry shared the same travel weary look. "I think we're
back," Henry quipped. "I'm too tired to tell for sure though."

Pablo laughed, "Come in. I will have Ignacio bring you some food.
Did it go well?"

"In part," Henry answered.

"You still have your home and half the hacienda," Jean added.

Pablo lent a hand turning the horses into their stalls and feeding
them. Once finished he said, "Come in, I know you are tired, but I
must know what happened."

"We're not too tired to talk," Jean replied.

Pablo led the way into the house where Ignacio met them. "Please,
Ignacio, food for Jean and Henry."

Ignacio hurried toward the kitchen.

Catherine and Angelina, both wrapped in their robes, came out
of their rooms at the sound of the voices. They hugged their husbands before they all entered the dining room to sit down. Ignacio
brought plates of cold meat and bread to the table. "I can make
coffee if you wish," Ignacio volunteered.

Jean and Henry both shook their heads, "This will do, thank you
Ignacio," Jean answered.

Pablo smiled at the houseman, "Thank you Ignacio. I am sorry to
have disturbed your sleep."

"It is my duty to serve," Ignacio responded. He stood for another
moment as if wishing to ask a question.

Henry read the worry in the old man's eyes. "We were not able to
get back the entire hacienda Ignacio, but your home and life here
is saved."

The old man's brown eyes showed relief as the wrinkles that ran deep in his dark skin bunched at his smile. He turned his eyes toward the ceiling, "*Gracias a Dios.*" He then left the room.

Jean and Henry took turns relating the details of the meeting with Endicott and the resulting purchase of the southern half of the hacienda.

"We took the paperwork to Beckett," Jean explained. "He said the forms came from the Washington land office and were legal."

Henry added, "Now, we just need to find a way to get the rest of it. Beckett is working on that."

Pablo's tense body began to relax at the news that at least his family home was saved and his people could live on here. "I cannot express my gratitude deep enough for what you have done."

"Wish we could have gotten it all though," Henry frowned.

"But, you saved the most important part, and I can still do well with twenty-five thousand acres. We will continue to try and get the rest of it back, but if we do not I am still a happy man with what I have. You have my eternal gratitude."

"We're family," Jean said. "You and Sebastian rode without hesitation to retrieve Angelina and my granddaughter."

Pablo smiled, "We could not have done otherwise."

"Neither could we."

"The drive went off to a good start," Pablo said. "The men arrived the day after you left and two days later had the cattle moving."

"We heard. One of Endicott's people came to his house while we were there carrying on about the cattle being driven off the hacienda."

"The local spies," Pablo commented.

"This man said he was going to send some of his men to stop it."

Pablo chuckled, "He had better send an army. That is one of the roughest crews I have ever seen. Four of my men are with them and I know what they are capable of."

"Yeah, they won't make much of a dent against that bunch."

"I met Clint Rush and feel confident in him as a partner. He and Ian did quite well purchasing the land. Ian bought out a three thousand acre ranch adjoining his and thinks his wife might have gotten more during his absence. Clint bought five thousand acres. I will see what can be done to purchase more in both places. The partnerships will be greatly beneficial for us all."

"Glad to hear that went off well. How many head did you send up the trail?"

"Sixteen hundred."

Jean whistled, "Wow."

"I still have over three thousand head here and the horses. I will have my men drive them all to this section that we own. There is plenty of graze and water to increase the herd."

"Sounds like you'll have your hands full with three operations," Henry remarked.

Pablo shrugged, "It will be a lot, but I will figure it out as I go. I wish I had my father's sense of business."

"You do," Henry said. "You just never had to use it before."

Jean agreed with Henry, "You'll do fine."

Jean turned his attention to Catherine. "Who all came up for the drive?"

"All of our boys, plus Clint Rush, and a new man Ian had hired."

"Jeb was with them?"

Catherine nodded, "We spoke together about what happened to Jenny. I will be paying a visit to some people in town when we return. What happened was disgraceful and inexcusable, the town believing the lies of a no good reprobate simply because it made for good gossip." Clenching her jaw she spit out, "Disgusting."

"Sounds like Jeb shut him up though."

"I cannot say I approve of seeking out a fight, however, under the circumstances Jeb was left with little choice."

"It was either that or tuck his tail and run away leaving the lies to stand as truth."

"As if one of our boys would ever do that."

"It would be a first."

Jean looked across the table at Pablo, "Well, this old man's about wore out and I hear a bed calling my name." He stood up. "I'll say my goodnights."

All at the table said goodnight to him and Catherine as they left the room.

Henry put his hand on Angelina's, "I have something I want to talk over with you."

She nodded, "I am tired and I know you are as well, but we can talk and then sleep."

Henry stood up, "Goodnight, Pablo. We will talk more in the morning." They left the room with Pablo sitting alone under the glow of the two oil lamps.

Pablo stared at the polished tabletop thankful that his friends had saved what they did and wondering what was to come next. He had a huge job confronting him. He lifted his eyes to the ceiling. "So much is depending on me Papa, please tell me what to do." His heart ached at missing the most important person who had ever been in his life.

He sat in the silence for several more minutes then slowly stood up. In a whisper he said, "I miss you Papa." He blew out the first lamp as he wiped tears from his eyes. It would never do for anyone to see the *patron* weep like a woman. He took up the second lamp and headed to his bedroom.

In the morning Jean and Catherine made their way to the dining room. Henry and Angelina were in the sitting room discussing something with Pablo. At seeing the elder Pelletiers, the three stood up to join them. Pablo shook Henry's hand and then hugged his sister. They sat down together around the dining table.

"I trust you slept well?" Pablo asked Jean and Catherine.

Jean chuckled, "I don't recall; I was asleep."

Catherine smiled, "He snored like an old bear."

Jean laughed, "You should be used to that by now."

She laughed in return, "I have learned to sleep in spite of you, mountain man."

Jean began to fill his plate, "Catherine and I will be heading home tomorrow morning."

"Yes, I am sure there is much to do and new matters to deal with," Pablo said with a hint of sly smile.

Jean glanced at Pablo, "Yeah, I suppose new matters could spring up, as long as they're good ones."

Pablo grinned, "I am sure they will be."

Jean wondered at the comment, but let it go as Pablo was simply wishing them well.

Henry and Angelina sat silent appearing nervous.

Jean looked across the table at them. "You will be staying, I assume."

Henry smiled, it was his father's gift for knowing what was to come or had happened already.

Catherine looked anxiously at Henry and Angelina, "You are not coming home?"

Henry's eyes showed sadness, "We will be staying here to help Pablo. He has more to do than one man can handle. He will need our help."

"Not to mention the property is in your name now," Jean added.

"In name only," Henry replied. "The hacienda is Pablo's, he is the *patron* and no one needs to ever know otherwise."

"I agree."

Catherine stared dumbstruck at Henry and Angelina. "I don't know what to say. We have all been so close for so long."

"And we will remain so," Henry assured his mother. "Pablo needs us here though."

"Yes, of course, I understand. It is just hard for a mother to see her children scatter so."

"Andrew and his family are a fixture on the Poudre Canyon ranch," Henry said. "They will never leave."

Catherine sighed as her eyes glistened with moisture, "Time does change much. We must do what is needed and you are needed here."

Pablo spoke in a soft voice, "I am sorry *Señora* to break up your family."

"No, Henry is right, he is needed here. You will have your hands full."

"Thank you for understanding."

Catherine dabbed at her eyes, "Perhaps one day the train will cover this entire country and coming to visit will be much easier."

"There is talk of the train running from Denver to Santa Fe in the next few years," Pablo encouraged her.

Catherine smiled at him, "That will certainly make the trip quicker."

"My home is always yours, *Señora*."

"Gracious as always, thank you Pablo."

––––––––––––

The next morning Jean and Catherine stood beside their wagon. Catherine cried at leaving more of her family behind. She hugged Henry and Angelina. Alicia cried as she hugged her grandmother and grandfather goodbye. Marcus fought back the tears not wishing to cry in front of the men. He hugged his grandmother then put his hand out to his grandfather who took it and they shook hands like men.

Jean and Henry looked each other in the eyes as they shook hands. With a burst of emotion Henry enveloped his father in an embrace and then stepped back. "I will be up soon to pick up our personal affects, and I will need to visit our partners regularly so you will be seeing me again."

"The door is always open, son."

Jean helped Catherine up onto the wagon seat. He climbed up beside her and picked up the reins. With calls of farewell and waves he started the horses for home.

"Shifting trails," Catherine whispered as the tears flowed down her cheeks.

"What's that?" Jean asked.

"Oh, just something Jeb said, "Shifting trails. Life has a way of moving us from where we think we are going to a new trail."

Jean nodded, "Very true, very true."

CHAPTER TWENTY-TWO

The night guard around the herd was stepped up to change every three hours rather than every four. Should they be set upon by a gang of outlaws they needed to be fresh for the fight not dragging from lack of sleep. It also helped those on watch to stay more alert. The night passed without incident.

The men ate a predawn breakfast and started the herd early. They moved through the morning, reaching the trace of the Goodnight Trail and moving due north toward the mountains and Trincheras Pass. The cattle had accepted the journey and struck a good pace following the cream colored bull.

They had wrapped biscuits and bacon in bandanas and stuffed them in their saddlebags. With filled canteens they could eat in the saddle and keep the herd moving past noon and on into evening. The further and faster they got from New Mexico the better. The mountains were in sight when the expected riders made their first attempt.

Four armed men rode in from behind the herd so they would be hidden in the dust and not spotted by any of the riders. Their intent was to force the rear animals to stampede into the animals before them. It was their lack of cattle knowledge that fouled the plan.

Red Horse and Jeb had rotated to the drag positions. Their mouths and noses were covered by dirt coated bandanas and their eyes red and burning from squinting against the sun and dust. The dust, heat, and noise from the cattle blocked their senses. They had no indication of the attack until the riders struck the rear of the herd shouting and shooting off their guns.

The laziest cattle were the ones in the rear and reacted to the attack with bovine indifference. The startled cattle did no more than jump into the cattle directly in front of them. Those cattle refused to move faster. The riders' horses hit the stalled cattle like a wall. Not being cattle horses, the mounts of the would-be stampeders fought the bits in an attempt to turn away from the tangle of animals they were being forced up against.

Jeb and Red Horse reacted immediately. Red Horse ripped his

rifle from the scabbard and in one smooth motion shouldered the rifle and shot the man closest to him dropping him from his horse. Jeb spurred his horse to his left, pulled his revolver and fired at the man to his left. The man slumped in the saddle but hung onto the horn. The plan foiled and two men shot, one dead, caused the remaining riders to turn and flee.

The rear-most swing riders, two of Pablo's men, along with Pete and Will, charged back to the fracas. They saw the fleeing riders. Rather than give chase they rode directly up to Jeb and Red Horse.

"What was that all about?" Will shouted to Jeb.

"Guess they wanted to stampede the herd."

One of the vaqueros laughed, "They must have been *loco* to think they could stampede sixteen hundred cows by charging the rear of the drive."

"My bet is they have no idea what they're doing," Jeb responded.

Pete stepped out of the saddle to look at the man on the ground. Pushing him over with his foot he shouted out, "This one's dead."

"Leave him," Jeb called back.

"I'll ride up and let Clint and Booker know," Pete volunteered. He swung back into the saddle, turned his horse and skirted around the cattle headed to the front.

As the swing riders returned to their positions they alerted the others who had not left their positions to ride to the shooting. Eugenio rode back to where Jeb and Red Horse were following the still moving herd. "I am going to ride a ways behind to watch for attacks." He kept moving past them.

The sun was balanced on the western ridge tops when they bunched the herd for the night. Three of the vaqueros stayed with the herd taking the first guard rotation while the pack horses were unloaded and camp set. Tom and Joe had religiously stayed with the horses and kept them moving with the herd. They rode to the camp to check in with the rest of the crew.

Andrew walked over to his son as the boys pulled in. "Were you two informed of the attack on the herd today?"

Tom stretched his tired legs, "Yeah, Will swung by and told us to watch ourselves."

"Push the horses up tight with the herd for tonight so the guards can circle them."

"Joe and me figured to take turns watching them tonight."

"Okay, but neither one of you has a gun so at the first hint of anything odd get to the closest guard."

"We will."

Cooking was a chore no one relished so it was also put into a rotation with two men at a time working on it. This night the job fell to Will and Pete.

"Who's got the cooking tonight?" Tom asked.

Andrew grinned, "Will and Pete."

Tom laughed, "Knowing those two they'll probably invent something scary."

"Remember the rule."

"Yeah, I know, first one to complain gets to cook next."

"Even if they've got prickly pear you say, 'yes sir, best prickly pear I ever ate.'"

Tom and Joe both laughed and agreed to say something good even if it wasn't. They mounted back up to check the horses and move them in closer.

Marty got the nightly cooking fire going as Will and Pete rode in from the herd. Andrew watched them dismount. "You boys have the chore tonight."

Pete frowned, "Are you sure? I could have sworn it was you and Ian."

"Nice try. You have a lot of menu choices. Bacon, dried beef, or bacon. Then there's beans and some more beans. Personally, I prefer bacon and beans, but you suit yourselves."

Will opened one of the packs and grumbled, "At least it's not complicated."

Jeb poked his thumb over his shoulder, "The herd trampled a rattler back a ways. I could get that if you want."

Will looked up from the pack, "Go get it."

Andrew snapped, "No! You cook a darned snake and I'll chain that iron skillet around your neck."

Pete grinned at Will, "Well, it it ain't mister snooty high society over there."

Will shook his head, "Mister-too-good-to eat trampled rattlesnake snooty high society to be exact. Fine then, you can eat bacon and beans." He pulled a sack of dried beans out of the pack.

Clint rode in from scouting and dismounted next to Ian and Booker, "See anything up front?" Ian asked.

Clint answered, "Just what should be there."

"What do you make of that bunch that hit the herd?" Pete asked as he threw a slab of bacon down on a square of canvas to cut it.

"I figure they're idiots," Booker said. "First they come up with the marshal on a load of nonsense and then attack the end of the line. They got about as much smarts as tree bark."

Clint agreed, "They're idiots alright, but idiots can be plenty dangerous. They've been sent to take the herd back. They don't know what they're doing which means they might pull anything, so be on the alert for *anything*."

"Pablo did warn us about that," Andrew added.

Eugenio rode into the camp hearing Clint and Andrew's last comments. "*Si, Senor* Ruiz was worried that there would be such an effort. The cattle belong to him, not these people who have claimed the Ruiz hacienda. My *compadres* and I will fight for his cattle." He paused for a moment as he corrected himself, "Excuse me, *your* cattle now as well."

"Don't worry Eugenio," Ian assured the vaquero, "We came down here to fight for Pablo and no one is riding away with this herd."

Eugenio bowed his head slightly toward Ian, "I did not mean to say you would not fight."

"It's okay, I know what you meant. You were fiercely loyal to Sebastian and now you are to Pablo as well. He is our friend too."

"He is a good man and as fine a *patron* as his father. We will fight for him as we did for Don Sebastian."

"So will we. I'm sure Pa and Henry will get the land back and that makes these cattle part of it. Anyone tries to take them will be rustling."

"And we don't like rustlers," Pete said from his place at the fire.

"I am glad to hear that," Eugenio chuckled. "I will join my *compadres* for the guard." He spurred his horse and rode off toward the herd.

Night fell as the conversation continued with the beans and coffee boiling on the fire. Ian wrapped a glove around the coffee pot handle and poured a cup. He scowled at the black liquid running out of the spout, "Good grief, Pete I need an axe to chop off a chunk of this tar."

Andrew forced a cough catching Ian's attention. Ian put the pot back on the fire, "But, that's exactly how I like my coffee . . . tarry." He rolled his eyes and sat back down using his saddle as a backrest.

Pete studied Ian from across the fire, "The bacon that fell in the dirt is yours, Ian."

"As black as it is it won't make much difference."

Will tossed a wry smile at Ian, "Guess who cooks breakfast?"

"It's not my turn," Ian growled.

"We just made it your turn."

Clint laughed, "Those are the rules. You should have just chewed your coffee and ate your dirt bacon."

Ian snorted, "Well, at least I know how to cook bacon."

"Good," Pete grinned, "you can show us in the morning."

"If he's good enough," Will put in, "maybe he can get on at one of those fancy Denver hotels."

Ian slurped his coffee, "Shut up."

Will shook his head, "And here we thought he was turning all nice."

"Nah," Pete said, "he's still a nasty old badger."

Without warning two men stepped suddenly out of the darkness and into the glow cast off by the fire. Those who were sitting sprang to their feet.

"Easy boys," the lead man said.

Clint recognized the men as two of the three who had been with the marshal. "You again? What do you want now?"

The two men stood an arm's length apart across the fire from the Pelletiers, Clint, and Booker. They had not drawn guns or showed an inclination of starting a fight. The vaqueros still had an hour on their watch, Tom and Joe had gone back to the horses. Red Horse had wandered off as he often did, and Marty had not been seen for a while.

"We've come peaceable," the man began. "You boys have a herd of cattle that doesn't belong to you and we've been sent to return it. We'd rather have a nice easy turnover here."

"Well, that's not going to happen," Ian snarled.

"I thought we got all that squared away with the marshal," Clint said.

The man grinned, "You had some papers, but we both know the cattle belong on that ranch back yonder, and there's another who owns it now and that includes these cattle."

Jeb stepped closer to the two men. "That land still belongs to Ruiz until the government says otherwise, and these cattle belong to Ruiz and us. You best go back and tell whoever sent you that none of us are going to buckle under just because they say so."

With a tsking sound and an exaggerated head shake the man said, "We was hoping you'd just do the right thing here without us having to resort to harsher tactics."

"The right thing," Ian shot back, "is for you little dogs to turn around and head back to your master before you get your ears pinned back."

The man called out, "Dirk, Shorty, bring 'em on in."

Jeb and Booker kept their eyes on the two men while the others turned their faces in the direction the man had called out. The sound of sliding boots in the sand and grass drifted out of the dark and then Tom and Joe were pushed into the firelight. A man stood behind each of them holding tightly to their upper arms with one hand and a drawn pistol in the other.

"If you don't want these kids hurt you'd better saddle your horses and ride away."

Andrew's temper flared as he took a quick step toward his son. Clint slipped the loop off his revolver and stared hard at the man holding Joe. At Clint's move the man lifted his gun toward Joe's head.

The talker continued, "It's really pretty simple, the boys for the cattle."

Andrew growled, "You hurt that kid and there won't be a hole big or small enough for you to hide in."

A chuckle sounded from the talker, "You're in no position to bargain, friend."

The man holding onto Tom's arm suddenly howled out in pain as Tom rocked back and crushed his capturer's foot with a hard driven boot heel. He followed it up by slamming his spur into the man's shin eliciting a second scream of pain.

Joe imitated his friend and slammed his heel down on the man's foot behind him. Both boys leapt forward away from the men. Andrew stepped forward and slammed a fist into the face of the man who had held his son. He put all his muscle behind it. The man's head snapped back as he fell sprawled out on the ground.

The leader went for his gun but stopped when he saw Jeb holding his gun on him. He couldn't believe how fast the kid had pulled that gun. A whisper of sliding leather and he was a finger twitch away from filling a hole. He lowered his gun hand to his thigh. The man standing next to him never moved a muscle.

Clint was standing with the bore of his cocked revolver pressed against the forehead of the man who had held Joe. The man was frozen in place, half bent over in pain, yet terrified to move.

Four more men, one with a bandaged arm, were marched into the firelight with Red Horse and Marty following them with rifles pointed at their backs. Marty said, "We found these coyotes slinking around in the dark."

The man Andrew had knocked down was sitting up groaning as blood dribbled from his nose. The hired outlaws stared back at the men who had so quickly turned the tables on them.

"Throw down your guns," Jeb ordered.

The guns fell to the ground without hesitation.

Ian looked over the men, "I swear, did you all run away from a circus? I've never seen such a pack of clowns in my life."

"Should we shoot 'em, boss?" Booker asked.

Ian shifted his gaze from one face to the next of the now nervous and frightened men. "It would seem proper don't you think?"

Booker agreed, "It is, but maybe we could hang 'em instead. There's a couple of nice trees yonder."

"Hang us for what?" the leader asked with a tremble in his voice.

"Cattle rustling," Booker answered.

"But, we didn't steal any cattle."

"You intended to, that's good enough."

"For kidnapping then," Andrew snarled.

"I think we should send these little dogs back home with a message for their master," Ian concluded.

"You want to just let them ride out of here?" Will asked incredulous.

Ian fixed a glare on the leader, "You want to be shot, hung, or go back with a message?"

The man looked at the hard faces in front of him and the gun in Jeb's hand. "I'll take the message."

"Okay, all of you take your boots off and toss 'em out into the dark."

The men all looked at him like he was crazy.

"Why?" the leader demanded.

"Cause you agreed to take the message rather than be hung or shot. We never discussed conditions."

The men looked at each other, but didn't move.

"Booker," Ian called out, "get the ropes."

The outlaws quickly dropped to the ground and pulled off their boots.

"Throw 'em over your heads," Ian commanded.

The boots flew through the air landing with thuds in the darkness.

"Now, start walking."

"*What?*" the leader screamed.

"Walk!"

"What about our horses?"

"We'll turn 'em loose tomorrow. For now you start walking south and tell your employer that he'd better pack his freight and forget about the Ruiz outfit."

"*This is nuts,*" the man shouted.

Ian said calmly, "Jeb, shoot him, maybe the others will be more agreeable."

"Okay." The man thrust his hands out in front of him as if to stop the oncoming bullet. "We're going, we're going, relax."

The men walked into the darkness. Their voices were heard cussing and yelling in pain as they stepped on prickly pear and sharp rocks in the dark. Their voices eventually faded away.

Will laughed, "I should have known you had something special planned for them."

Andrew looked Tom over, "You don't look any worse for the wear."

"Nah, Joe and me are fine. We were sitting and watching the horses when that whole bunch showed up with guns drawn and grabbed ahold of us."

"That was a pretty smart move stomping on that fella's foot like that," Ian praised his nephew.

"It just seemed like the Pelletier thing to do," Tom grinned.

Ian and Jeb burst out laughing.

Clint slapped Joe on the back, "Nice going partner. You handled that with a cool head."

"I just did what Tom did."

Red Horse and Marty collected the guns and laid them with the packs. "No sense in wastin' perfectly good guns," Marty grinned.

Ian turned his attention to Red Horse and Marty, "Nice going you two. How did you happen on those boys you gathered up?"

Red horse answered, "I was scouting around the camp in the dark when I met Marty. He said he had heard some funny noises while checking on his horses and was looking for what made it. We went looking together and found them standing out in the dark."

"They weren't doin' nothin' but standin' out there waitin'," Marty added.

Ian snorted, "Waiting to jump us, good catch."

Booker silently studied Jeb, he had seen the draw. What he had heard about Jeb being a fast gun was sure enough true. He wondered if anyone could beat that draw. Offhand he couldn't think of anyone that fast and he'd been around enough to know.

"Who taught you to handle a gun like that?" Booker asked Jeb in a low voice the others couldn't hear.

"Been shooting since I was six. Clint taught me the finer points."

Booker nodded, "It shows."

Ian walked to his horse. "Jeb, Andrew, Booker, we have the next watch." The three followed him, mounted their horses and rode into the dark to relieve the vaqueros.

Joe looked at Clint, "Think we've seen the last of those men?"

"They won't be back. Now, you boys get some grub and sleep. We're pushing this herd into Colorado tomorrow."

CHAPTER TWENTY-THREE

Ida Webster heard the cattle coming before she saw them. She looked to the south and saw a long dust cloud rising into the blue sky, the lowing of cattle on the move drifted with it. She felt a thrill of excitement run through her. The cattle meant success for them and she had had little of that in her life. More importantly the son she loved, and the man she had come to love were almost home.

She watched and saw the point riders first and then the lead cattle. A light colored bull walked behind the riders swinging his big head back and forth. Clint waved to her as they continued to push the herd past the house and on to the new five thousand acre section where they were halted and held.

Clint and Joe rode back to the house to see Ida while the crew began to separate the cattle into Clint and Ian's herds. Ida's smile filled her face as she embraced her son and husband to be. They told her about the trip leaving out the confrontation where Joe ended up a hostage. He told her about Marty, that there would be one more at the table. Ida was anxious to meet him.

She asked about Pablo, what he was like. Clint assured her he was an honest man and the partnership was a good one. He told her about Jean and Henry working out a plan to get Pablo's land back and hoped they had succeeded. If they had not, Pablo at least had the two partnerships to keep him afloat. Clint and Joe returned to the herd to help with the work.

It took well into the next day to cut out the two herds. Clint's herd was pushed across the range to create a separation between his and Ian's herds so Clint's wouldn't follow Ian's cattle when they moved on. The two hundred head of young animals that had the yellow slashes on them were held in their own group.

At dawn the next morning the men gathered to shake hands and say their goodbyes as Ian prepared to move his herd on. Clint had ridden back to the herd from the house with Ida and Joe along. Marty had spent the night at the house, but rode out ahead of the family to help.

Ida was overwhelmed at the number of animals before her. "What happens now?" she asked Clint.

"Joe, Marty, and me will stay here to take care of our stock. Ian and his group will continue on with the rest of the cattle to Ian's ranch."

Ida pointed at the cattle with the yellow slashes. "What about those, why are they painted?"

"They're a special gift from Pablo to Jean for all his help." Clint grinned, "Except Jean doesn't know about it yet. The vaqueros will drive those up to the Pelletier ranch and then head back home."

"I thought the Pelletiers only raised horses?"

"Not anymore. I was told that Pablo and Henry were talking Jean into raising cattle, but he couldn't afford the breed stock."

Ida smiled, "So, Pablo gave him these as a thank you gift."

"Yes. That's the kind of man Pablo Ruiz is."

"And a very generous one. I can see where our partnership with him is going to be a good one."

Clint nodded, "A *very* good one."

Eugenio and his vaqueros tightened up the group of Jean's cattle. Andrew met with them before they left letting them know that Tom would guide them to the ranch as he was going to stick with his brothers and help get Ian's herd home. The four vaqueros started the two hundred head moving, letting Tom take the point.

Ian's crew bunched his cattle and began pushing them north with the cream bull again taking the lead. Clint, Joe, and Marty positioned themselves between their herd and Ian's departing cattle to turn back any animals that thought they were supposed to follow along. Once Ian's crew was out of site with his seven hundred head Clint and his boys went to work among their own cattle.

Jean and Catherine had been home for three days. Catherine was adjusting to having another one of her children move beyond their reach and was in her house visiting with Sarah and Blue Flower. Jean was with Andre checking over the pregnant mares being held in the barn. Two of the mares had thrown foals while he was away. Three more were close and being watched.

Jean studied the horses, considering what Henry and Pablo had said about horses possibly becoming a thing of the past. Once again he thought about the cattle and how much it would cost to buy the stock. It was the cost that held him back; it would take all they had in savings.

"Pablo and Henry wanted me to go into cattle," Jean told his brother. "Henry thought we should spread out and not just count on the horses for income. I don't know though. It sounds like a good idea and we certainly have the good graze and water for cattle."

"If it sounds like a good idea, why the hesitation?"

"The cost. I can't afford enough breeding animals to make it pay anything. I'd be forever getting it back."

Andre shrugged, "You just have to start small and build up. I have some money that I can throw in."

Jean stared at the mare in front of him. "If I was younger maybe, but I'm a little long in the tooth now and don't have a lot of years left to start small and build up."

Andre laughed, "You sound like you're planning your funeral already."

"Just being realistic."

Andre snorted, "Since when have we worried about the end?"

"Since I started getting closer to it."

"Would you like me to wrap a shawl around you and warm some milk while you sit in your rocking chair?"

Jean scowled at his brother and then sighed, "Do I sound that pathetic?"

"Yes."

Jean stared into Andre's eyes, "I haven't gone soft, just thinking ahead."

"Sounds like soft to me. So, how long would it take to raise enough calves to make money at it?"

Jean frowned at the comment, but then considered the question. "With what I can afford, five years at least."

"And if you don't do it how many cattle will you have in five years?"

Jean let out a sigh of surrender, "None."

"So?"

"So, I guess we raise some cattle."

"Do you know where to get breed stock?"

"I'm sure I could buy some from Pablo, but I don't want to make that trip again anytime soon."

Andre stopped and turned his head.

Jean looked at him, "Hear something?"

Andre walked out of the barn and stared off down the river. "You hear that?"

Jean strained to listen. He heard the river, ravens squawking, and something he couldn't identify. "Something's moving this way."

"A lot of somethings moving this way," Andre remarked.

The lowing of cattle was heard before they were seen. "What the heck?" Jean whispered.

"Sounds like cattle," Andre said.

The first person they saw was Tom and then the cattle following him. Jean stood with his jaw slack watching as the cattle continued to move along, strung out in a line. He then saw Eugenio and the other three vaqueros he recognized as Pablo's men.

They pushed the cattle into the green lush pasture down from the house and rode back to where Jean and Andre stood watching.

Eugenio stepped off his horse as Catherine left the house to see what the commotion was about. Eugenio swept off his wide sombrero and bowed slightly to Catherine, "*Senora* Pelletier, a pleasure to see you again."

Catherine nodded toward him, "Thank you."

Eugenio grinned at Jean's confused expression. "*Senor* Pelletier, a gift from my *patron.*"

Jean looked at him, "A gift?"

"*Si*, it is *Señor Ruiz'* way of showing his gratitude to you for saving the hacienda. There are two hundred head of the finest young heifers, cows, and bulls from the Ruiz hacienda."

"I don't know what to say."

"There is nothing to say, simply accept my *patron's* gratitude."

"Yes, I accept. Please thank Pablo for his generous gift, but he doesn't need to thank me. I helped because he is my friend and his father was my friend before him."

"True, however, his gift is not from necessity to thank, but from gratitude and from one friend to another."

"Thank you for bringing them."

"My pleasure. My *compadres* and I will be returning to the hacienda now that our job is completed."

Catherine stepped in, "It is late in the day, please spend the night and take supper with us."

"*Gracias señora*, we accept if it is not too much trouble."

"No trouble at all."

Eugenio spoke in Spanish to his friends regarding their invitation. They all thanked Catherine and dismounted.

"How did the drive go?" Jean asked.

"It went well. *Señor* Rush has his cattle and your sons are heading north with those for the rancho in Wyoming."

"Did anyone try to stop the drive?"

"Three times." Eugenio laughed, "The third time they were captured and Ian made them take off their boots and walk back to where they came from . . . barefoot."

Jean laughed, "That sounds like Ian alright. Anyone get hurt?"

"One of theirs was killed and another wounded. Ask your grandson about the one with the broken foot," he laughed again. "That young man is an *hombre*. *Señor*, you should be proud of him."

"I am." Jean looked at Tom who was standing off to the side and saw him visibly stand straighter and fight back a smile.

"We will care for our horses now. Can we put them in the corral right there?"

"Sure, there's hay and feed in the barn."

The vaqueros walked away leading their horses into the corral.

Andre moved up close to Jean's side. "Want me to warm your milk now?"

Catherine looked at Andre with a raised eyebrow, "What is that all about?"

"Nothing," Jean snapped.

Andre laughed as he walked away, "I will get my sons and be back to help you with the cattle."

Ian and his crew were trail weary and worn down when they reached the ranch. Anne and Jenny rushed from the house to look over the cattle and greet their sorely missed husbands. Ian called from the saddle, "We're going to push them on to the McKenzie place and be back."

Driving the cattle through the main ranch they left them to graze and water on the newly acquired property. As the men rode back to Ian and Anne's house, Ian took Jeb on a side trip to the house Duncan McKenzie and his wife had occupied. The house was empty. They dismounted and went up to the door. Finding it unlocked they went in and looked around.

Ian looked the house over. Most of the furniture had been left.

"Nice place. Do you think you and Jenny would like to live here?"

The offer took Jeb by surprise. The house was solidly built with two stories, and three times larger than the little house they had in Fort Collins. "We'd love it."

"Then it's yours. You can keep an eye on the operation from this end of the ranch while I cover the original side."

Jeb smiled, "Wow, thank you brother."

Ian shrugged, "No problem. I'm glad to have you here to help and Anne really likes Jenny. It gets lonely for a woman out here. She needed a friend."

"Yeah, it's a good setup all around for Jenny and me. A lot better than putting up with what we did before. Guess I'm not all that social."

Ian laughed, "Wonder who you take after."

Jeb looked down at the floor and formed his words, "I'm sorry I talked to you like I did when you were warning me about the gunfighter thing."

"Ah, don't worry about it. You and me, little brother, we don't like people telling us what to do."

"Maybe, but I had no business talking to you like that. I knew that you were right. I guess that's why I got my hackles up."

"You're my brother, Jeb, I want to help you wherever I can. Sometimes we can't see where we're heading and need someone to tell us to watch out."

Jeb smiled, "Like when Pete and Will said you were a grouchy badger?"

Ian chuckled, "Yeah, like that."

They walked back outside and looked around. Jeb pointed at a building alongside a barn and a couple of sheds, "Is that a bunk house?"

"Looks like one, doesn't it? Let's take a look."

They pushed open the door of the building to see six bunks, a table, chairs, and a wood stove. "It's a bunkhouse alright," Ian said.

"We could put Booker and Owl in here," Jeb said as he looked around the place. "It's better than what they've got now and pretty much in the middle of things."

"That would put the burden of feeding them on Jenny though."

"We could set in a store of food for them and they could make their own breakfast and noon meals. That way Jenny would only have to cook supper."

"You'd better talk to her first," Ian warned.

"I will. We'll get everything worked out eventually."

They rode back to the house where the rest of the crew had already stripped the tack off their horses and Will was forking hay to them in the corral. Ian and Jeb tended to their horses and then went into the house to see their wives.

Anne and Jenny were busy preparing supper for the crew. Anne smiled at Ian, "Guess what? I found us another five hundred acres."

"Good," Ian beamed, "where? Babcock's town?"

"No, some government land at a dollar and two-bits an acre and it adjoins the McKenzie property. I used the rest of the money to lay in a stock of food for the crew. I know the money was for land, but we need to feed the crew too."

Ian nodded, "Yeah, I think that would be okay with Pablo."

Red Horse walked in with Owl. They sat down alongside Ian and Jeb. "Red Horse wants to stay here and work. Do you approve?" Owl asked.

Ian agreed, "Sure, we can use the help."

Jeb looked at Ian from across the table, "We're going to need that bunkhouse."

"Looks like it. We'll have to work that out."

"Jeb, we saw the McKenzie house," Jenny said with excitement. "It is so nice."

Jeb smiled, "I know, Ian just gave it to us."

Jenny jumped and squealed with delight, "Anne had thought it would be okay with Ian and we were going to talk about it."

Ian grinned, "Consider it talked about."

Jenny hurried over to Ian and gave him a hard hug, "Thank you."

"Watch out there pretty girl or your husband might get jealous."

Jenny let go of him and laughed, "Oh, I don't think he'll get jealous because I hugged my brother."

"Even if he is a cranky old badger?" Pete asked as he walked in the door.

Jenny smiled, "Oh, he is not."

"Yes, he is."

"Is there someone else you could annoy for a while?" Ian asked Pete.

"I could annoy Jeb, but he'd probably shoot me."

"Now there's a thought," Ian grinned.

Jenny wrapped her arms around Jeb's neck, "What a wonderful family. Everything is going to be so good here."

Jeb put his arm around her, "Yes, it is."

Summer was waning into fall. The leaves on the aspen turning to September yellow. Talk in Bitter Creek regarding the killing of Dick Norton was still as fresh as the day it happened.

The livery hostler in Bitter Creek stepped into Mike's saloon for a beer and to sit with his friends. He had repeated the story over and again of how Dick Norton and Ralph Todd met their end. The shooting and scare he received from Ian Pelletier made him cautious about the origins of any horses he'd bought since then, but he told the story as if he had not been afraid.

The horse trader again made mention of the fight which caused a hard eyed man leaning on the bar to turn his attention to him. He pushed off the bar and walked slowly to the table where the hostler sat with his friends. The stranger stopped and looked down at the man, showing no hint of friendliness. "What do you know about Dick Norton?" he asked.

The hostler looked up at the man and froze with his mouth half open as if to answer. The man's face was lean, chiseled like granite, and equally cold. It had been days since he shaved and the scar down the side of his right eye made him look fierce. He coughed nervously, "He was killed in a gunfight."

"So I heard. Why?"

The hostler figured it would not be in his best interest to say that Norton had been killed for stealing horses. "I'm not sure."

"Who did it? Must have been backshot or bushwhacked 'cause he was too fast to ever be beat to the draw."

With a silent shiver the hostler remembered the coolness of the young man who outdrew Norton and his friend. "It really was a gunfight, I saw it."

The man glared at the hostler.

"Was Dick Norton a friend of yours?"

"My brother. I asked who did it."

"A gunhand from Colorado."

"*Name?*" the man growled.

"Jeb Pelletier. He runs a ranch with his brother up by South Pass."

"Pretty fast is he?"

The hostler nodded, "Oh, yeah. Hear tell he killed Alex Cassidy up Fort Collins way."

"Is that a fact? Guess I'll head out and pay him a visit." The man walked out the door of the saloon.

About the Author
Dave P. Fisher

Mountain men, Voyageurs, pioneers, and explorers make up the branches of Dave's family tree. His mother's side was from Canada where the men plied the fur trade in the Canadian wilderness. Others moved down into the wilds of Northern Minnesota and established trading posts among the Chippewa.

On his father's side were veterans of the War of 1812, and the Spanish American War. His natural grandfather died out West while working as a telegrapher for the railroad. His step grandfather, born in the 1800's, was Blackfoot Indian from Montana. He was a hunter and horseman who brought a great deal of Old West influence into the Fisher family.

As a lifelong Westerner Dave inherited that pioneer blood and followed in the footsteps of his ancestors. Originally from Oregon, he worked cattle and rode saddle broncs in rodeos. His adventures have taken him across the wilds of Alaska as a horsepacker and hunting guide, through the Rocky Mountains of Montana, Wyoming, and Colorado where he wrangled, guided and packed for a variety of outfitters.

Dave weaves his experience into each story. His writing, steeped in historical accuracy and drawing on extensive research, draws his readers into the story by their realism and Dave's personal knowledge of the West, its people, and character. As an example the inspiration for his popular *Poudre Canyon Saga* series came from an ancestral Canadian family of twelve sons, all voyageurs and trappers. Two of the sons ventured to the Rocky Mountain West in the 1820's to trap and were never heard from again. The Saga is based on what might have become of those two men.

With over 400 works published, Dave's accomplishments and credits include: Winning two *Will Rogers Medallion Awards*, one for Western Fiction with his collection of short stories *Bronc Buster – Short Stories of the American West* and again for Western Humor with *The Auction Horse*. In addition he has won 8 People's Choice Awards for western short stories. He is also the author of 13 novels and books, over 70 published short stories, and has been included in 15 anthologies.

You can learn more about Dave's background and writing at his website:

www.davepfisher.com